A DARING TÊTE-À-TÊTE

If Bigelow entertained any thought of the impropriety of a tête-à-tête between Miss Weldon and Mr. Haverill, he repressed it manfully. He inclined his head, led them across the hall, and closed them into the dimness of the dining parlor with a sigh which no one heard but which relieved Bigelow immensely.

Mr. Haverill turned her gently toward him. "Miss Weldon—Carolina—"

Finding himself deserted by the English language, he did what he had been wanting to do for a long time. He bent his head and kissed her.

When Mr. Haverill raised his head, Miss Weldon made no attempt to draw away, but stood gazing up at him, her mouth parted, her face suffused with pink.

Mr. Haverill was not made of iron. He dropped his hands to her waist, drew her close, and kissed her with increased warmth—not so much passion as to alarm an innocent young lady, but enough, at the same time, to exhilerate a gentleman. When this kiss ended, Miss Weldon hid her face against his chest and Mr. Haverill laid his cheek against her hair.

"Do you find this pleasant?" he asked in tender, if ragged, tones.

"Yes," said Miss Weldon baldly to Mr. Haverill's waistcoat.

Praise for GENTLEMAN'S CHOICE by Dorothea Donley:

"A lively tale."

—*Romantic Times*

"A classic Regency filled with humor and a heroine you'll just love."

—*Rendezvous*

A SINGLE SEASON

Dorothea Donley

Zebra Books
Kensington Publishing Corp.

http://www.zebrabooks.com

ZEBRA BOOKS are published by

Kensington Publishing Corp.
850 Third Avenue
New York, NY 10022

First Printing: June, 1997
10 9 8 7 6 5 4 3 2 1

Printed in the United States of America

One

.Miss Carolina Weldon had not intended to be late for breakfast. Miss Weldon was a most responsible daughter. She was also the mainstay of the household, which meant that this morning she had been obliged to rap twice on Cedric's door with commands for him to get *up*. There was a ribbon hiding from Susan and a sash of Charlotte's that refused to tie itself. There was a very contrary snarl to be coaxed from Melissa's curls. Well, she had sent them all down, and as she came last of all into the breakfast parlor, the vicar sent her a reproachful glance.

Poor, dear Papa! He did like Order in his home! Tall, handsome, and vigorous, his feet planted firmly on the Solid Rock, the vicar was a towering force in Dolden Overhill. He thrived on service to his fellow man. All he asked for himself, all he asked was Order in his home. And for seventeen years of married life all he had had was chaos. Then Miss Weldon turned sixteen, and having long recognized Papa's dilemma, calmly assumed the management of the vicarage. Now, three years later, all was running smoothly and no one objected, least of all Mama, who was totally immersed in parish needs. Hardly a day went by that someone did not breathe thankfully, "Mrs. Weldon is such a comfort!" It did not matter at all that she forgot to gather the eggs until the hens were almost crowded out of their nests, or to mend the linens so the vicar's toe would not go *through*. She never forgot a soul in need. Mrs. Weldon was the perfect helpmeet for a country cleric . . . besides being the darling of his heart.

"Only see, Carolina," she exclaimed, "I have a letter!"

At a table of handsome people she was not least in looks, having sparkling eyes, a faultless complexion, and—happiest of all—an amiable expression. "It's not Harriet's writing . . . I wonder who sent it."

"I hope," said the vicar kindly, but firmly, "that a letter from your sister need not disturb our breakfast."

Mrs. Weldon and her daughter exchanged amused glances.

"No, indeed," said Mrs. Weldon meekly, putting the interesting letter resolutely aside. She buttered toast and handed it to her spouse.

Between bites the vicar surveyed his family. Fortunately, an honest faith saved him from the deadly sin of Pride. A lesser man would have been insufferably puffed by the contemplation of so much pulchritude and good nature. Miss Weldon's eyes followed his; they were green like her mother's, but they viewed life like the vicar.

Susan was eating, as she did everything, with exquisite grace. She was gentle, tender-hearted as her mama, impossible to anger, and easy to please. Her nature was retiring, and while all persons were received into her presence with pleasure, she truly preferred solitary pursuits such as sewing. Like a good general, Miss Carolina had delegated family mending to Miss Susan who contentedly restored everything with the smallest of stitches. If she had a special joy it was cutting into new fabric to create an elegant frock for her mother or one of her sisters. Sometimes it was necessary to restrain Susan's romantic taste for lace-edged flounces and clutches of ribbon. However, Lady Luce was generous in lending her London journals, so that the vicarage ladies were able to keep aware of the latest fashions, and even imitate them when fabric came their way.

Charlotte and Melissa were yet children, sunny and neat. It was too soon to tell much about Melissa's character—except, of course, that it would be molded by the Book of Proverbs. Although only nine, she had her share of family duties and performed them willingly. Charlotte was a young miss of a less docile stamp. She had utmost faith in Papa's wisdom, Mama's love, Carolina's good sense, and her own capabilities. She was as orderly as Papa could wish. It was probable that in a few years she would be able to manage the household as well as her older sister, especially since Miss Weldon had already made up *her* mind to that end.

The four Weldon sisters were everything agreeable . . . if only their Papa were less impecunious.

About the scion of the vicarage there were no "ifs." This morning, as often happened, he sat wrapped in a cloud, eating, but tasting little, and hearing nothing. At seventeen Cedric was tall and comely, well-mannered and well-read. He was also very confused about himself. Since he did not understand himself at all, it was fortunate his mama, his papa, and his eldest sister understood him perfectly. Moreover, they were in complete agreement that Cedric Must Go To Oxford. By age, scholarship and inclination, Cedric was prepared to do so . . . although sometimes he liked to lie out in the pasture behind the stable. When the grass was deep no one could see him—or even think of looking for him there—and he could stare up into the immensity of the sky and dream.

"Will you visit Mrs. Hackett today?" Mrs. Weldon asked her husband.

The vicar shook his head ruefully. "Poor soul! I should— she needs looking after, being so old and weak. But I have a meeting with Sir John and his bailiff about those deplorable hovels people are trying to live in behind the Feather and Thistle."

"Then I will go to Mrs. Hackett for you," said Mrs. Weldon immediately.

"Bless you!" exclaimed Mr. Weldon. He stretched out his hand to his wife and she placed hers into it. They smiled into each other's eyes, oblivious to the children and Annie, who had come in to set down a fresh pot of tea.

Mr. Weldon resumed his perusal of the morning post. There were several ecclesiastical journals, the butcher's bill (which was passed to Carolina), and a London newspaper. Nothing to hold his attention long. He therefore applied himself to a substantial breakfast and was just finishing when Annie came in again to report that the stable boy thought Nellie might be raising a blister.

"I will come at once," said the vicar.

The fall of his napkin to the table top was the signal for all heads (including Annie's) to bow. The vicar offered a fervent prayer of praise and thanksgiving, committed each person in the breakfast parlor, by name, to the care of the Lord, said a resounding "amen," and departed for the stable.

Annie returned to an un-plucked chicken, and Mrs. Weldon reached for her enticing letter.

"Dear Mrs. Weldon," she read aloud, "Lady Tufton has asked me to write you. . . ." She turned to the end of the epistle, exclaiming, "Why, it is from Brother Tufton's secretary." Returning again to the salutation, she continued to read silently, while the children watched with curiosity. At last she raised her head. "How kind of Harriet! She invites Carolina to visit her for the Season. . . . But there is no offer of help for Cedric. Oh, dear. And it would mean so much!"

"Me?" cried Carolina in astonishment. She was not offended by her mother's lack of enthusiasm as she very well understood and endorsed Cedric's claim upon the family fortunes.

Hearing his name, Cedric came out of his fog and said, "What? What?" And the younger Misses Weldon waited alertly for more information, while their mama reread her letter.

"Yes," said Mrs. Weldon. "Harriet has invited Carolina for the Season."

"She must go!" said Charlotte stoutly. "Caro *deserves* to go."

Mrs. Weldon came back into focus upon her offspring. "Yes, indeed. I did not mean—you understand, dearest?" She looked remorsefully at Carolina.

"Of course, Mama," replied Miss Weldon calmly. "It is Cedric that matters. Had you asked my aunt for help with his education?"

"Not directly," admitted Mrs. Weldon, "for Papa would not allow it. But I did hint that, that—very mildly, you know—"

"Too mildly," said Carolina, smiling.

"So it seems," agreed her mama ruefully. "But this offer of my sister's, for you, is very kind."

The children of the vicarage, having no knowledge of their aunt's character, were prepared to accept their mama's evaluation of her kindness.

"Well," said Mrs. Weldon, rising, "we shall see what Papa says. What is there for me to take Mrs. Hackett, Carolina?"

"Some calves' foot jelly, Mama," said Miss Weldon, following her mother to the larder.

The vicar was as ready as his wife to exclaim over Lady Tufton's attention to his daughter, if with less enthusiasm. He had a well-founded suspicion of the worldliness and evil to be encountered in Town Life. Although he did not begrudge his daughter a few weeks of pleasure, it was necessary to persuade him that genuine (and harmless) pleasure did exist in balls, dinners, and conversation of an indolent and extravagant Society.

Miss Weldon, being torn between anticipation and alarm, said not a thing, leaving all argument to the generous nature of Susan, the verve of Charlotte, and the fond aspirations of her mama. The vicar was won and a thankful note dispatched to London. Of course the exciting news must be speedily relayed to Lady Luce and Sir John. This was easily accomplished without any Weldon walking a step, writing a note, or speaking a word outside the vicarage portals, for Annie's brother arrived soon after breakfast with a load of firewood. As his next call was at Luce House, where he dallied as often as possible with a bouncing kitchen maid, and as the kitchen maid was triumphant to pass on to Lady Luce's dresser a piece of information unknown to that august London female, and as *she* knew it was her duty to regale Lady Luce—well, almost before Mr. Weldon had given his reluctant approval, Sir John Luce was so obliging as to offer the loan of a team for the trip.

"If you don't push them, they'll be good for two stages," he said.

The vicar, after all, was a gentleman's younger son, and a tolerable whip. He was also a better judge of horse-flesh than Sir John, who plumped for endurance instead of speed. However, the vicar was long past the day of "springing" his horses. Sir John's sturdy team was entirely to his taste and he accepted the loan gratefully.

Lady Luce was delighted at the good fortune of her young friend. Not to be outdone by her husband, she sent down two lengths of cloth that brought a gleam to Susan's eyes. Jealousy was unknown in the vicarage. The rich green crepe and pale apricot taffeta would be dashing for Miss Weldon, Susan declared. None of the family doubted her judgment or her talent for design.

Carolina owned two walking-dresses which could be refurbished. Also, both Mrs. Weldon and Susan could contribute a muslin frock, Mrs. Weldon's blue and Susan's white with blue ribbons which Caro could change to her favorite green. Altogether they could assemble a wardrobe quite dazzling to one whose life had been quite simple.

"A presentation gown is out of the question, you understand, dearest?" Mrs. Weldon explained. "I am sure your aunt will take you to some delightful entertainments, but presentation at Court is not for persons of our means."

"No, indeed, Mama."

"It is really most obliging of your aunt," Mrs. Weldon went on. "I hope you will be suitably appreciative and biddable—there! What am I saying? Of course you will! But do not forget to put your aunt's wishes first at all times. You must accept her judgment in every matter, unless—you see—Harriet is different from me, from us. Her—er, standards are different. Indeed, I do not know what they may be! I do know I can count upon you to act always in accordance with Papa's precepts."

Miss Weldon smiled. "And yours, Mama."

Mrs. Weldon gave a small, deprecating shake of her head, but did not offer a verbal denial.

Since March had already begun when the invitation to Carolina came, and since it urged an early arrival, in scarcely more than a week, the vicar's curricle, relic of his bachelor days, was washed down by the stableboy, Miss Weldon's trunk strapped on, and Sir John's team hitched up, and the vicar had set out with his elated daughter.

England was at her best that day for Miss Carolina Weldon. It was cool, but clear, the road free of puddles. A gentle wind brought agreeable scents of thawing earth. Papa had every expectation of reaching London that afternoon.

They had gone a mere mile from Dolden Overhill, when around a sweeping bend they saw approaching a sporting vehicle drawn by a spanking team. Slowing his horses, the vicar looked with interest at a sight to gladden any horse-lover, while his daughter, who had seen assorted horses every day of her life, observed with astonishment and pleasure two gentlemen such as she had never before encountered.

At the reins was a distinguished gentleman in a many-caped driving coat; his skill was patent. Beside him rode a handsome young man, and perched behind was a diminutive tiger in green livery. The sight was splendid. Both the vicar and his daughter watched the approaching rig without alarm.

On the other hand, Sir John's horses, having eyes in the sides of their heads, and consequently viewing everything quite differently, took exception. Just as the strangers swept neatly past, with two inches to spare, Sir John's pair whinnied and lurched. Miss Weldon, who had been holding on with one hand, was tumbled to the flooring-boards. A wheel went into the ditch, and Mr. Weldon sailed into the hedge.

"Lord, Lawrence! You ditched them!" cried the younger gentleman who had turned his head to look back.

"Never touched them," objected the driver, but he was slowing his horses. "Have a look, James."

The young man needed no instruction. He jumped down and ran back along the road.

Miss Weldon had already scrambled from her father's curricle and was attempting to soothe the frightened animals.

"Oh, I say," exclaimed the stranger. "Let me help. Surely we didn't touch you!"

"No," agreed Miss Weldon cheerfully. "These absurd creatures took the notion they were blood-cattle."

By this time the tiger had the other team in hand and the distinguished gentleman was approaching. "Are you injured, sir?" he asked the vicar, who had not emerged from the hedge.

"No," replied Mr. Weldon. "That is—er, I very much fear I have split my breeches."

Miss Weldon cried, "Oh, *Papa,*" gave a gasp, and burst out laughing. Her father rolled his eyes and began to shake with mirth.

The strangers exchanged looks. Then the younger one, clearly bedazzled by dancing green eyes, began to laugh also. The other gentleman permitted himself to smile.

"My name is Haverill," he said. "And this is my cousin."

"*James* Haverill," added the young man.

"Charles Weldon," said that stricken cleric. "Vicar of Dolden Overhill."

"You cannot be far from home," observed Mr. Haverill.

"About a mile," replied the vicar.

Mr. Haverill then proposed that he drive the young lady home, while James Haverill should follow along with the vicar in the curricle.

"There's a wide place there, ahead, James, where you can turn," he said.

James would have preferred to drive the young lady, but he was quick to see they would reach the same destination in a very short time. It was settled. Since Sir John's team was now placidly waiting as though some *other* horses had caused all the excitement, Miss Weldon surrendered them to James Haverill, went down the road with Mr. Haverill, was handed into his dashing vehicle, and soon found herself returning in style from her journey to London not many minutes after she had started out.

Two

Dolden Overhill rested in a shallow saucer of meadowland fanning from an oak-shaded green which fronted the church. Across the park, facing the church as a challenge to it—or possibly a rebuke—was that establishment of vice (indolence) and sin (cool ale), called the Feather and Thistle. Bounce, the innkeeper, was an honest-enough fellow who came to Sunday worship regularly and gave his bit for expenses, even though the vicar was unable to convince him that the selling of alcohol was reprehensible. Almost as though they were taking sides in the contest between church and inn, houses of the gentry flanked the church, while those of tradespeople shouldered each other across the way. Behind the inn a ragged lane held several miserable cots that had long disturbed the vicar's mind and heart. There was also a smithy, and a small lumberyard where village children spent happy hours storming and defending wooden citadels.

When they had reached the church, Miss Weldon directed Mr. Haverill into a side lane, and presently they had come upon the vicarage and swung into its curving drive. From the vantage point of a new and elegant curricle, Miss Weldon for the first time was able to see the unkemptness of the grounds and the subtle deterioration of the house itself. Being her father's daughter, she did not apologize to the smart London gentleman or even, in her mind, dwell upon it. The vicarage was Home. There was love in it.

At the sound of wheels, Mr. Weldon's stableboy came running around the house.

"You can trust Jem with your horses," Miss Weldon told Mr. Haverill. "He is very good."

Something suspiciously like "Arrr!" could be heard from the rear of the curricle, and for an awful moment Miss Weldon thought there might be a disagreeable confrontation of boys, but Jem's face, as his eyes fell on the splendor of Mr. Haverill's tiger, revealed the most gratifying awe.

"Jem will have your father's team to deal with in a few moments," said Mr. Haverill smoothly. "Wallace knows what I like with mine."

Wallace had already jumped down and gone to the horses' heads. Since Jem was so obviously ready to lick his boots, his chest swelled inside its bottle-green coat, and he inclined his head and emitted a civil remark that could only, by a country bumpkin, be interpreted as encouraging.

Mr. Haverill handed Miss Weldon from the curricle and she led him into the house.

"If you will wait here, sir," she said, throwing open the door of the drawing room, "I will see if I can find my mother. She will want to thank you."

"For ditching you?" asked Mr. Haverill with a crooked smile.

Miss Weldon replied that Sir John's horses had done *that*. She then went from the room, leaving him to wonder who Sir John was and how he entered the matter.

Through a front window he could see James bringing the vicar's vehicle into the crescent of the vicarage drive. The vicar descended clutching a cloak about him, and presently the two gentlemen could be heard in the hallway.

"Mr. Haverill will be in there," he heard the vicar say, and James opened the drawing room door to join him.

"Wait till your friends in the Four Horse Club hear about this!" said James with a twinkle in his eye.

Mr. Haverill regarded him disapprovingly. "But out of courtesy to Mr. Weldon they will *not* hear," he murmured.

"Oh," said James, chagrined, "I had not thought of that."

"Well, you have now," replied his cousin, "and I am sure I can depend on your good manners."

"Quite. Yes, yes," James responded hastily. He was too cast down by Lawrence Haverill's chastening attitude to venture into further conversation. The gentlemen sat in silence, until presently they heard footsteps approaching and Miss Weldon came into the room followed by Miss Susan Weldon.

The gentlemen, being presented to the vicar's second daughter, bowed gracefully, but Susan, who was carrying a tray and so could not curtsy, merely nodded her head and smiled angelically. James's spirits were immediately revived and he hastened to assist her with the tray.

While Miss Weldon explained that her mother had gone into the village for an all-day sewing party, the younger sister served the gentlemen with hot chocolate. Even Mr. Haverill, whose tastes ran to more sophisticated beverages, seemed to enjoy a hot drink on such a crisp day.

Their duties done, the ladies sat down and talked easily and politely with the strangers. That is to say, Miss Weldon talked with James Haverill. Susan was her usual quiet self.

Mr. Lawrence Haverill, looking from one young lady to the other, could not fail to notice the calm self-possession with which they filled their parents' shoes. These were no simpering misses. Nor did they put themselves forward. He was not surprised that James found them charming.

At last the vicar joined them, newly breeched, had a cup of chocolate, and chuckled that he was thankful his parishioners had not witnessed his Fall from Grace. Then he consulted the gentlemen as to whether they thought he could still reach Town before dark. Mr. Haverill, who was well acquainted with the route, and James who had tried out Sir John's team, both assured him it could be done.

"So we will not delay you further," said Mr. Haverill, rising. "We are for Kole."

The party moved into the hall exchanging thanks and good wishes for respective journeys.

It was at this point that a ball rolled down the stairs, passed between their feet and bounced against the front door. All eyes turned upward to discover a pair of very young ladies sitting on the landing with obvious intent to examine the strangers in the house. James picked up the ball, smiling, and called out:

"Can you catch it?"

"Certainly," said Charlotte, and stood up.

James lobbed the ball gently toward her and she managed to catch it nicely.

Melissa's mouth rounded into a pretty "O."

Meanwhile, Mr. Haverill was interested to observe upon the faces of his three hosts not embarrassment, but fond smiles.

"Ready, James?" he reminded gently.

The adieus were concluded and the gentlemen stepped outside. Wallaee, who had been slowly walking Mr. Haverill's bays, and who was now in the lane, quickened his stride and brought the curricle into the driveway. With civil nods on both sides, the strangers departed.

"I say," exclaimed James as soon as they were out of hearing, "What a deuced pretty girl!"

"Which one?" asked Mr. Haverill.

James chuckled. "All four that we saw, of course, but I meant Miss Weldon."

"Charming," agreed Mr. Haverill, who knew a diamond when he saw one. "But I advise you not to toss your handkerchief too hastily. Chances are she won't have a sixpence."

"Must I admire a lady only according to her riches?" James asked irritably.

"Dear boy, your mother would say you must," replied Mr. Haverill in a bored voice.

James frowned. *"I* am not hanging out for a rich wife!"

"I hope you aren't hanging out for a wife at all," his cousin said. "Not for several years, anyway."

James grinned suddenly. "There are too many mills to see yet? And too many balls to be enjoyed? And races cheered?"

"Exactly," said Mr. Haverill.

"Nevertheless," said James firmly, "I shall call on Miss Weldon when we get back to London. Mr. Weldon told me she is to spend the season with her uncle."

"Who is her uncle?" asked Mr. Haverill.

"Your friend, Lord Tufton."

"Gilly's niece? Never heard he had one."

"Well, Lady Tufton's, to be exact."

"Ah," said Mr. Haverill. "That explains it. I thought there was something familiar about Miss Weldon. Her mother will be Lady Tufton's sister."

"Quite acceptable," James pointed out.

"If penniless," replied Mr. Haverill, having the last word, but not altering James's intentions in the slightest.

When the gentlemen had passed from view, the vicar sent for his rig, Carolina embraced her sisters again, and they set out once more for London.

"Were they not very elegant gentlemen, Papa?" said Miss Weldon in much the tone that James had described *her* to Mr. Haverill.

"Indeed, they were. But do not lose your heart, my dear, for such are above your touch. I hope you will someday attach a gentleman of honor and kindness and respectability, but affluence such as I suspect belongs to the Haverills is not for a country cleric's daughter," the vicar explained unhappily.

"Of course not, Papa. I understand perfectly. I hope I would never indulge in unfruitful and worldly fancies. Besides, it's unlikely I will ever see the Misters Haverill again in intimate society."

"On the contrary," said the vicar heavily, "You will be sure to. Mr. James Haverill tells me his cousin is a close friend of your uncle."

They rode a time in silence, but it became clear what path the vicar's thoughts followed when he said with a sigh: "At least I need not worry about fortunehunters dangling after you."

Miss Weldon made no comment.

"It would be deceitful," he went on, "not to admit that the purpose of this visit is to find you a suitable husband. However, I, for one, am not eager to lose you."

"You mustn't worry, Papa," said Miss Weldon. "Charlotte will soon be capable of keeping your home in perfect order."

The vicar shot her a reproachful look. "I was not thinking of domestic convenience. I enjoy your company, Daughter."

"Thank you, Papa," she replied gratefully.

"Do not, I beg you, give your hand where you cannot give your respect."

"I will not be easily satisfied, Papa, for you are my standard," she told him roundly. The vicar's eyes misted. He reached out and squeezed her hand.

After a few moments, he said: "Never act in haste. That is a good rule." It was a rule she had heard many times. He now added: "Never act or speak in haste or anger. I make it a practice to close my eyes and count to ten. It helps astonishingly."

"I have never seen you angry, Papa," she observed.

He chuckled. "I had counted, you see," he said.

When they were at last threading their way through the streets of London, Mr. Weldon returned to his veiled admonitions. It was always difficult for him to speak ill of anyone.

"I fear, Carolina," he said, "Lord Tufton's household will be quite outside your experience. Your aunt is not—is not—the woman your mother is. She will necessarily be your guide for a few weeks, but you must never ignore the dictates of your conscience."

"No, Papa," she agreed.

"Love not the world," he reminded.

"A wise child heareth its father's instructions," she responded promptly.

Warm with mutual affection they drew up at last before Lord Tufton's door.

Although Bigelow, Lord Tufton's butler, received them with perfect deference, their arrival was dampened by the fact that Lady Tufton had not waited at home to receive them, but was lending her lustre to a soirée. However, his lordship was reading in his library and sprang up when Bigelow announced them to greet them with every appearance of pleasure.

Gilbert Maxwell, the Viscount Tufton, had kind eyes, Miss Weldon thought as she watched him welcome her father. She, herself, remained demurely silent until addressed by her uncle. Then she curtsied gracefully and thanked him for his generosity in having her to visit. Clearly, Lord Tufton was pleased, but neither Mr. Weldon nor his daughter suspected the pang with which he studied her face, seeing in her the young Harriet he had wedded and who had now somehow been replaced by a spoiled and fashionable young matron.

Had the travelers dined? They had not.

"Ah," said Lord Tufton, "I held my own dinner on the chance of this. Half an hour, Bigelow. And send in Mrs. Moffitt."

Mrs. Moffitt was the housekeeper. Like her employer, she saw Miss Weldon's resemblance to her aunt and prepared to assign her a similar temperament. Somewhat haughtily she escorted Miss Weldon to her bedchamber. By the time they had climbed two flights of stairs and traversed a hall, however, Miss Weldon's earnest apologies to the cook and thanks to herself had disarmed Mrs. Moffit completely.

An elderly woman of ample bosom and somber eyes was waiting to take Miss Weldon in charge.

"I'm Nannie, miss," she said stiffly. "I will be waiting on you while you are here."

"Nannie?" exclaimed Carolina, advancing with a smile and her hand held out. "My mama's dear Nannie?"

"Yes, miss," said Nannie, thawing as Miss Weldon's hand clasped hers.

"But I thought you were Aunt Harriet's maid."

Nannie sniffed, "From the day she was born, miss, until him lordship unexpectedly came into the title, and then I wasn't good enough."

Miss Weldon was not a vicar's daughter for nothing. "How fortunate for me," she cried immediately.

"My lady has a *dresser* now," Nannie said, getting it off her chest in a terse sentence.

"Well, I would be very uncomfortable with a dresser," Miss Weldon declared sincerely. "Oh, Nannie, there is so much for me to learn. I will depend on you utterly."

"Like your mama, you are," said Nannie, wiping the corner of her eye.

"I hope so," said Carolina. "Now, Nannie, Lord Tufton is waiting dinner. Can we do something about my hair?"

Mr. Weldon departed the next day without ever seeing his sister-in-law. She returned to the house after he had retired to bed and was still enjoying her beauty sleep when he set out the next morning on his long drive home.

It was nearly noon before Carolina was summoned to her aunt's chamber by a sober footman.

"Oh, thank you," said Carolina, rising immediately from the windowseat where she had been moping with inactivity. She bestowed such a radiant smile on the young man that he, who seldom received thanks in this house, began to unbend, and when she asked if he would kindly show her the way, went so far as to say, "A pleasure, miss."

They went down a flight to the first floor where the footman rapped gently at a carved door. Admission being granted by a muffled voice, he opened the door and deposited Miss Weldon before a beautiful young woman.

"Miss Weldon, my Lady."

The door closed softly and for a moment no word was spoken as the two ladies stared at each other in astonishment.

Miss Weldon thought at first that Lady Tufton was the duplicate of her mother and as a consequence opened her heart to her immediately. Then she perceived that although Lady Tufton's eyes were blue, and although she was taller by several inches than her niece, the resemblance to herself was startling.

"Good God!" exclaimed her ladyship. "A twin."

It was true the likeness was great. In calling them twins, however, Lady Tufton flattered herself. She was not quite twenty-nine, and a youthful twenty-nine; Carolina at nineteen had a serenity of manner beyond her years. Nevertheless, there were unmistakably years between them. Not enough for mother and daughter. Sisters, perhaps.

"Your Ladyship is generous," Carolina murmured.

Taking no notice of the words, Lady Tufton drew her to a mirror and they stood before it, contemplating themselves.

Carolina, who in innocence thought that anyone who looked like her enchanting mama must be of equally warm disposition, waited for a greeting of affection. She could not know that Lady Tufton was far from pleased to have thrust upon her a niece as beautiful as herself and noticeably youthful.

There were those who might expect Lady Tufton, who was without daughters, to welcome so charming a niece to sponsor. What a joy it should be to dress and direct and comfortably dispose her! The truth was that Lady Tufton, somewhere in that chilly region that was her selfish heart, felt only apprehension.

"So," she said at last, "you are your mother's child."

It would seem so, of course. She could not know on a momentary acquaintance that Miss Weldon also had her papa's self-possession and strength of character.

"We all are, more or less," Carolina answered. "Susan and Charlotte are fair like Papa, but Mama really *must* claim us all."

"Five?" said Lady Tufton in minatory accents.

"Four girls. Cedric truly resembles Papa. In brain as well as looks. We expect wonderful things of Cedric."

Lady Tufton frowned, remembering her sister's timid hints about the boy. "Well, that is neither here nor there. We are concerned with your come-out. It is very generous of your uncle, you know, to have you here."

"Yes, indeed," agreed Carolina. "So kind of him!"

"You must not expect too much—either in the way of entertainment or marital prospects," her aunt said. "Your uncle cannot be expected to provide a dowry. I hope you understand this."

Carolina was shocked. No Weldon ever expected anything material of anybody. It had been instilled in them to be content with what they had received and where they were placed. "Certainly not," she cried fervently.

Satisfied that nothing would impinge upon her wants, needs, or desires, her ladyship then allowed: "Well, I expect we shall rub along together well enough. You may go now."

Carolina curtsied. Still having not received the welcome that might have been expected by a niece, and wondering exactly where she was to *go,* she exited from the presence of the Incomparable Lady Tufton, beginning to understand what her parents had meant when they said her ladyship was not like them.

Lord Tufton came along the hall opportunely then and carried her off to his ground-floor study for a comfortable chat which passed the time pleasantly and added to each's admiration of the other. The other members of the family, The Honorable Masters Roddy and Hugh Maxwell, were

not presented to their cousin until after the dinner hour,
when they were brought to the drawing room by a timid
nurse-maid.

Tufton House was a handsome town residence. To one
side of the marble-floored entrance hall was a fine library,
with Lord Tufton's study behind it, facing on a small unin-
teresting garden and a view of the carriage house in the
mews behind. On the other side of the hallway lay a long
dining room whose table was as lengthy as Lady Luce's in
the manor house at Dolden Overhill. As this one customarily
stood, it could seat twenty-four, and most likely could be
stretched to more. Behind the dining parlor was a serving
pantry with narrow stairs to the kitchen realms below—
gloomy, but walled around with capacious presses. Also on
this level was a morning room which viewed the same dull
garden plot, but by its situation caught the early sun and
was therefore quite cozy.

A fine, broad stairway led via two landings to the first
floor, which was occupied by the drawing room, two small
parlors, a sitting room for Lord and Lady Tufton, and their
private suites. Often Lady Tufton deplored the lack of a ballroom, but at least her drawing room was immense, stretching across the front of the house. At the second story, the
stairway effaced itself against one wall before continuing to
the servants' rooms and attics under the roof. Carolina's
chamber on the second floor was one of three commodious
and austere guest rooms. Mrs. Moffitt had her quarters on
this level, and a nursery suite on a side corridor filled the
remaining space.

All was washed, waxed, and solid. Except for the dining
parlor with its pale green panelling and Adams mantel, and
Lady Tufton's chamber, all azure and gilt, the house was
somber without being unpleasing.

The Viscount Tufton, having so newly come into title and
wealth he had never expected, was cautious with both. By
nature he was modest, and a sudden elevation to the peerage

effected no change in his personality, although her ladyship, already spoiled by the attention she had received since her debut, became overbearing. Too late did Lord Tufton discover that the indulgent lover he had been when they first married was now a slave. Lady Tufton *must* command every luxury. He could not refuse her gowns, jewels, carriages, bibelots, and pin money. Otherwise, Lord Tufton kept careful rein on expenses. In Mrs. Moffitt, who was both frugal and zealous, he had an able ally. There was no penny-pinching on quality, but wastefulness was not tolerated. The estate, Lord Tufton determined, must pass unencumbered to Roddy some day.

If Lady Tufton had known (or cared) about the opinions of her employees, she might have moderated her demands. But Lady Tufton, who had married for love, or so she thought, soon concluded love was an over-rated emotion compared with power. How she had chafed at the limitations of *Mister* Maxwell's pocket and the humiliating lack of precedence accorded Mrs. Maxwell! By the time his lordship had come into the title, her ambition could be satisfied with nothing less than supremacy. Family sentiment such as kept her sister chained to a country vicarage she could only regard as maudlin.

Lucky lady! Her astonishing good looks and exquisite figure, unaltered by the presentation to her husband of two sons, together with Lord Tufton's new affluence, placed her where she wished to be, and if few persons felt affection for her, she did not comprehend it and consequently did not care.

Master Roddy and Master Hugh were all but exiled to the nursery, and their mother saw exactly enough of their scrubbed faces and goffered collars to remind herself that she had contributed to the marriage.

Of his sons Lord Tufton saw almost as little. A nursery was not the proper field of action for a gentleman; the servants would have been scandalized. And as Lady Tufton discouraged any interference with the nursery routine in case it might interfere also with herself, the little fellows grew up in the shade of the second story, as little heard as seen.

Once when his lordship spied the children being placidly walked about the square, he joined them on the spur of the moment and was warmly received. He obligingly held the acorns that the boys had gathered and had the felicitous honor of telling them how trees began in just this way. The children prattled happily, so that Lord Tufton enjoyed the half-hour with them enormously and promised himself to arrange more of the same, only it was not as easy as one might think.

The governess who had been engaged was delayed by illness of a parent. Until she was able to take up her post, Betty continued Nursery Duty, but she could not respond more than monosyllabically "yes, m'lord" and "no, m'lord." He missed the conversation he might have had with an educated governess.

Lord Gilbert Tufton, himself, had been the only child of a father who was smitten with debilitating disease before small Gilbert was out of his cradle; consequently, he had no model of a father to imitate. The teaching of a governess and the doting of a nursery maid seemed natural to *him*. It was lonely, yet he knew no other life.

Carolina's view was quite different. Had she not caressed and cuddled her younger siblings? Had she not fed, bathed, dressed, and admonished them, augmenting the fond attentions of her busy parents? She quite looked forward to meeting these new little cousins.

Three

Dinner that second night was held early since Lord and Lady Tufton were to attend the theatre with friends. There was no blessing, and very trivial conversation. At least the food was delicious, and Carolina marvelled over the eggs and butter and heavy cream that had gone into it. She was shocked when her aunt sent back a luscious custard with instructions to throw out the tasteless thing.

His lordship did not linger alone over the port, but accompanied the ladies to the drawing room where they were joined by Masters Roddy and Hughie.

The children came in with their nursemaid, and Roddy went trotting to his mother shouting that there were kittens in the stable. He was large for his age, handsome and irrepressible.

"Mind your manners," reproved her ladyship, fending him off from her elegant gown.

Lord Tufton, who had been in the act of kicking a reluctant coal in the fireplace, looked up, but saw nothing to condemn in his son's enthusiasm. "Kittens, Roddy?"

"Oh, yes, Papa. But we have not seen them yet. Betty *told* us."

Lord Tufton turned him gently toward Carolina. "You must tell your cousin," he said. "Carolina, this is our Roderick. And our Hugh."

Roddy at once executed a small bow which, while it was

not polished, was endearing. Miss Weldon held out her hand to him.

"How do you do, cousin? Kittens are much more interesting than strange ladies, are they not?"

At this point, Hugh abandoned the folds of Betty's skirt to hurl himself against Carolina's knee. "Kitty says me-ow," he announced.

"Indeed kitty does," agreed Carolina, drawing both boys to sit beside her. "And sometimes purrrr, and pft! and hith." She imitated cat sounds so dramatically that the young gentlemen were enthralled.

"Do *you* like cats?" Roddy asked.

Carolina nodded. "I certainly do. As a matter of fact, I am missing my own dear Tabby Four Toes very much! Will you take me to visit your kittens?"

The boys immediately shrieked, "Yes!" and their mother frowned.

"But they are not our kitties," Roddy explained. "They belong to John Coachman, and he said he would give us one, only—"

"Ugh," interrupted her ladyship. "Nasty, sneaking things. Why ever did you tell them, Nurse?"

Betty looked ready to melt into the carpet and drip through to the cellar. "I am sorry, ma'am. I thought—"

"You thought wrong," snapped Lady Tufton.

"Oh, Aunt," cried Carolina, "Papa always says cats are the best possible pets for children for they are so fastidious."

Master Roddy and Master Hughie had no idea what "fastidious" meant, but it sounded agreeable, so they shouted, "Yes, yes!"

"I will not have the sinister things lurking under furniture in my house," declared Lady Tufton. "I. Will. Not."

Four faces immediately recorded the finality of that. Carolina was astonished; then noticing Hughie's trembling lower lip, she said in a conciliating tone: "A number of people feel as you do, Aunt. We would not want you to be uncomfortable.

May I take the children to the stable one day soon? It would be educational for them, would it not? City children miss some of what country children learn so easily."

Lady Tufton, not wanting to be convicted of impairing her sons' education, hesitated just long enough for her spouse to regroup his forces.

"That would be kind, Carolina," he said. "You must arrange a time with Nurse."

The boys were bouncing beside her. Carolina said: "Tomorrow morning, then, Nurse? Shall I have breakfast in the nursery?"

"Oh, yes, miss. The young gentlemen would like that, I'm sure."

Master Hughie liked the idea so well that he felt compelled to stand on his head, and obviously must be removed. Betty clucked anxiously and tugged at the seat of his pants.

Carolina winked at Roddy. "Early to bed/ and lots of rest/ is sure to bring/ a breakfast guest. I am your cousin, remember. You must call me Caro. And if Hughie will stand up tall like a man and mind Nurse, Caro will tell stories about all the animals of Dolden."

Hughie's posterior went down, and his head came up. "Stories?"

"Yes, silly," said Master Six-years-old. "Come on."

"I'll tell stories, and you must tell me *exactly* how to get along in the city."

The boys saw nothing illogical in that. "We will," they promised. After all, Caro would need to know how to walk on cobbles, and where the gate to the park stood, and which crossing-sweep was friendly. She hugged both, and they went off docilely with a bemused Nurse.

As promised, Carolina took her breakfast in the nursery with Master Roddy and Master Hugh, telling them enchanting tales of Tabby Four Toes and her grand total of eighty-two offspring. It was a number beyond the comprehension of small boys, but as anything over ten was Enormous, they were agreeably awed and did not think John Coachman's cat with four children would have anything to act proud about.

The trip to the stable was delayed until afternoon, because Lady Tufton required the presence of her niece on the urgent matter of clothing. Miss Weldon had been included in a dinner invitation that very night, and her ladyship wished to examine Miss Weldon's wardrobe and choose what she must wear.

The pretty dresses from Dolden Overhill did not impress Lady Tufton. Well, no one was pretending they were Paris originals! And at least Lady Tufton could not quarrel with their neatness and suitability for a young miss. To Carolina's consternation, she chose the apricot taffeta that Mama had intended for Carolina's best and moot formal frock. If this were worn to a small dinner, what would meet the demands of a London ball?

"My best frock?" cried Carolina.

"And why not? Lady Franklin is very high in the instep," replied her aunt. "The people you will meet in her house will be of the first stare. Besides, this is your first appearance in London society. Every reason, you see, to look your best."

Carolina was willing to look her best. What troubled her was that her best might not stretch very far. Since she had been told to be guided by her aunt, she said: "Yes, ma'am." And rather thoughtfully began to hang away her dresses in the huge carved press. When Lady Tufton, satisfied with her arrangements, had departed on a shopping expedition, Carolina was left to a doleful scrutiny of her meager wardrobe.

Lady Tufton positively *wallowed* in a plethora of tippets and shawls; lavendar gloves and beaded reticules; negligees, petticoats and unmentionables of gossamer silk; silver, gilt, and rainbow slippers; cloaks, bonnets, and dresses, dresses, dresses. Carolina had never seen so many clothes. It seemed wicked. She should think the servants would be goaded to rebellion.

What the servants thought of their mistress's extravagance there was none to say. Her ladyship's dresser had no such reticence. *She* considered the lavish array her due. To attend a lady less well equipped would be unthinkably lowering. She delighted to brag about her ladyship's latest frivolity and was happy to swish before Carolina's shocked gaze the most elaborate and daring of frocks.

"There's not many could wear *this,* miss," she would say. "My Lady has the perfect bearing and *élan.*"

So my lady did. Even a country miss could see that. But Papa's daughter could not understand a lady's taking more interest in fashion than in her household.

As Lady Franklin dwelt only two doors from the Maxwell's home in London, and as her coachman often smoked a pipe with Lord Tufton's man, the news of Miss Weldon's arrival had reached her ladyship promptly. Lady Franklin was, as Lady Tufton had said, a high stickler. At the same time, she was a skillful hostess and knew how to assemble a crackling party. Harriet she considered to be ornamental (besides having blood that was satisfactorily blue). It always went down well with the gentlemen if there was a lady pleasing to look at, so Harriet won a place on her lists. With Lord Tufton the matter was different. For him she had a fondness that dated to their childhood in Shropshire. Nor had she forgotten the faithfulness with which this old friend presented himself as a partner at every ball when she made her come-out to society.

Lady Tufton was invited for her looks, the viscount for *himself.* And if back-door gossip could be relied upon, the visiting niece was a happy combination of her relatives' best features. The three had therefore been bid to dinner.

When they wore announced at the door of Lady Franklin's drawing room, their hostess, opulent in plum silk and diamonds, surged toward them graciously.

"Harriet. My dear. All the crack as usual."

The ladies exchanged near-kisses, and Harriet presented her niece.

"You will know everyone, I think," continued Lady Franklin to Lady Tufton with a friendly smile to Miss Weldon.

Lady Tufton's eyes swept the room, and singling out the most important guest in view, she said; "Why, yes. There is dear Princess Esterhazy. I have been wanting to speak with her." She thereupon advanced across the room toward her quarry, leaving Lord Tufton to look after Miss Weldon.

Lady Franklin did not miss Lord Tufton's mortification at his wife's behavior.

"A little leeway is allowed Beauties, you know," she said mildly to him.

His lordship was not obliged to reply, for that moment a deep voice said: "What, Gilly? Is not one Incomparable enough for you?"

"Ah," replied Lord Tufton, "you are seeing double, perhaps?"

Mr. Haverill stood before them.

"James will damn me for not bringing him tonight," he said. "He admires, he tells me, green eyes excessively."

Lord Tufton, smiling, presented Mr. Haverill to his niece.

To Miss Weldon's astonishment, the gentleman bowed and gave no indication of having met her before. She replied with a brief how-do-you-do, wondering if he ran so many people off the road that he had gotten into the habit of forgetting them promptly.

"You remember I invited James," Lady Franklin said.

"Yes, and he knows your reputation as a hostess as well as I do. Unfortunately, he was engaged. Shall you invite him another time?"

Her ladyship chuckled. "You know I will. I have a soft spot in my heart for bonny young gentlemen."

"And when they pass thirty, ma'am?" asked Mr. Haverill.

"Then," declared his hostess, "I am on my guard." To Miss Weldon she added: "That is a wise word to you, my dear. The older gentlemen grow, the more dangerous they become."

"And more foolish, my lady. Admit that too," said Haverill.

"Oh, I will admit it, but what gentleman ever did? Do you speak for yourself? And Tufton? I think not."

Lord Tufton said he would admit to being dull, to which Lady Franklin replied, nonsense, and took Miss Weldon off to introduce her to other guests.

"You will have your hands full, Gilly," warned Mr. Haverill, for he envisioned the attention that such a lovely girl would attract. "Guardian to a Belle is no sinecure, as you should know." The lightness of his tone relieved his words of any sarcasm. Lord Tufton understood him perfectly.

"At least I have had experience," he replied with a wry smile. "And this miss is a biddable one, I think. You should see her with my sons—so friendly and amusing. Her sweetness to such little fellows must indicate a warm heart."

"I would say ingratiating."

Lord Tufton looked severely at his friend. "Do not be cynical."

Mr. Haverill raised one shoulder in as much of a shrug as the perfection of his coat would permit. "This season should be interesting," he murmured.

Lady Franklin was thinking the same thing. Like everyone else she saw the similarity between Miss Weldon and her aunt. Lady Franklin, as her fond husband could tell, was a perspicacious woman. She knew at once that there was also a difference.

She led Miss Weldon about the room, slanting clues to her *sotto voce,* as she presented her to key people: "Almacks. Watch it . . . Lady Jersey, have you met dear Harriet's niece?"

This name Carolina recognized as belonging to one of the famed Patronesses.

"How do you do, Lady Jersey? You knew my mother, I believe."

"I did. A charmer, she was," asserted Sally Jersey. "But I have not seen her for a very long time because she fell in love with your papa and allowed him to bury her away in the country."

"He is very persuasive," Miss Weldon said with a twinkle. "She still loves him very much."

"Not surprising. I had a *tendre* for him myself."

The guests were all above thirty years. Only one was anywhere near Carolina's age, and him Lady Franklin characterized in an aside: "Plump in the pocket." The gentleman bowed stiffly but seemed interested to meet Miss Weldon. "My dear, may I make known to you Lord Dooly?"

In the most adroit manner Lady Franklin then extricated herself, leaving the young couple to make what conversation they might under the scrutiny of at least a dozen people, one of whom was Lord Dooly's mother, a gaunt female who sniffed constantly and kept dabbing her nose with a wrinkled handkerchief.

The young gentleman's figure was the converse of his mother's and his conversation was as expansive as his coat, so that dialogue between them was no problem. Miss Weldon had learned long ago at the vicarage that self-interest (alas!) is of driving concern to all persons at all levels. In two sentences, she had discovered Lord Dooly considered himself a scholar (Latin *and* Greek), and one more was all she needed to determine that he thought very little of George Byron ("conceited ass . . . setting the women all on end"). His lordship launched happily into vehement and repetitive opinions. Miss Weldon needed only to look attentive and supply trivia such as "Indeed?" and "You are right!" and (best of all) "Can you explain . . . ?"

It was not often that beautiful young ladies, even pauperous ones, hung upon his words. He enjoyed himself thoroughly, and assumed Miss Weldon was equally delighted with his pontifications.

She was glad for him to talk, since it spared her the necessity of doing so. Delight was hardly her emotion, however. Having an uncritical spirit, she found boredom no hardship, but merely thought him an "unfortunate" young man.

Dinner was announced, and Lady Tufton, not ill-pleased with Carolina's favorable impression upon Lord Dooly, allowed herself to be pried from her station beside Princess Esterhazy by an asthmatic but admiring gentleman and passed into Lady Franklin's dining room to find that the elegant Mr. Haverill was to be seated at her right hand. This was enough to drive all consideration of Miss Weldon from her mind.

Miss Weldon, who had no claim to fame or fortune, found herself situated about midway along the table, with Lord Dooly at her right, a view of which was mercifully blocked from Lady Dooly by a large epergne. If she was a tiny bit dismayed, she concealed it well, winning thereby the praise of Lady Jersey.

"Too bad," whispered her ladyship to Lord Tufton, "that your niece has to be saddled with that blockhead. We will have to find her something better."

"At Almack's?" asked Lord Tufton, seizing the bull by the horns.

"To be sure. I will send a voucher," promised Sally Jersey. "Well, Gilly, you will have your hands full this season."

"That is what Haverill tells me, but somehow I cannot see myself as the stern papa."

Lady Jersey, who could not see Gilbert Maxwell being a stern anything, assented.

"I do not go into society a great deal, you know," he continued. "It is really Harriet's duty to shepherd Carolina through her first season."

"But Harriet is a Belle herself," reminded Lady Jersey. "I do not think you can depend upon her to—to—remember."

They both looked down the table to where Harriet was engaged in a flirtation with Mr. Haverill.

"You may be right," Lord Tufton conceded in a colorless voice.

"You spoil her, Gilly," said Lady Jersey, which was rather outrageous of her, but her ladyship was known to chatter more than she should, and Lord Tufton took no offense.

"Yes," he said, "though you will allow she is a glorious creature."

Lady Jersey would, and did, adding firmly that Lady Tufton was also a very fortunate woman.

Their host was a taciturn man. Nevertheless, since Lady Franklin had planned well, conversation flourished about the table as one magnificent French dish followed another. It was possible she had Miss Weldon's welfare in mind when she assigned Lord Dooly as her dinner partner. He had a great deal of wealth and position to recommend him—if one could discount a parent who clung like a barnacle, and a tendency on his own part to drive his hearers into somnambulism. The whole of Miss Weldon's dinner was enlivened by the details of Lord Dooly's personal ordeal in the translation of Ovid's *Metamorphoses*.

"Is there not already an English translation?" Miss Weldon asked, with a small hope of a fresh subject.

"Oh, yes, but not at all satisfactory. Quite misses the author's artistry, don't you know? A deep study of vocabulary is necessary to *me*. I fear other translators have been careless."

"Inaccurate, do you mean?" Miss Weldon prodded, although her own acquaintance with Ovid had been congenial.

Lord Dooly shot her a quelling glance.

"My dear Miss Weldon! Not inaccurate, exactly, but lacking in flavor—tonal balance—ah, alliteration and such. Paltry use of our versatile English language. Paltry!"

It was a relief to Miss Weldon to withdraw with the ladies to the drawing room, even though Lady Dooly snatched the opportunity to blight her pretensions by deliberately ignoring her.

This was the time of evening that Lady Tufton especially abhorred, and to console herself for the lack of masculine attention, she ensconced herself again by Princess Esterhazy.

Lady Franklin, mercifully, took charge of a rather fatigued young lady.

"I am going to call you Carolina," she announced. "I did not know your mama, but always heard the most agreeable things about her."

Miss Weldon thanked her gratefully. Lady Franklin might, as her aunt had implied, be a snob, but Miss Weldon rather thought she was a person of character who adhered to Standards, which was an entirely different matter. Papa had often said a man without standards was like a ship without a rudder. Of course, Bible standards were what mattered at the vicarage, but if they were *ethical* ones—well, it was a step in the right direction. She liked Lady Franklin and was prepared to see only good in her.

"I hope you are going to let me be a friend to you," said Lady Franklin with a smile. "I have no daughters—or any children at all, for that matter—and have often envied the mothers of debutantes. The foolish ones moan about their duty and burden, but I think it would be diverting—especially if my daughter were as beautiful as Lydia Weldon's."

Miss Weldon colored faintly, rising a notch in her ladyship's estimation.

"Of course Harriet is too—er, youthful to see this as I do. She has great engagements of her own. I hope you will call on me any time you need advice—or a chaperone."

"It is very good of you, my lady. It sounds pleasant as well as helpful," Carolina responded fervently.

"I'll tell Gilly too, so he will know he can depend upon me. He and I are very old friends, you see. We don't stand on ceremony with each other. Next to my own dear Franklin, he is my favorite gentleman."

Carolina nodded in agreement. "One of the best things about my visit is the opportunity to know Uncle Tufton."

"Here come the gentlemen now. I expect you have had enough of Dooly. Well, well. I shall steer him off. . . . Lord Dooly, your mama has been asking for you. You see her? There beside Mrs. Peckinridge. Pray ask if she is feeling a draught."

Since Lady Franklin was generally believed to be a superior hostess, the evening must be declared a success. Carolina had met with the approval of Lady Jersey (even Princess Esterhazy conceded her to be a prettily behaved young woman), had received attention from a promising suitor, had acquired a powerful friend, and had made the discovery that people in London were little different from people in a village—that is to say, equally concerned with the big fish in their particular pond.

Lady Tufton was not sure in her own mind whether to be thankful her niece was no embarrassment or to be indignant that a green girl should conduct herself with enough poise to draw admiration from persons whom one might expect to prefer more mature charms. On the whole, she had to be pleased with her niece. Her own impact on the male gender seemed unimpaired. And she did not miss the fact that both men and women held her husband in respect. When Lord Tufton announced his satisfaction with the evening, she assented.

The next morning a more positive confirmation awaited Lady Tufton. She had made a leisurely toilet and had just joined Carolina in the drawing room, when Mr. Haverill was announced. The excuse for his visit was to bring his cousin Mr. James Haverill to be presented to Miss Weldon, but Harriet, recollecting the arrows she had fired at him the night before, felt all the elation of triumph. To reduce Mr. Haverill to slavery was the personal ambition of every London Belle—so urbane he was, so rich, so handsome—and so elusive.

Carolina, astonished by her aunt's upsurge of spirits and sudden sparkle of eye, had barely time to note the remarkable fact of Mr. James Haverill's introduction as a *stranger.* She did not understand it, but could only be thankful she did not have to explain to her aunt that one had met the Haverill gentlemen in a ditch.

The conversation was at first general, with Lady Tufton and Mr. Haverill agreeing that Lady Franklin's party was "delightful" and James Haverill, his gaze fixed on Miss Weldon, declaring he was devastated to have missed it.

"Lady Franklin is a very good sort," James opined.

Mr. Haverill looked amused. "You think that," he said, "because she indulges affable young men."

Rushing to the defense of James, who seemed discomposed, Miss Weldon said she, too, found Lady Franklin very easy and winning.

"My aunt warned me that she is most—proper—and indeed that is a quality to be admired. At the same time I found her gracious and kind."

Lady Tufton was not pleased with this speech. She was about to deliver a setdown, when Mr. Haverill interposed: "I believe Miss Weldon did not understand that I was teasing James. Lady Franklin is too well-known and too widely admired to need our defense!"

Lady Tufton was even less pleased with this. Her indignation was complete When Mr. Haverill added that Gilly had long been an admirer of Lady Franklin.

"Gilbert's opinion must always count with me," she responded in honeyed accents.

Mr. Haverill inclined his head.

"Well, enough of a party I did not attend!" exclaimed James with youthful impatience. "The weather, Lawrence. Speak about the weather."

Lady Tufton looked at him in some surprise, and Carolina

looked out the window. The day was bright and clear. James's glance followed hers.

"Yes, Miss Weldon, the sun is daring to show itself," he said.

Mr. Haverill addressed Lady Tufton: "We came to bespeak your company, my lady—yours and Miss Weldon's—in a drive about Hyde Park. James will make himself useful by pointing out to Miss Weldon the most interesting Londoners and the most dashing vehicles."

This was more to Lady Tufton's liking. She was being invited to sit beside Mr. Haverill in his well-known landau—a position offered few ladies—while James amused Carolina in the opposite seat. Gilbert would be complimented by such attention to his wife and London would know she was still a diamond of the first water!

She accepted immediately.

Mr. Haverill then suggested that very afternoon as a suitable time, and Lady Tufton was unhappily obliged to plead another engagement.

"Then tomorrow afternoon?" persisted James. "If the weather holds? You are available, Lawrence?"

Whether he was available or not, Mr. Haverill must say he was. The appointment was made, and the gentlemen took their leave.

"I hope," said her ladyship to Carolina, "that you comprehend the honor of this invitation. To be seen in Mr. Haverill's landau will certainly add to your consequence."

Carolina, who had already ridden in Mr. Haverill's curricle and experienced only convenience was not impressed. She was wise enough, however, to say, "Yes, ma'am."

"You must not presume upon this, though, Carolina," Lady Tufton continued. "Lawrence Haverill will never permit his cousin to become serious about you."

"Is he looking for money?" Carolina asked. A lady of greater sensitivity than Lady Tufton might have been shocked.

"James doesn't need it," Lady Tufton admitted. "But he will expect it—at least, his mother will. It is a distinguished family. The Haverills can look very high. Very high indeed. They would never accept you."

With some understanding of what her papa had meant about counting in a tense moment, Carolina bit her lip.

"Please explain, Aunt, to what *may* I look forward. Lord Dooly and Mr. James Haverill have been most cordial, yet you say they are not for me. I have too much common sense, I hope, to build upon casual flattery. But tell me, pray, why I came here to make a come-out if no gentleman will consider me a tolerable marriage risk."

Realizing now that she had been too blunt, Lady Tufton said unctuously: "My dear child, I warn you for your own good! And you will notice that I speak only of Expectations. Of course anything could happen. The danger lies in setting your heart on a splendid match. Your uncle and I will see that you meet many gentlemen. We have some confidence that there will be *one* so comfortably circumstanced as to be able to marry you for your looks."

"I would rather be chosen for my *self*," Carolina said, looking rather wilted.

"That," declared Lady Tufton positively, "never happens. Rid yourself of any romantic notions. You must do the best you can with your only asset, which is beauty."

"I can read Latin and speak French, and I am a very competent housekeeper," Carolina offered hopefully.

"None of which are of any use at a ball or formal dinner. Good god! Don't ever mention Latin!"

The corners of Carolina's mouth lifted. "Lord Dooly is a scholar of the classics," she pointed out.

Lady Tufton rolled her eyes heavenward. "Then correct his declensions," she snapped, "and see what happens!"

"Of course I would not be such a goose," Carolina replied in a mollifying tone.

By now Lady Tufton was reckless in her impatience.

"Your mother was certainly one. Let me tell you she declined a very fine offer to marry your papa instead. Our parents were exceedingly angry with her."

"They *liked* Papa," cried Carolina. "Mama always said so."

"To be sure they liked him. Everyone does. But what has that to say to anything? Five children and not a prayer of settling one of them!"

"You are wrong!" protested Carolina, bursting with emotions she had never before experienced. "In my Papa's house there's a great deal of prayer—only not for worldly things."

"The more fool he, then. If you cannot pay attention to what I tell you for your own good, I will wash my hands of you."

Struck by the horrible vision of being sent home in disgrace—unattached and unattachable—a permanent burden to the vicarage and an impediment on Cedric's path—Carolina forced herself to respond meekly.

"Mama said I should be guided by you, Aunt."

"Very well. Mind your manners, then, and leave your uncle to find a husband for you. If he can bring Dooly up to scratch he will do so. It would be beyond anything great."

Carolina would have preferred to reject Lord Dooly on the spot. Lifetime bondage to a crushing bore would be beyond anything hideous, she thought. However, it was also extremely improbable. Lady Dooly's attitude had been made clear already. Carolina did not think his lordship had strong enough fibre to defy his mama; nor was she, Miss Weldon, of sufficient beauty to launch a thousand ships.

"I see," said Miss Weldon, and her aunt was satisfied, although what Carolina *saw* was altogether different from what her ladyship intended.

Lady Tufton's temper would have been restored, had not Carolina rashly burst out on a matter that had puzzled her for the whole of her visit: "It is so confusing. Money appears to mean everything. But I know Mama's portion was small and so—if I understand the family situation—yours must have been likewise. And yet you were able to attach my uncle who is most handsome—and—and admired and—kind. Why is there no hope for me?"

Lady Tufton opened and shut her mouth several times, being at a total loss for words. It was her inclination, naturally, to exhibit herself in the best light, but how to do so without diminishing the husband who was now Lord Tufton—widely respected, as Carolina had said—or odiously bleating about her own charms and conquests, she did not know. Harriet might deal contemptuously with her sweet-tempered husband, but she knew his worth better than Carolina. As far as beauty was concerned, Carolina had ample, and to dwell too much on the fact would defeat her argument.

"To be sure there is hope," she said finally. "Otherwise your papa would not have sent you to us. Allow me, pray, to be the judge of what is best for you. *Your* part is that of a charming Innocent. Your uncle and I will find a husband for you as soon as possible."

Carolina assented meekly. She would have liked to have said she would choose her own husband, but the shocked voice of Mama was saying in one ear, "It is rude to argue with your elders!", while Papa's voice assailed the other with, ". . . long-suffering, gentleness, goodness, faith, meekness, self-control; against such there is no law. . . ."

Four

The drive with the Misters Haverill was a success from all points of view. Mr. Haverill's horses performed magnificently, and his coachman's handling of them was topnotch. Lady Tufton flirted to her heart's content, while the young people enjoyed an unaffected companionship.

"Does James admire my little puss?" Gilly asked Haverill afterwards.

"To be sure he does," replied Lawrence, languidly. "One wonders about the secret of your finding charmers."

Gilly chuckled. He knew his wife's penchant for flirtation, but he was perfectly secure in the knowledge of his friend's character, and consequently suffered no anguish of jealousy.

"I daresay my ladies did you credit," he observed.

"Just so," agreed Haverill. "I seldom drive ladies about. They must be diamonds of the first water when I do."

"Then you can appreciate my concern for the proper setting of my—er—diamonds."

"Yes," said Haverill. "A concern I share. James is still a boy, Gilly. Only twenty. I hope you haven't been indulging in fruitless. . . ."

"No, no," interrupted his lordship. But he *had*. And continued to do so. To settle Carolina with James would be so agreeable that he could not relinquish the idea.

About one thing were Miss Weldon, her aunt and uncle of one mind. No offer was seriously expected from Lord Dooly.

Which of the three, therefore, was most surprised when Dooly regularly presented himself in the Tufton drawing room it was difficult to say. By the time he had heavy-footedly danced with Miss Weldon at two evening parties, even Lady Tufton was beginning to think a Splendid Alliance might be possible.

Because she saw all the advantages of such a connection (Lord Dooly's mama was a social force to be respected), Lady Tufton's hopes rose and she chose to ignore the fact that James Haverill appeared equally often, guarded by his cousin, it was true, but beaming upon Miss Weldon.

What she saw her husband did also. The points of view diverged widely. Bemused by his fondness for Lawrence Haverill, Lord Tufton favored James, admired his attentiveness, and saw nothing significant in Dooly's taking Carolina to see Westminster Abbey, and prosing away about Greek lyric poetry. Lord Tufton was a scholar himself and knew something of poetry—Greek, Roman, or any other—but he did not think it was anything by which to woo a green-eyed young lady.

Gilbert Maxwell, now the Viscount Tufton, had not won a reigning belle for his wife without the exercise of charm. In his bachelor days, he lacked the self-confidence and dash of a great beau, but his agreeable ways and sensitive understanding of the interests and emotions of ladies consistently drew their approbation. His attention to their fashions and furbelows had made him something of a connoisseur.

It was not surprising, then, that when Lord Tufton had escorted Carolina's apricot silk to several dinners and a reception his lordship observed to his wife that their niece needed more clothes. Buy her a few pretty things, he said. One must not put a lily in a clay pot!

Lady Tufton, having discovered a ruby necklace which she hoped to wheedle her husband into buying, recognized the wisdom of appearing to acquiesce to his lordship's plans for Carolina. Sacrificing some of the time customarily spent in contemplating her reflection in the mirror, she began to calculate muslims and ribbons for her niece. Although the whole business was galling, at least satins and furs and jewels need not enter into it.

Then her dresser, unawares, presented a delightful solution by laying out a gown she did not like.

"Not that," snapped her ladyship, who was dressing for a reception where the competition would be fierce.

"Oh, my lady, you have not worn this above once!"

"Well, I detest it."

To argue with her employer was seldom wise, but Mrs. Gibbs had some hope of being offered the rejected garment for her own use, so she murmured, "Such beautiful fabric . . . it would be a shame to waste. . . ."

Lady Tufton raised her head and stared critically at the gown as it drooped dispiritedly over Gibbs's arm. A gleam came into her eye.

"So it would," she agreed, and rising suddenly followed Mrs. Gibbs into the dressing closet.

This interesting chamber was equipped with broad presses on three sides. The fourth was occupied by two windows flanking a small grate where fire smouldered summer and winter. Several irons waited expectantly on the hearth to attack any presumptuous wrinkle, and a pressing-board presented its back obligingly in the center of the room. Even such a utilitarian place must not offend her ladyship's sensibilities: the window hangings were azure velvet, and the cabinets had moldings of gold and blue.

Lady Tufton trod carelessly across fawn carpeting and threw open doors. With speed and precision she selected and tossed out garments.

"Oh, my lady," breathed the dresser, swimming in happy misapprehension.

Her mistress moved to the next cabinet, choosing dresses she did not like, was tired of, or knew to be spotted.

"There!" she announced. "That should take care of Miss Carolina's needs! Pray call Nannie to take them."

"Oh, my lady," said Gibbs in quite an altered tone.

But her ladyship had already swept from the chamber, leaving Gibbs to a crushed contemplation of What Might Have Been. Some of the clothes would have done so splendidly for her own use, and others she might comfortably have sold. It spoke well for Miss Weldon that the dresser harbored no grudge. Indeed, she was able to console herself with the thought of poor Miss Weldon making her come-out in hand-me-downs.

"Bring the ivory lutestring, Gibbs," her ladyship called impatiently.

Nannie, when presented later with the clothing, looked disapproving. She accepted six dresses and a cloak from the reluctant Gibbs and carried them to her young mistress.

Carolina was bedazzled.

"For me? Such magnificence?"

"That's yet to be seen," responded Nannie. "Let us try them on and see."

Two morning dresses, with alterations, would do nicely. They were soiled about the hems, but since Carolina was shorter than her aunt, Nannie was confident she could cut away the offending parts. Three party frocks posed more of a problem, as they were entirely too sophisticated for a debutante. Swathed in green silk, Carolina contemplated herself in a long mirror.

"Oh, Nannie," she sighed, "Papa would be shocked."

Hesitantly, Nannie reminded her that London fashions were considerably more daring than country ones.

Carolina shook her head. "I couldn't appear in this. It is kind of my aunt, but I should feel indecent. What can I do?"

Nannie patted her bracingly.

"Leave it to me, missy," she said. "Many's the dresses I stitched for your mama. Yes, and for her ladyship too. I will remake these. See. The primrose has a rent panel. I can remove that section—it's too full for you anyway—and there ought to be enough fabric in the torn part to reshape the bodice. Do not be troubled, missy. You'll go out indecent over Nannie's dead body."

"How good you are!" cried Carolina, giving her a hug.

"Fiddle-faddle," objected Nannie. But she accepted the embrace, twitched her nose, and reached for the sixth dress, which was of heavy grey silk. "Now this will not become you, miss. With your permission, I will return it to Gibbs. For her own use, you understand. A thank you, so to speak."

Since Carolina had no knowledge of the etiquette of dressers, she was grateful for Nannie's guidance and agreed immediately. Thus Gibbs was rewarded for her tolerance by receiving the very gown she coveted most.

While Lady Tufton congratulated herself on garbing her niece without the expenditure of a farthing, Nannie embarked on a sewing orgy. Carolina wished briefly for Susan's clever fingers, but when she saw Nannie's first recreation she was able, she discovered, to anticipate a stunning wardrobe. Long acquainted with hand-me-downs, and having at that moment in her possession a gown of her mama's and another of Susan's, she was not the least reluctant to accept her aunt's elegant cast-offs.

Lord Tufton remained serenely unaware that his orders had been thus economically bent.

The viscount was so gratified by the prompt arrival of Carolina's voucher to attend the assemblies at Almack's that he stunned and disconcerted his wife by announcing he would accompany the ladies for Miss Weldon's first appearance. Lady Tufton heard this with misgiving; an attentive husband was certain to cramp the style of an Incomparable. She tried to dissuade him, but his lordship, having made up his mind that Miss Weldon must not be allowed to hold up the wall and that he would himself lead her out in her first figure, remained adamant. While Lady Tufton was promising herself that no one should impose on *her,* her husband was resolving to lend their niece every possible support.

Accordingly, when Miss Weldon came downstairs in an evening frock cleverly contrived by Nannie, Lord Tufton, himself elegant in evening attire, was waiting to assure her she looked charming. Lady Tufton's sea-green silk had been stripped of *diamante*-sparkled flounces, nipped at the waist and bosom, and draped discreetly about the neckline with excess inches trimmed from the bottom. Miss Weldon was in very good looks.

"You did not show me that gown," Lady Tufton said sharply.

"Oh, Aunt," cried Carolina with a small indulgent laugh, "do you not recognize your beautiful gown? Nannie has made it perfect for me, you see."

"What?" interrupted Lord Gilbert. "It was my understanding, Harriet, that you would purchase Carolina an appropriate frock."

Lady Tufton offered the hurried explanation that it had seemed a shame to waste a gown which would so enhance Carolina's green eyes. Her husband pursed his lips disapprovingly, but said nothing further except, "Let us be on our way."

In the carriage Miss Weldon rode with happy anticipation. At the same time, a few needles of apprehension pricked her, for her aunt had made it clear she would be the focus of many critical eyes—patronesses, matchmaking mamas, surfeited gentlemen. Lady Tufton was too preoccupied with her own social affairs to have encouragement to spare, and although Nannie and his lordship had fondly *said* she looked well, Miss Weldon suspected they would have said the same if she had spots and a squint.

When they came into the assembly rooms James Haverill, who had badgered Mr. Haverill into coming early so he could claim Miss Weldon's first dance, began to make his way toward her. Neither he nor Lord Tufton, however, was privileged to lead her out, for no sooner had she made curt-sies to the patronesses than a young lieutenant in splendid Life Guards uniform sought her for the figure just forming, and she went off with him, chatting easily as though, James thought, she had known him all her life.

So she had. The officer was Rob Luce, second son of Sir John and Lady Luce, and an old friend.

"A good beginning," said Lord Tufton with satisfaction.

"That will never come to anything," said Harriet. "Sir John will never approve the connection even if Robert is not his heir."

"We are not at the altar yet, Harriet," reminded Lord Tufton. "Do allow the child a friend!"

He then sought amusement in a card room and Lady Tufton was spared the humiliation of having to join the dowagers around the wall by a gentleman's coming up to ask her to dance. Across the room she could see Mr. Haverill and she sent him an encouraging glance, but he did not appear to catch it, so she turned her attention to her partner and became very gay—as well as very beautiful.

It was some time before James was able to approach Miss Weldon. Like the kind and affectionate friend he was, Rob Luce was pleased to present as partners several of his comrades-in-arms, jolly young men who liked green eyes and who delighted in frivolous conversation with a pretty girl.

Miss Weldon was glowing with pleasure when James at last led her into a set. Success was not an experience new to her, for the small balls and routs of county society had already established her claims to masculine attention. Also, she had enjoyed nineteen years of Christian indoctrination into the evils of vanity. *Her* head was in no danger of being turned.

James Haverill, on the other hand, found his head was spinning. He might not be "hanging out for a wife," but for the first time in his life he was confronted with that powerful force called Competition. His admiration of Miss Weldon, together with disappointed intentions and diminished self-esteem, made him flushed and anxious.

Luckily, both lady and gentleman were accomplished dancers, moving easily and responsively about the room. In addition, Miss Weldon's manner was so serene and friendly that in a few turns James was able to relax and enjoy the dance.

"I had hoped," he said, "to have your first dance."

"Did you? How kind of you," said Miss Weldon. "But this music is so perfectly suited to our steps—is it not?—that *this* dance becomes special."

James found her opinion restorative. When he discovered bystanders admiring their performance, he was able to dismiss his chagrin.

"I had hoped to be of service to you," he persisted, still remembering his blasted scheme.

"Well, I thank you for the thought," responded Miss Weldon.

"I would like to do *some*thing," James declared. "Can you think of something? Slaying a dragon, perhaps? Or swimming the Eske River where ford there was none?"

At this point Miss Weldon's eyes fell upon a wan young lady against the wall. "Well . . . there *is*," she said.

James pressed for her commission.

"You can ask Miss Lessenover to dance."

Such a remarkable request nearly caused James Haverill to miss a beat. "I do not know any Miss Lessenover," he said.

"Yes, you do. You were presented to her two nights ago at Lady Heathwhite's drum." She smiled encouragingly. "It would give her so much pleasure."

As James had never heretofore considered the pleasure of a dancing partner versus his own, he was hard-pressed to reply.

"It is very painful, you see, to sit out when everyone else is dancing."

"Is it? By jove!" He looked without enthusiasm at the young lady Miss Weldon indicated, and reluctantly agreed.

The set ended and James returned Miss Weldon to Lady Tufton's side. The word of a Haverill being good, he then made his way to an astonished and grateful Miss Lessenover and secured her for the next dance. Miss Lessenover was no beauty. Being very musical, however, she had a splendid sense of rhythm and was able to perform well on the dance floor, and James discovered to his surprise that he was enjoying their dance. Miss Lessenover was painfully shy, but endeavored to respond when James addressed her. She said enough for James to discover that she possessed a melodious voice.

Afterwards, at the punch table when Mr. Haverill commented on his surprising choice of partners, James said, oh, well, she was a good sort of girl. A neat goer. Which Lawrence Haverill interpreted to mean Miss Lessenover danced well—not that she was horselike. "Musical voice too," he added, permitting, though not intending, Lawrence to think the girl a singer.

"It was all Miss Weldon's idea," James explained, "but I liked the lady after all."

"What do you mean, 'all Miss Weldon's idea?' " asked Mr. Haverill.

"Put me up to it. Said it's pretty beastly sitting out without a partner."

"I doubt," objected Mr. Haverill, "Miss Weldon has ever had such an unpleasant experience."

"No," agreed James. "Taking little creature, ain't she? Well, that's what she said. . . . Sensitive, I expect."

Mr. Haverill said, "Hm," to which James was not listening anyway. They parted company. After exchanging some words with Lady Jersey in the doorway of the ballroom, Mr. Haverill made his way to where Lady Tufton was seated with her niece.

He greeted both ladies and stood some minutes in civil conversation with Harriet, who laughed and used her fine eyes enticingly and open and shut her fan. Miss Weldon sat quietly listening to what she supposed was sophisticated flirting at its finest. She was expecting Mr. Haverill to ask her aunt to dance, so that she was dumbfounded at the first notes of music to have him hold out his hand to her and say: "May I have the pleasure, Miss Weldon?"

"It is a waltz, Haverill. Carolina is not approved," Lady Tufton interceded immediately.

"On the contrary, I have Lady Jersey's permission," Mr. Haverill replied firmly.

Lady Tufton's eyes flew across the room to discover Lady Jersey standing beside Lady Tufton's own husband. Sally Jersey nodded and smiled.

"You can't want to trouble with the child," Lady Tufton countered.

With a nuance Carolina did not understand, Mr. Haverill replied: "You know I do not do things unless I wish to, Lady Tufton." He drew Miss Weldon from her chair. "You have no objection, Miss Weldon?"

"Oh, no. Thank you . . . most kind." She had the sensation of a tempest brewing in low clouds behind her as they went onto the floor.

If the patronesses watched Miss Weldon critically, they found nothing exceptionable in her waltz. Lady Luce, that kind friend and leader of all society within ten miles of Dolden Overhill, had out of fondness for the vicar's daughter schooled her well in timing, steps, and decorum.

"A charming young lady," Sally Jersey said to Lord Tufton. "Too bad she has no money."

"Does not seem to keep the partners away," he answered.

"No," agreed Lady Jersey. "But life-partners are another matter."

The lady seated next to Lady Tufton was saying the same thing. Her ladyship, seething at the slight from Mr. Haverill, asked sharply the source of her information, and learned it was the lady's son, via James Haverill.

Lady Tufton, wondering how one secured a husband for a miss who was thought to be destitute, said piously that she intended to do her best for the girl. As her best consisted of accompanying a gentleman into the refreshment room and leaving Miss Weldon to fend for herself, the dowager said to the lady on her *other* side: "Handsome is as handsome does" and that lady, who had a homely daughter to fire off, agreed fervently.

The assembly rooms at Almack's were genteel and pleasing; they were far from magnificent. No one was critical of the fact, for every person of discrimination knew elegance was not to be confused with lavish display. Only those accepted by the patronesses were allowed to enter those hallowed portals. Inebriation was unknown there. Matchmaking mamas might safely bring their fledgling daughters; they did so eagerly. Why gentlemen cared to come where orgeat was the beverage and whist stakes were minimal remained a perpetual mystery.

Tonight Mr. Haverill was there because James coerced him, or so he would have James believe. Since he was generally known to be a close friend of Lord Tufton, his dancing with Tufton's niece caused scarcely a ripple. If onlookers could have heard his conversation with Miss Weldon, they might have been surprised.

"Miss Lessenover is a friend of yours?" he asked.

"A very new one," replied his partner. "I met her when Mr. Haverill did, at Lady Heathwhite's drum."

"Ah, James," murmured Mr. Haverill. "I believe you found it necessary to remind him of his manners."

Miss Weldon colored slightly. "I hope he did not think that! It was only that I wished Miss Lessenover to have as much pleasure as myself."

"Indeed?" said Mr. Haverill. His face was solemn, but a

twinkle could be detected in his eye. "I understood that you commanded—"

"Certainly not," cried Miss Weldon. "I did not—"

"Commanded," repeated Mr. Haverill firmly. The close approach of another couple at that point ended the conversation and Miss Weldon hoped the subject had died.

It had not. When a neat turn had gained them space, Mr. Haverill asked: "Do you command me likewise, Miss Weldon?"

She was indignant but unruffled. "It would be improper of me, sir."

"Nevertheless, I must not let James exceed me in civility, must I?" he asked.

"I cannot think he would ever do so," she responded, and raised her eyes to look at him challengingly.

In the carriage, going home, Lady Tufton remarked waspishly that one never *knew* with Haverill. "Very condescending to dance with Carolina."

"Did you find Haverill condescending, Carolina?" his lordship asked.

"Oh, no, sir. Very kind and easy," Caro replied.

"Well, he must have thought it a dead bore," said Lady Tufton.

"The other young gentlemen did not seem to," Lord Tufton pointed out. "Lawrence enjoyed it, I expect. And James too."

"Well, you cannot think it meant anything," objected his wife. "I saw them dancing with the Lessenover girl too."

"But our girl was the belle of the evening," said his lordship.

"Everyone was very kind. . . ." Caro ventured.

Lady Tufton now splashed cold water liberally: "I hope you will not set your sights too high. You will not be able to deceive anyone about your lack of dowry."

"I would never want to deceive anyone," Carolina said in a small voice.

"What are you saying, Harriet?" demanded his lordship. "Surely you cannot have been discussing Carolina's circumstances with anyone!"

Stung into defending a difficult position, Lady Tufton declared Mrs. Pettigrew had talked to *her,* and after all, everyone knew the situation.

Lord Tufton said depressingly that he was not acquainted with any Mrs. Pettigrew. His tone implied he did not wish for the acquaintance. "How could she know anything?" he asked.

"Very simply," snapped Harriet. "James Haverill has been pleased to tell young Pettigrew that our niece is an impoverished country parson's daughter. Very likely he has told *every*one."

Shocked and hurt, Carolina shrank unspeaking into her corner of the carriage. She had looked upon James Haverill as a friend; she could not credit he would speak demeaningly of her (even if it was the truth). To her astonishment, she heard her uncle chuckle.

"So that is it!" he said. "Mrs. Pettigrew is a fool. James makes his admiration of Carolina quite obvious. Would he malign her? Never! Besides, he is a gentleman. Depend upon it, James dropped something casually to discourage competition from this young Pettigrew. Did you meet Pettigrew, child?"

"Yes, sir," whispered Carolina.

"There. You see? Must expect Haverill to defend his interests. Pettigrew a pretty fellow? Dandy, eh?"

"Yes, sir."

"Well, then. No doubt James was defending you as well as himself. Harriet, you will have to choose your friends more cautiously."

Lady Tufton angrily denied any friendship with the Pettigrews.

"But you cannot ignore the fact that Carolina is a vicar's daughter," she insisted.

"Why should I?" he responded. "The patronesses know. *They* do not condemn her. Good God, Harriet. Such a tempest over nothing! Half the people at Almack's must know Charles Weldon personally. And Lydia too. Carolina has nothing to blush for!"

Carolina's heart was overflowing with gratitude to her forthright uncle.

"But it is true, sir," she said tremblingly. "I haven't any money."

"Who is to know that?"

"Anyone might guess," said Lady Tufton.

"Obsession with money," replied the viscount, "is uncouth." Which reduced his wife to seething silence.

It was not Lord Tufton's nature or habit to quarrel with his wife. Tonight, however, faulting her on two counts, he sent Carolina to bed and invited his wife into his study with a flat, "A word with you, Harriet, if you please."

Indignant, and a little alarmed, yet managing to look supremely beautiful and desirable, Harriet went as bid, and his lordship closed the door.

Miss Weldon climbed to her room with no interest or knowledge about what was passing below. Papa *never* upbraided Mama, so she had no understanding of the Words with which husbands were obliged to secure peace and obedience from spoiled beauties.

Her thoughts, her emotions were absorbed by the questionable behavior of James Haverill. *Had* he spoken slightingly of Papa? Had he ridiculed her poverty? Already Carolina was learning to discount much that her aunt said in her stinging moods. James was so open—so amiable—so admiring. She wished to think her uncle's interpretation was correct. And there was the matter of James's cousin. *He* was a man of experience. He would notice the shabbiness of her home and the unworldliness of her parent. *He* had not spurned the Weldons. It was true Mr. Haverill watched over James as a guardian might, but had he not brought James to call? And had he not danced with the vicar's daughter *himself*?

Downstairs the interview between Lord and Lady Tufton proceeded without gunfire. It was not so alarming as supposed by one, nor as chastening as intended by the other.

Lord Tufton did not berate his wife for her errors. He assumed that she recognized the unbecomingness of her attitude. He therefore addressed himself to making it plain Carolina would be treated as a daughter of the house.

Thankful to escape a frightful scolding, Harriet looked up at him beguilingly through her lashes and murmured, of course, whatever Gilly wished. Then she sighed artistically and asked, "I wonder if you realize how young and uncertain I feel to act the part of a chaperone?"

"I do, Harriet," he answered kindly, adding with classic male density, "But you ought to enjoy the companionship of such a charming young lady. You ought to have much in common."

Harriet gritted her teeth, smiled gently, and allowed that Carolina was most agreeable.

"The thing is," she confided alluringly, "all these young men—these young beaux—are so *callow*. I find them dull compared with real men."

His lordship, who was ten years her senior, recognized the strategy, but was not secure against it.

"Well, small matter. It is only for a few weeks. Your sister will be grateful for kindness to her child. I, too, will be grateful."

Having some hope, now, of her ruby necklace, Harriet glowed upon him and presented her cheek for his kiss.

Although his lordship's anger and disgust had been subdued, he felt singularly unloving. He coolly kissed her cheek and her hand and bowed her from the room.

Five

The assemblies at Almack's were dignified affairs; the jaded might even say insipid. Nothing, at any rate, to exhaust a healthy young lady, even though she might dance every dance. Yet the cup of chocolate which Nannie brought quietly was cold beside Miss Weldon's bed when she awoke. The heartache of James's callous behavior, which had kept her sleepless so long, came rushing upon her when she opened her eyes. It was Nannie's re-entry with fresh chocolate and apologies that finally drew her attention to the hour.

"Were you sleeping, miss? That is lucky, for all is sixes and sevens belowstairs."

Carolina sat up, accepted the cup, and allowed Nannie to wrap a shawl about her shoulders.

"Is something wrong?" she asked.

Nannie folded her hands under her apron and announced with satisfaction: "Everything."

It sounded very familiar—as though Annie's stove were smoking or Jem had dropped the pail of fresh milk.

"Ominous," said Miss Weldon. "Better tell the whole."

"Well," related Nannie, "Bigelow cut his hand on a broken glass—not deeply, you know—but very bloody which made the scullery maid (silly chit) quite hysterical, and *that*—or so Cook says—is why his lordship's porridge is lumpy. Very humiliating for Cook, you see, although likely his lordship won't complain, being such a kind gentleman.

Cook is That Upset, and Mrs. Moffett has been laid on her bed the whole time with a Tooth."

Halfway through this discourse Miss Weldon was coming from her bed, personal anxieties driven to Outer Mongolia. It was clear that Nannie, best of nannies, could not cope with a household crisis (or did not wish to), and Miss Weldon (who *could* and whose talents were atrophying without exercise) rejoiced to feel useful.

She demanded a dressing gown and astonished Nannie, who trailed protestingly behind, by descending immediately to Bigelow's pantry where he was discovered holding a gory napkin to his hand as he directed a footman in the collection of glass fragments. The high-pitched lament of the sensitive scullery maid rose up the kitchen stairwell, punctuated by vituperation from Cook.

Bigelow, both shocked and gratified by Miss Weldon's interest in his wound, insisted it was a mere scratch, even though his blood was spattered on the floor.

"I will see for myself," she said firmly.

Expecting to have a beautiful young lady drop fainting at their feet, Bigelow, Nannie, and the gaping footman watched with awe as Miss Weldon drew aside the napkin, examined the cut carefully, and risked contamination of her pretty little hand by pressing the napkin back into place when fresh blood welled up.

"I do not believe there are any glass particles remaining," she opined.

Nannie recovered her voice now and began to expostulate on the advisability of protecting a young lady's sensibilities. "No sight for you, missy. No sight at all," she declared.

"Well, I have seen it now," Miss Weldon answered calmly. "Please fetch some linen, Nannie."

Peace settled on the pantry with Nannie's grumbling departure. The footman, who knew better than to open *his* mouth in such exalted company, resumed sweeping with increased vigor.

"While Nannie is finding what we need, I will have a word below," Miss Weldon said.

Bigelow nodded mutely, as Miss Weldon caught up her dressing gown and continued to the kitchen.

At the unprecedented appearance of a lady in their territory both Cook and maid were struck dumb. Hostilities ceased. The servants drew closer to each other. But the young lady, whom neither had seen before, and about whom both had heard much, was actually smiling!

With superb inspiration she announced: "All is well."

If she said so, it must be so. They relaxed visibly—although the lumpy porridge sat irrefutably on the range.

"Now, my girl, what is your name?"

The scullery maid wiped her sniffly nose and owned to the dignity of "Marlene."

"Marlene? Very pretty," said Miss Weldon. "Would you be so kind, Marlene, as to go to the storeroom and count the jars of preserves?"

Marlene gaped. She had never in her life been asked to be so kind as to draw a breath. "Preserves, miss? *Count* them?"

"Yes," affirmed that amazing young lady. "I would like to know the exact number of each sort."

"Yes, miss." Marlene bobbed an abbreviated curtsy and fled, mumbling, "There is strawberry, I know, and gooseberry. . . ."

Cook eyed Miss Weldon with respect. A decided twinkle could be detected in Miss Weldon's eye as she said, "That should take some time, I think."

"That it should," agreed Cook.

"Then we can forget about porridge for his lordship. The delicious meals you have prepared during my visit give me every confidence that you will think of something better."

"Certainly, miss." Buttered and roasted to tenderness by one adroit sentence, Cook swelled like a plump capon.

As Miss Weldon retreated upstairs she could hear pots

dancing energetically while Cook rendered *This is the Day That The Lord Hath Made* largely, and rather well.

Nannie had brought Basilicum powder and lint, as well as linen, and was awaiting Miss Weldon's instructions.

"Do not be alarmed, Bigelow," said Miss Weldon. "I have helped the apothecary many times to bandage village children, not to mention my brother and sisters." She then proceeded to tie him up neatly.

"Like a proper midwife," reported the interested footman afterwards, and his hearers understood that approbation was intended, though Miss Weldon would have shuddered at the comparison.

If Nannie was surprised to see a young lady one third her age deal competently with several crises, she concealed it. Since Order had been established, however, she returned to her admonitions, saying his lordship would soon be down and would not be pleased to discover his niece entertaining the servants in her negligé.

Bigelow, to whom Miss Weldon now resembled a ministering angel, defended her hotly, announcing she was a Real Lady Who Could Do No Wrong.

Miss Weldon rewarded him with a beatific smile. Then she yielded to Nannie's entreaties and went upstairs to dress. Mrs. Moffett remained to be dealt with. She, Carolina thought, would expect more formality. Her superior position would demand a greater (though not more kindly) condescension.

Nannie was just buttoning the last of tiny pearl buttons down Caro's back, when a timid knock sounded and Marlene bobbed in the doorway.

"If you please, mum, it's forty-seven."

With some effort Carolina kept her face composed. "Thank you, Marlene. Does pantry-work interest you?"

"Well, yes, mum. That is, it doesn't intrist me heggsactly. Better than slops and swills, though, if you take me meaning."

Both Miss Weldon and Nannie took her meaning very well, and Nannie was scandalized. She opened her mouth to blast such plain-speaking from one at the bottom of the service ladder, but a signal from her young mistress muffled the words.

"There's twelve strawberry, an' eleven blackberry," Marlene continued relentlessly. "Only seven cherry, but Cook says that's on account it's his lordship's favorite and we can't keep it *in*. And the gooseberry—"

"Stop!" protested Miss Weldon. "I cannot keep it all in my head. Suppose you—suppose you find Lord Tufton's secretary and ask him to write it down."

"Yes, mum." Marlene bobbed again and vanished.

"Well, I never!" declared Nannie. "What rubbish was that?"

Carolina chuckled. "Not rubbish. Preserves."

She went out the door and along the corridor to Mrs. Moffett's suite.

Mrs. Moffett was not, as reported, laid upon her bed. She—poor soul—was walking the floor with swollen face and glassy eye.

"Mrs. Moffett! You are suffering!" cried Carolina, drawing her to the light of a window.

The woman could not deny it.

"Open your mouth," said Miss Weldon.

"Oh, no!" gasped Mrs. Moffett. "It wouldn't be seemly."

Papa's daughter had learned to be firm with villagers.

"Open," she commanded, and explained: "I have whisked out a lot of baby teeth. Always such a relief to the little tots—especially when they are abcessed. I am sorry, Mrs. Moffett, but your gum is very inflamed. I am afraid you will have to have the tooth drawn."

The housekeeper groaned.

"Lord Tufton will tell us the best man. Can you tidy your hair? Do not worry. I will go with you."

While Carolina was ministering to the anguished woman, his lordship had sat down to breakfast.

"What is this?" he asked in some surprise as Bigelow's bandaged hand set a dish before him.

"An omelet, my lord. Miss Weldon ordered it for you, I believe."

"Omelet?" said his lordship, regarding with interest the golden mound from which mushrooms and cheese oozed seductively. "Miss Weldon?"

"There was an Accident, my lord," Bigelow reported. "And some Confusion, due to Mrs. Moffett's being laid on her bed with a Tooth. Miss Weldon arranged matters for us."

"Did, eh? This looks very good."

His lordship had just cut into the omelet when Miss Weldon came purposefully into the room.

"Poor Mrs. Moffett," she said immediately. "Such a bad tooth. Oh, do eat while your breakfast is hot, sir. I only came to ask if I might order out the carriage to take us to the dentist."

"Carriage? Us? Dentist?" Lord Tufton abandoned his food reluctantly.

"Do eat, Uncle! Mrs. Moffett is in such pain, sir, and I think the tooth must be drawn. Of course I must go with her."

"Why must you? Send one of the maids, child."

"But I promised."

The viscount shook his head ruefully. "A slim creature like you support that Valkyrie? What is needed is a man."

"Yes, to be sure," agreed Carolina. "That would be better. Oh, would you, Uncle? How thoughtful of you! You will know the proper man to take us to—one who will accord *your* housekeeper every attention"

His lordship avoided Bigelow's eye.

"Very well," he said heavily.

"If I may suggest, sir," ventured Bigelow. "Brandy."

"Brandy? Oh, yes, certainly. Brandy. Just the thing."

Bigelow's imperative hand dispatched a footman to the cellar, during which interlude Lord Tufton was allowed to finish his breakfast and gulp a cup of coffee. Soon thereafter he found himself shut behind the crest of Tufton with an earnest young lady and a large, semi-inebriated housekeeper who leaned on him heavily throughout the whole ordeal.

When the awful deed had been done and the agonizing pressure of the abcess relieved, Mrs. Moffett was able to pour out her gratitude to the Sweet Little Miss and the Kind Gentleman. Then she tottered to her room where additional brandy put her to sleep for the rest of the day.

Miss Weldon next conferred with Bigelow. Although a dozen guests were expected that evening, menu, seating, setting, and wines were settled between them before Lady Tufton appeared from her boudoir.

Meanwhile his lordship lost no time in escaping to his club where he regaled Mr. Haverill and another gentleman with all the finer details of the morning. He shook his head over the affair, but was obviously very pleased with his Little Puss. If the gentlemen thought he sounded doting, they were generous enough not to say so. Later in the afternoon Mr. Lawrence Haverill and Mr. James Haverill called upon the ladies. Neither mentioned the events of the morning, James because of not knowing, Mr. Haverill out of caution.

As he exchanged pleasantries with Lady Tufton, Mr. Haverill looked with some interest at Miss Weldon where she sat surrounded by James and two other young sprigs who had also come to call. When he somewhat reconciled in his mind the demure miss one *saw* with the heroine Gilly had described, he detached himself gracefully and made his way to Gilly's study. Here Gilly welcomed him, repeated his adventure, and added the information that Bigelow reported a smashing-fine dinner had been arranged (by Carolina) to climax the trying day. Because he saw no connection, he did not report the perplexing list of jams and jellies which had been furnished him by his secretary.

Perhaps Lady Tufton was learning to appreciate callow swains whose ages were not far from her own. At any rate, when Mr. Haverill had decamped she changed seats and made herself agreeable to James, Rob Luce, and Rob's fresh-faced friend.

The three gentlemen were comely and exuberant. Lady Tufton might be pardoned for classifying them as friendly pups. If she thought this, she hid it well, so that Carolina, who had seen many faces on her aunt, discovered yet another, and thereby a clue to her allure. She smiled and teased and was as light-hearted as carefree young men could wish.

"Your aunt is charming," whispered Rob's friend. "I declare I could easily fall in love with her myself."

Fortunately, Carolina had been long enough on the town to know such falling in love was empty sentiment. She did not think the young man was in any danger of a crushing passion, even though he remembered from time to time to cast soulful looks upon her ladyship.

Presently Lord Tufton came in with Mr. Haverill who extracted James from the merry group and took him away. The other gentlemen soon followed suit.

In the ensuing lull Lord Tufton warmed his back before the fire and regarded his wife thoughtfully.

"Lawrence asked if we plan a ball for Carolina," he said finally.

"A ball!" cried Lady Tufton. "What a shocking extravagance!" Her amiability could almost be seen peeling from her in sheets. Only that morning she had made the mistake of rushing her fences. She had asked for the ruby necklace and been refused. It was the first time such had happened, and Lady Tufton laid the blame upon her niece.

Actually, she was not far wrong. Carolina knew nothing of rubies and would have thought them a wicked substitute for education (Cedric's). She had not interfered, or even thought of doing so. However, her sweet temper and undemanding nature presented his lordship with an awful comparison.

To make matters worse, Carolina now blurted: "Oh, no! You have been so generous! I could not bear to accept more when Cedric needs—"

Lady Tufton ground her teeth and snapped, "Cedric's education is his father's responsibility," thereby alerting her husband to a need which she had heretofore skillfully concealed.

The fat was in the fire. A disconnected discussion followed during which his lordship probed the depths of Cedric's finances at the same time Carolina earnestly declared her gratitude for cast-off clothing and minor social whirl. Lady Tufton was extremely angry at her own slip and therefore even angrier at Carolina, who stood, all unknowing, between her and the jewels she craved. She found herself arguing from several diverse positions and was finally led into proposing alternate parties in an attempt to turn her husband's thoughts.

Lord Gilly was mild and kind, but he was not a feather cushion. He had a keen mind. What was more, he had a generous heart which, though in thrall to his beautiful wife, was large enough to embrace others than himself and Harriet. It was all very well to bear an old title, to enjoy the elegant fineries of life, but deep within that heart of his lurked a wistful longing for the sort of home Charles Weldon maintained in Dolden Overhill. A home where prestige did not matter, where wife labored side by side with husband, where a sister put her brother's interests before her own.

"Enough is enough," he said. "I have decided we will give Carolina a ball. If you do not wish to arrange it, Harriet, I will have my secretary do so."

What he did not say was that Lawrence Haverill had offered to give one.

"For Carolina?" Lady Tufton had exclaimed. "You know it would not be proper!"

"True enough," Mr. Haverill agreed. "I had in mind a ball for—er—one of my nieces—or James's sister who should be old enough by now, though James has all the family looks and Miss Weldon would ruin her evening by outshining her."

No, Gilly had responded, any ball would be his undertaking.

Lady Tufton, seeing she had been out-generaled, now raised her favorite complaint: "But we have no ballroom."

"We have a very large drawing room which will do perfectly if some furniture is removed," his lordship responded. "Carolina, my dear, you will write to Cedric at once and ask him to come. You will want him with you for your ball, and we shall take the opportunity to know him."

"Oh, but you must not—Cedric must not—" she protested.

"But I must," he said, patting her cheek. "Bigelow has been expecting it."

Carolina inhaled with a small gasp. "The servants! Oh, what a burden for them!"

"Burden? They will enjoy it! You will see."

Lady Tufton said suddenly, "I shall need a new gown."

"Certainly, my dear," he agreed. "And Carolina also. I shall choose hers myself."

Harriet's eyes flicked, but she said silkily, "I wish you would choose mine too, Gilly."

He replied that he would. "I wager James will want your first dance, Carolina," he added complacently.

"If Lord Dooly does not ask before him," said her ladyship.

Carolina blushed rosily and said she rather expected her *host* to lead her out.

Lord Tufton chuckled in appreciation. "Aye! He may. He may. Indeed, shall we count it settled?"

Since the arrangement sounded dull to Harriet, she raised no objection. The following morning saw her restored to good temper by the receipt of a note from Mr. Haverill's secretary. The presence of herself, Lord Tufton, and Miss Weldon was graciously requested for dinner a week thence.

Carolina took breakfast in the nursery again, at which time Master Roddy explained the necessity of chimney sweeps and related a story about a shower of Black Snow on the nursery floor the last time a boy climbed the flue.

Between black snow and a visit from Caro, Master Hugh lost all appetite. His porridge sat cooling (though smoother than velvet) until Caro explained that a visit to the stable could not be made on an empty stomach.

An observer might have said four children went out to the stable, for Betty was only fifteen and combined affection for wee furry creatures with reverential awe for John Coachman. Miss Weldon, her hair tied back with a green ribbon and her face glowing with animation, looked scarcely older.

The boys romped ahead, hopping and skipping with excitement.

"Come on, Caro," cried Hugh.

Roddy said, "Pokey Betty!" But he smiled beguilingly and Betty was not offended.

Either John Coachman was expecting them or he kept a vigil, for he met them at the garden door and conveyed them to the stall his cat had appropriated for her nursery, an adroit manner allowing him to bring up the rear with Betty. Miss Weldon and her cousins immediately fell to their knees in the straw to fondle the infants.

Betty did not warn Miss Weldon about soiling her dress, because she had done so the first time and had been silenced with an impatient, though kindly, "Fustian!"

That Betty's interests were not entirely in cats became marked when Lady Franklin's man who must have had an ear cocked strolled casually into the stable and engaged Betty in discreet banter. John Coachman did his duty by

Family, but it was plain his attention was upon Betty's blushes.

In any case Betty said little, and Miss Weldon clearly saw *her* duty to distract the younger gentlemen of the party. It was better than a novel (of which she had only read one or two—surreptitiously lent by Lady Luce) to see the courting of Betty by two men who were otherwise friends, and whose style was an interesting blend of directness and subtlety. Betty, showing a radiance that was not visible in Lady Tufton's drawing room, appeared to encourage neither, which had the effect of encouraging both. Miss Weldon was fascinated. She thought the ladies of the Upper Orders could well take lessons from the Lower. And, she told herself, Lord Dooly could learn a lot of address from the coachmen! Even their clothing, their magnificent livery, was more dazzling than the best regalia of a Bond Street Beau.

Somewhat wistfully Miss Weldon reflected that a lady of quality could not enjoy the same flirtation as her maid. There was dalliance enough, but the romantic exchange between ladies and gentlemen (at least in London society) seemed fraught with practicality—titles bartered for wealth, beauty for power. Even without her papa's admonitions, Miss Weldon knew she could not enter into matrimony with any man whose sole concern was to add a branch to the family tree, or to bolster his own sagging ego by attaching an ornamental wife. The Bettys of the world were better off than she!

Miss Weldon knew, of course, that marriage was not easily financed by the serving classes, and that their hours were utterly dependent upon the whims and needs of their employers. Only now she focused upon admiration of Betty's Bettiness, and her thoughts were so muddled that she did not realize that the vicar's daughter might be valued for her uncalculating self.

Master Roddy was in raptures over the kittens, taking up first one and then another, demanding which Caro thought prettiest and suggesting various names as though they were his cats and not John Coachman's. Master Hugh, who thought creatures that purred in addition to mewing were worthier of his attention, pursued Mother Cat around the stall until he captured her, and clutched her to his chest from which disadvantaged point she cast beseeching looks at the adults but submitted in the understanding way animals have with children.

Betty remained neat as a daisy in spring, while Miss Weldon and the children soiled themselves shockingly with straw and hairs of black, white, and orange. All occupants of the stable including the horses might have remained contented for the entire morning had not Lady Tufton ordered out her carriage and brought all to awareness of their obligations, so that they hastily dispersed.

When Carolina went in to her aunt's boudoir to see if she were wanted on the projected outing, she found Lady Franklin sitting with her, watching preparations for a foray to the stylish shops of town.

Carolina curtsied prettily and greeted Lady Franklin with unfeigned pleasure which Lady Tufton soon dampened by exclaiming: "Good God, child! Your gown! What will her ladyship think?"

Remembering, then, her mussed and littered frock, Carolina gasped in dismay and brushed ineffectually at the front of her skirt until Lady Tufton said, "No, no. Not straw on my carpet, please! Ask Lady Franklin to excuse you, miss."

Carolina stammered apologies, but Lady Franklin said no sensible lady visited a stable wearing a ball dress and that she was sure young gentlemen of six and three had no inclinations to formality.

Lady Tufton nodded agreement. "Very true. My boudoir is not a stable, however. You may go, Carolina. I will not be needing you."

Carolina curtsied and went hastily from the room.

"Are you trying to break her spirit?" Lady Franklin asked.

Lady Tufton looked taken aback. "Not at all. I concern myself only with deportment."

"Of a servant? That is how you speak to her, you know."

There were not many who would dare to speak so critically to the Viscountess Tufton. She did not like it at all.

"Beauty is as beauty does. I mean, beauty does not excuse everything," she said, wanting to defy Lady Franklin without offending her.

"Indeed," said her ladyship pointedly, "I am glad you understand that."

She then suddenly recollected an appointment which would prevent her accompanying Harriet to the shops and departed.

Lady Tufton found herself reduced to taking her maid or waiting for Carolina to dress. Being impatient with people, the day, the room, and the hour—though never with herself—she summoned her maid and set off crossly to find solace in a straw bonnet lined with celestial blue silk and ornamented with curls of blue ribbon.

Six

Carolina's letter to Cedric became, after she had given the matter some thought, a letter to her parents with fond messages to her brother. The invitation for Cedric to attend the prospective ball at Tufton House was simply set forth. As Lord Tufton said, she would enjoy having Cedric with her for the event. Carolina nibbled her pen. "Our uncle wishes to become acquainted with Cedric," she wrote. "I believe he means to do something helpful about his education. He is a very kind and generous man." The ink on that had long dried when she added, under some compunction to speak favorably about Lady Tufton, "My aunt is very beautiful. She is invited everywhere."

Feeling closer through writing and at the same time farther away and therefore a tiny bit homesick, she reassured her loved ones (and herself) by praising Nannie and saying what a comfort and help she was. The vicar and his wife exchanged wry smiles when they received this missive. They read a great deal more from it than Carolina wrote, and sent Cedric off at once to join her.

Mr. Weldon was hesitant to accept funds from his brother-in-law, but having long preached that it was more blessed to give than to receive was obliged by necessity to receive aid and let his kinsman enjoy, his proper blessings. Mrs. Weldon said, "Thank you, Lord," and entrusted her son with her pearls (which were a wedding gift from Papa) for Caro to wear at the ball.

Lord Tufton was so enjoying himself with a foster daughter that his ideas grew larger and larger. It was well Harriet did not know. In addition to a ball dress, he intended to choose a necklace as his particular debut present to Caro. When Lydia Weldon's pearls arrived he realized at once that both Lydia's and Carolina's sentiments required the wearing of them, so he contented himself with buying a pretty pair of pearl earrings with small diamonds glistening at the ends. For his wife he chose a dress of sapphire with demi-train and deep cut neckline; it was sure to please Lady Tufton for there were unmistakable signs she and Madam Celeste had already agreed upon it.

Neither Madam Celeste nor Lady Tufton had any say-so in Carolina's dress. A Mrs. Holder, known to London's most charmingly garbed ladies, though not patronized by the dashers, was his choice of modiste, and between them they composed an exquisite garment of spider gauze with raindrops of seed pearl over a satin underdress. Mrs. Holder was heard to say several times that *white* was customary for young ladies making their debuts, but his lordship, whose taste was excellent, and who was vindicated by the results, approved white gauze but insisted on shell-pink satin for the underdress. Since he talked happily and openly about his choices to Lawrence Haverill, James had no difficulty in planning a suitable bouquet of pink rose buds in a silver holder to send Miss Weldon.

Lord Dooly also made up his mind to "do something" for Miss Weldon, and as his consequence required something large, he sent to his greenhouses in Hampshire for an immense basket of orchids. His gardener came close to tears over cutting them, but who was to know or care for that?

The arrival of Cedric Weldon had a singular impact on Tufton House. Lady Tufton awaited his coming with mounting indignation, only to be completely won in less than a day by his pleasing person and sweetness of temper.

Cedric had the felicity of being nurtured by a wise and

godly father, a fond mother, and four adoring sisters—not to mention Annie, who knew he was a Prince in Disguise—Sir John who admired his accuracy with a shotgun (taught along with the Luce boys by Sir John himself), Lady Luce, whose affection for Lydia Weldon overflowed to all her family, and all the females of the village who naturally could not resist the combination of beauty and amiability in a young gentleman. The miracle was that he was not spoiled. Not at all. Because everyone had always dealt kindly with him he simply and whole-heartedly believed that *everyone* was a good fellow.

When he saw the glamorous Lady Tufton resembling his Mama, he knew she must be nice and—she was! To him (at least) she was consistently charming. She could no more resist his appeal than could the ladies of Dolden Overhill. Mr. and Mrs. Weldon's earnest explanation of Caro's "difficult situation" faded from his mind. He detected no flaw in Lady Tufton, and naturally Carolina said nothing to disillusion him. She saw almost as little evil in her fellow man as Cedric did, which is why her aunt perplexed her mightily.

No one would replace Carolina in Lord Tufton's affections, but he was extremely pleased with Cedric and soon resolved to see him through Oxford. There remained only Master Roddy and Master Hugh to be cajoled. They were uncritical gentlemen. When he had made for them his funny little drawings that the family chuckled over—little sketches of Tabby Four Toes dozing on the vicar's lap, a malevolent badger peeking from his hole, and the goat chasing Annie about the kitchen garden—they received him joyfully into the Stable Club, introduced him to John Coachman, and generally prepared to worship this new cousin almost as much as they did Caro.

"He's a pretty fellow," James opined to Mr. Haverill after meeting Cedric, "but a Right One. I like him." He was quite willing to take Cedric about—to Jackson's Boxing Saloon, to gaming hells, and to the opera where Cedric could look his fill at pretty ladybirds.

None of these things appealed to Cedric. He saw nothing scientific in the science of pugilism, had been raised with a thorough understanding of hell (any sort), and thought no opera dancer could be as pretty as his aunt. What he wanted, if James didn't mind, was to see the Royal Academy.

"A museum!" James exclaimed. Then the thought occurred to him that the museum was a suitable place to take Carolina, and he immediately said, "Oh, the museum. To be sure. Miss Weldon will like that. Of course I will take you. Lawrence will lend me his landau. Not the bays, you understand, but another team. Paltry city horses with no nerves, but you will not regard that, I expect."

Cedric assured him he would not. They set a day.

It may be that Lady Tufton was right. The Haverills would not countenance a match between James and Miss Weldon. At any rate, in his familiar role of guardian, Mr. Haverill said he would join the museum party and that naturally they would use his bays. James accepted the alteration good-humoredly, for he had not read Mr. Haverill's mind or Lady Tufton's, and he liked his cousin excessively. Since neither lady was consulted, Harriet did not insinuate herself into the group, and Miss Weldon proceeded to make plans of her own for the specified day.

Each gentleman, it seemed, had counted on another to arrange matters with Miss Weldon, with the result that the outing was planned without its ornament being aware.

Roddy had imparted to Caro most glowing reports of the menagerie at Exeter 'Change and the wild animals to be seen there. It sounded interesting, but mostly she was motivated by Roddy's burning desire when she said of course they must go there, and she approached her uncle to take them.

With powerful memories of the dental jaunt arranged by his niece, Lord Tufton would have liked to say no. However, as his friends had noticed, he had become dotingly fond of her, and since she seemed always to ask for someone else's need or pleasure, he found it difficult to refuse. When she pointed out it was a splendid opportunity for him to enjoy the company of his sons, he capitulated. The viscountess, informed of this scheme, said only, "What a bore!" and declined to be one of the group.

Thus it was, when the Misters Haverill arrived to take up Miss and Mr. Weldon, they found Miss Weldon waiting in the hallway with her uncle and her cousins for Lord Tufton's coach to be brought around. Cedric came downstairs, dismay written on his face as James expostulated with Miss Weldon.

"We were counting on you!"

Miss Weldon was very sorry, she would have enjoyed seeing the Royal Academy about which Papa had told her so much and about which she had read. Hugh pressed himself anxiously against her as Lord Tufton offered to continue with the children while she joined the other group. Miss Weldon's cheeks grew quite pink. She patted Hugh reassuringly. She was very sorry, but she had *promised*.

Mr. Haverill, who had been a silent onlooker, was interested to see the strength of vicarage principles. He said smoothly: "Surely no one will be disappointed if today we visit the 'Change and tomorrow the museum. Promises must be kept. The children will enjoy the animals. Remember, James?"

"Lord, yes," said James. "It is ripping. I shan't mind going again. You will like it, Cedric."

Mr. Haverill glanced at his friend. "Gilly and I are not too jaded for—er—lions, are we?"

Lord Tufton smiled. "No, no. I live with two monkeys, don't I?"

Roddy and Hugh squealed, and Miss Weldon bestowed on Mr. Haverill a grateful smile, the beauty of which he found more valuable reward than words would have been.

"Tomorrow," continued that gentleman calmly, "I will

contract to take Miss Weldon and Cedric to the Academy at Somerset House."

"Well, I shan't mind that either," James assured them. "I said I'd go, and I will."

In no time at all, Miss Weldon had been handed into the seat next to Mr. Haverill with Lord Gilly and the boys facing them. James and Cedric climbed to the box, where James received the reins from Haverill's reluctant coachman. The horses danced a bit, then went off smartly, as Haverill's man swung up behind. At the slow pace of city traffic James managed the team without difficulty.

"Why ever do you want to visit the museum?" James asked Cedric.

"For the paintings," Cedric said.

"Such mouldy old things? I would rather see a fellow splashing on paint."

"Oh, yes," agreed Cedric. "I would like that best of all, only I've never known a painter."

"Well, it's easy enough to arrange," asserted James. "My brother—the baby one—is being done. His portrait, I mean. When my mother cannot take him for sittings she sends me along to see he behaves himself. You are welcome to go any time."

Evidently Cedric was much struck with the generosity of this offer, for he thanked James several times, and volunteered to go at the first opportunity.

"Not my cup of tea," James said. "I prefer mills and races. Be glad of your company, you know. Not that my brother isn't a jolly little nipperkin—because he *is*. It is just that I cannot see sitting in silence waiting for a fellow to decide when to put his brush to the canvas. Get to wanting to take the brush away and have a go at speeding matters up!"

"The results might not be the same," Cedric suggested with an apologetic smile.

James chuckled. "I expect you are right about that."

Meanwhile Miss Weldon was wondering why it felt different to ride behind Mr. Haverill's horses in London than what it felt in Dolden Overhill. Mr. Haverill's voice gently interrupted her thoughts:

"I hope you do not feel we have intruded on your outing."

"Oh, no," she responded. "Cedric will enjoy it so much. There is still a great deal of boy in him—although we must pretend there is not—and he will like the animals, I am sure. He is enjoying your cousin, too. You see, John Luce, who is his particular friend, went off to Oxford last year and there has been no one to—to—share things with him."

"He has been studying, I take it?"

"Yes, a great deal. He loves books, and good books are like close friends, only of course they cannot answer back or—or—punch one in the ribs."

They had reached a busy crossing and Mr. Haverill's attention was diverted to James's handling of his horses. When the congestion had been safely negotiated Haverill said civilly that he hoped Miss Weldon would bring her brother to his dinner that evening. She thanked him, explaining her uncle had bought seats for his secretary to take Cedric to see Mr. Kean perform.

"Papa has some reservations about the theatre," she said, "but my uncle feels Mr. Kean is an experience Cedric should not miss."

"Very true," agreed Mr. Haverill. Presently he continued: "My aunt—James's mother—is acting as my hostess. I believe she would like to meet your brother."

The only possible reason Carolina could see for Mrs. Haverill's wanting to meet her brother was because he was *her* brother, and the ramifications of this flushed her cheeks. She murmured, "So kind . . ." and was thankful when Lord Gilly drew his friend's attention. Soon they were approaching the menagerie.

It became apparent that the three years separating James and Cedric were very short years indeed. They had their heads together constantly and several times wandered off from their party. It was a strange way to court a young lady. Carolina concluded that the Haverills had nothing to fear from her!

If James was deficient as a beau, no one's day was ruined. At least five of the group enjoyed the spectacle, and the other two were able to enjoy their enjoyment.

"I am glad I came," Lord Tufton confided to Mr. Haverill. "Caro talked me into it. She said it was a splendid opportunity to fraternize with my sons and she was right. I wonder what she will require of me next."

"Something for your own good," Mr. Haverill said.

Lord Tufton nodded. "Yes, that is certain."

When Miss Weldon followed Lady Tufton into Mr. Haverill's drawing room that evening she found assembled a very select group, all of whom were known to her except one. As this lady bore a strong likeness to James Haverill she was easily identified as James's mother.

Mr. Haverill approached and bowed over Lady Tufton's hand with exquisite ease. He then adroitly conveyed her to the attention of the nearest titled gentlemen, employed an encouraging sentence to send Gilly off to his friend Sally Jersey, and drew Miss Weldon toward his aunt.

Mrs. Haverill greeted her with civility and a shrewd look. Carolina wondered what she sought. If it were money she would not see *that*. Then Mrs. Haverill said, "Lydia. Lydia's daughter. Lawrence told me you resemble Lady Tufton, but he is wrong about that. It is your mother."

"Are you acquainted with my mother, ma'am?" Carolina asked.

"Yes, but Lawrence is not, so how was he to know? . . . Have you met Miss Lessenover?"

With some surprise, Carolina now observed who was standing next to Mrs. Haverill. "Indeed, I have," she said, relieved to move along the room. "I am glad to see you again, Miss Lessenover."

Miss Lessenover whispered that Miss Weldon was very kind.

Behind her, Carolina heard James's mother say: "No wonder James is all upside down."

"Just so," murmured her nephew.

As Miss Lessenover's conversation seemed exhausted by one sentence, Carolina progressed to Mrs. Lessenover (who might be pardoned for looking with resentment at any beautiful debutante), and finally came into safe harbor beside Lady Franklin.

"Neat as wax," said her ladyship with a twinkle. "Nary a straw."

Carolina smiled ruefully. "I am afraid my aunt finds me a sad trial."

Lady Franklin said firmly that Lady Tufton did not know the meaning of the word. "I won't ask you to sit down, child. Here comes James and he will want your attention, I warrant."

What James wanted was to say that his cousin had said he might take Miss Weldon in to dinner. Wondering how it would affect Mrs. Haverill's digestion, Miss Weldon replied that she was agreeable to such a comfortable arrangement.

After dinner, when the gentlemen had joined the ladies in the drawing room, Mr. Haverill appeared briefly at Miss Weldon's elbow to ask, a gleam lurking in his eye, how her patients did.

"Patients?" said Miss Weldon. "Oh, you have heard about Bigelow and Mrs. Moffett! They have mended famously, which is a fortunate thing as I do not know where Tufton House would be without them."

"I am not acquainted with Mrs. Moffett," Mr. Haverill said, "but Bigelow is a prince."

"Yes, is he not? So efficient and so kind."

"My butler is also efficient, but he lacks Bigelow's—er—warmth."

"I expect it is his feet," Miss Weldon said.

"His *feet?*" repeated Mr. Haverill.

"Yes. Surely you have noticed that he limps."

"Does he indeed?"

"Yes. I saw it at once. Very likely his shoes do not fit, for there's a look on his face I see so often on the village children when they have outgrown their shoes. I expect if you buy him better ones he will become quite sunny. It is astonishing how shoes affect one's disposition."

Mr. Haverill regarded her as though he found *her* a matter for astonishment "You may be right," he said. "If you will excuse me. . . ."

And he went off to ask Lady Lloyd to favor them with a solo at the harp, while Miss Weldon berated herself for a wagging tongue and was thankful her aunt had not heard her being a silly.

Following the harp number, their host, still laboring under the illusion that Miss Lessenover possessed a Voice, asked that damsel to give them a song.

Miss Lessenover blushed, seemed reluctant but not alarmed, and looked to her mother, who nodded and beamed complacently. Plainly Miss Lessenover would be obliged to sing and the party would be obliged to listen.

Mr. Haverill withdrew to a window embrasure.

Miss Lessenover stood up before them, smiled shyly, requested the gentleman at the piano to play an Irish ballad, opened her mouth, and filled the room miraculously with clear and glistening notes.

When she had finished there was a sudden hush. Then applause erupted, many stood up, and several gentlemen surged forward to congratulate the pleased young lady. The only unsurprised occupant of the room was Mrs. Lessenover, who did not begrudge one penny paid to a very severe and competent singing master. She did not know why they had been invited to this house, for she barely knew the host. All this was insignificant, however, as victory was hers tonight!

"How did Lawrence know?" asked James, coming up to Miss Weldon.

"How did Lawrence know what?" asked Mr. Haverill, just behind him.

"That Miss Lessenover could sing so divinely."

"Why, you told me, James."

"*I* did? You are bamming me! *I* didn't know. Do not listen to him, Miss Weldon. This is one of Lawrence's jokes."

"It is not a joke at all," objected Miss Weldon. "It is a delightful surprise. Let us go to tell her so."

Whereupon James promptly offered his arm.

Mr. Haverill watched them walk away. Then he went toward his aunt, who had sent him several signals.

"Your Miss Weldon may be beautiful, but I wager she hasn't a voice like that," she said.

"Probably not," he agreed serenely. "Miss Lessenover's voice is exceptional. Do you aspire to a nightingale in the house?"

She eyed him sternly. "Ladybirds—nightingales—little nesting wrens! I don't aspire to any. James is still a *boy*."

"You will always think so," he pointed out.

"Perhaps," she conceded. "It is true now, at any rate."

"Yes, yes, I agree with you. Do not be exercised. I cannot see that Miss Weldon shows any *tendre* for James. Besides, he has powerful competition in Lord Dooly."

"Dooly?" Her brows shot up. "His mama will have something to say about that! Is the girl looking for a title?"

Mr. Haverill directed his gaze across the room to where Miss Weldon stood speaking with Miss Lessenover. "I do not know," he said.

"More likely it is money," she decided. "She will need it."

"Miss Weldon has more than looks to offer," he told her.

"If you came to know her better you would see this. Gilly quite idolizes her."

Mrs. Haverill said, "Miss Weldon has my permission to be as charming as she pleases as long as she doesn't trap James into matrimony. I depend upon you, Lawrence, to keep a check-rein on him."

"Better not," he responded. "Every man has to wear his own armour. And if you heed my advice, you will not nag James."

"Do you take me for a fool?"

"No," said Mr. Haverill with a slight smile. "More likely a drill sergeant."

His aunt was unoffended. "Rubbish," she replied. "James's tutor did the drilling—and very efficient he was, too. I, sir, am a mother who does not want her eldest to Throw Himself Away on the first pretty face that comes along."

"Suppose he loves her. Would you blight his happiness for lack of money? I have tried to tell you Miss Weldon has other qualities to offer, if you will only see them."

"I see a great deal more than you think, Haverill, and I am going to depend upon you, whatever you may say to put me off. Good God! Imagine having Harriet in the family."

"Appalling," agreed Mr. Haverill. "One hopes there is only one such . . . although I cannot say Gilly is *unhappy.*"

"Gilbert Maxwell," asserted Mrs. Haverill, "is a saint."

Since Mr. Haverill was in accord with that, he merely inclined his head, executed a slight bow, and went off to see to his guests. It was true, he did not hang upon Lady Tufton, but as she had been seated at his left at dinner (the Countess of Langley, who outranked her, being at his right), and as several gentlemen of assorted ages paid her court the entire evening, she was satisfied. At first she had been miffed not to be asked to play the pianoforte, at which she had some skill, but when Miss Lessenover had performed she was sharp enough to realize any display of hers would be anti-climactic and therefore out of the question.

Courtesy required that Lady Tufton be invited to join the expedition to Somerset House. Being engaged for an afternoon card party, she was obliged to decline, and dropped some hints that another day might find her available. She had no interest in Somerset House or paintings, but had not abandoned her scheme to subdue Mr. Haverill.

Mr. Haverill was very sorry. The outing could not be put off, as he understood Cedric would not be in London much longer.

"Yes," said her ladyship, "Cedric is to leave the day after our ball. I have urged him to stay for he is a dear boy and I quite dote on him." Her doting did not extend to approval of Gilly's paying his college expenses, but she was sincere in her liking for the vicar's heir.

Soon after this the guests began to call for their carriages. The last to leave were Lord and Lady Franklin.

"It was a charming evening, Lawrence," said Lady Franklin. "You were very clever to spring Miss Lessenover on us."

Mr. Haverill chuckled. "I was fortunate not to come a cropper! James had said something which I took to mean that Miss Lessenover had a Voice—which of course she has, only James knew nothing about it."

"I did not realize the Lessenovers were friends of yours."

"Barest acquaintances," he admitted. "Miss Weldon seems to have some interest in the daughter and I thought a—er—friend would not be amiss among so many strangers."

"Very thoughtful," approved Lord Franklin, who was generally silent in company, but not without sensitivity.

"And he was amply rewarded by the outcome," Lady Franklin said to her husband. "Pay him no more compliments."

Mr. Haverill followed them downstairs where a footman produced their cloaks and opened the door under the commanding eye of Mr. Haverill's butler. When the door had closed upon them, the butler turned and limped toward his employer, who was watching him critically. The man's expression was decidedly acid.

"Clawson," said Mr. Haverill suddenly, "are you in pain?"

"Beg pardon, sir?"

"Do your feet hurt?"

"Well, sir—yes." Clawson was looking faintly shocked and his astonishment grew when Mr. Haverill said:

"What is the trouble? Blisters? Calluses? Pinching shoes? Come, come, man. Tell me the situation."

"A bit of all, sir, I expect—though perhaps the shoes are the whole fault."

"Well," said Mr. Haverill, "I cannot have a butler with aching feet. Get yourself some new shoes and bring the bill to me. And thank Miss Weldon the next time you see her."

Clawson voiced his thanks and went off up the stairs to see that lights were being extinguished properly in the drawing room. What Miss Weldon had to do with his feet he could not comprehend.

Mr. Haverill walked into his study, where he poured himself a thimble of brandy and sat down thoughtfully before the dying flames of the grate. Presently the door opened and James came in saying, "There you are."

"Was I lost?" asked Mr. Haverill. "I thought you had gone."

"Oh, no. I wanted to speak with you. Put my mother in her carriage and sent her off. I'll walk home. It isn't far, you know, and will keep this town life from making me soft."

"You will have to watch those lobster patties," his cousin warned.

"I only ate two," objected James. "And that is not what I meant at all. Do not think I am not enjoying the Season, because I *am*. It is jolly kind of you to take me around. Only the mixed-up hours—breakfast at noon and dinner at mid-night—and over-heated rooms—and doing the pretty all the time! I positively hunger for a gallop over the downs!"

"Come along with me to Jackson's," suggested Mr. Haverill.

"What? Stand up to you? You'd floor me quicker than the cat could twitch his whisker."

"Suppose I promise not to."

"*Let* me win?" cried James, horrified.

"Oh, no. Not that." Mr. Haverill got up and punched the smouldering coals with a poker. "Gentleman Jim never lets us win, but he gives us a good match. I can do that for you, if you like."

"Famous," said James. "And I will take you up on it. But that is not what I wanted to talk about. Are you still going along to Somerset House tomorrow?"

"I contracted to do so."

"Well, then, have you any objection to including Miss Lessenover?"

Mr. Haverill turned in surprise, but he answered calmly, "Not at all. Did you wish to invite her?"

"I? No. That is, I do not mind, of course, but it was Miss Weldon's idea. She says the gel paints too, and that it would be civil to ask her."

"So it would," allowed Mr. Haverill, much struck.

"The thing is," explained James, "the children won't care about going and if Lord Tufton does not take his carriage, how shall we all crowd in?"

If James was angling for his cousin to bow out and leave a neat little foursome which reserved Miss Weldon to himself and allotted Miss Lessenover to Cedric, he was disappointed.

"Oh, I expect Lord Tufton will be glad to take the young ladies in his coach," Mr. Haverill said wickedly. As James's face fell, he added:

"You can take the landau, if you like, and I will bring the

curricle. But Miss Weldon can't be expected to perch on the box with you. Better let William drive."

James looked relieved. "That is all right, then. If Lord Tufton goes, he will want to ride with you, I expect."

Mr. Haverill nodded. "Undoubtedly he will. And now, James, you please go home. It has been a long day. In three more seconds I shall be yawning in your face."

James gave him a saucy grin and departed, very pleased with his arrangements for the immediate future.

Seven

In the morning young Haverill was disgruntled to find that his mother had delegated him to take Master David to the portraitist. He set off crossly with the boy skipping happily beside him, heading for a hackney stand at the corner of the street. By the time they had secured a hackney he had the consoling thought of taking Cedric along to while away his tedium. He therefore directed the driver to Tufton House. Master David, who thought two companions would certainly be twice as jolly as one, raised no objection. He liked his brother, he liked hackneys, he liked having his portrait painted.

Fortunately Cedric was both awake and dressed. James found him at his breakfast, convinced him he had eaten enough, and took him off willy-nilly.

It proved to be the highlight of Cedric's London visit.

The painter occupied two top floors of a large old house which had been made into flats. On the lower one, he (presumably) ate and slept, while on the topmost he *lived*.

The studio had oddly sloping ceilings common to attics, but its flavor was like none Cedric had encountered. A huge window had been let into one gable so that the light was fine. Canvases were stacked everywhere and some swung from rafters. Odors of paint and turpentine were delectable.

The painter greeted little David pleasantly enough, though he took no more notice of James and Cedric than he did of the students who waited at their own easels, whispering

among themselves. When little David, who was a coopera-
tive child, had been posed, a hush fell upon the attic and
brushes were plunged into oil.

Cedric was enthralled.

It was old hat to James, who was not artistic anyway, and
he would have liked to withdraw to a far gable where there
was a dusty view of the street so one could see something
happening and chat the time away. But Cedric could not be
budged. He watched everything—that is, he wished for six
eyes and watched as much as he could. The painters forgot
him and he forgot James, who was too good-hearted to be
cross, only bored.

"What," asked James as they made their way homeward,
"did you find so absorbing in that?"

"Well," Cedric answered slowly, "I think—it was—the
creation of something out of nothing. Something splendid,
you know. The portraitist seemed quite gifted. Even the students were skillful."

"I like to sketch with chalks," inserted Master David con-
fidingly.

"Do you?" said Cedric, looking down at the child. "So
do I. See here." He drew a bit of paper from his pocket and
a stub of charcoal wrapped in muslin. In quick strokes he
drew a boy stooping with a sailboat at the edge of a pond.

David thought it was better than a portrait any day and
said so.

Cedric laughed and handed him the paper.

"If I could do that I might be interested in art too," James
conceded. "Do not forget—Somerset House this afternoon.
Be sure Miss Weldon remembers."

Cedric was set down at Tufton House and the Haverills
proceeded to the house their mother had rented for the season.

It was a veritable cavalcade that assembled in Grosvenor
Square that afternoon. James, watched over by a disapproving William, brought the landau, driving tolerably well

though not up to the standard to which Mr. Haverill's coachman was accustomed. Mr. Haverill drove his curricle.

Soon after they reached Tufton House, Lord Tufton's carriage arrived bringing Miss Lessenover. It had delivered Lady Tufton to her card party and was able, with only a minor detour, to collect the young lady.

His lordship immediately appeared on the flagway by Miss Weldon, Cedric, Roddy, and Hugh.

"There must be something to interest the children," Lord Tufton explained. "How do you do, Miss Lessenover. Y'servant, Lawrence, James."

The children, who were delighted to go anywhere with their papa, bubbled with excitement.

The lack of vehicles that James had feared now became an excess. Everyone began to talk at once—except, of course, the timid Miss Lessenover and Cedric, who was used to his sister arranging everything for him.

The day was fine. Obviously James could never sustain the disappointment of not sitting with Miss Weldon.

"Lady Tufton may be wanting your carriage before we return, Gilly," Mr. Haverill said. "Let us take Roddy in my curricle, and tuck Hugh into the landau."

Miss Weldon, with no regard for wrinkles in her skirt, immediately offered to hold Hugh.

His lordship demurred. He thought Hugh's wriggling might make her uncomfortable. But as the child had already thrown himself rapturously upon Miss Weldon, she said encouragingly that she would hold him tightly and would promise not to let him fall out.

"William will drive," said James as though it were his own idea. "I'll help Miss Weldon with Hugh." Before Lord Tufton could think of objections Miss Weldon had handed her reticule and parasol to James, climbed to her seat, and received Hugh into her arms. James promptly followed.

With his ageless courtesy Cedric assisted Miss Lessenover to the opposite seat and joined her.

"Race you, coz," James called gaily.

"No you won't," replied his cousin firmly. "Come, Gilly. Hop up, Roddy. I depend upon you to tell me if my horses are well-matched."

It was at this moment that Lord Dooly's curricle drew up, a tiger in red and blue swinging behind. He nodded civilly enough to the various members of the party, but addressed himself to Miss Weldon:

"I had hoped, Miss Weldon, to take you driving in Hyde Park on this fine day."

Miss Weldon was so sorry. She appreciated his thought, for indeed the day was perfect. It then seemed only courtesy to include his lordship in the excursion.

He accepted. It remained to find a seat for him.

"I am sorry I haven't a seat to spare, Lord Dooly," said Mr. Haverill. "Or James either, have you, James? Will you not follow us?"

Even Lord Dooly could see there was no vacant seat, and as he could not expect Miss Weldon to descend from James's side in order to provide him with company, he reluctantly agreed, and the procession set out.

"Could the fellow not see he was not wanted?" grumbled James.

"Well, he was asked to join us," replied the authoress of the invitation, feeling guilty, but knowing it had been common courtesy.

"What will he find to interest him?" demanded James.

Lord Dooly found a great deal. He was well acquainted with the collection of documents at Somerset House and was sure Miss Weldon would benefit from seeing how they were preserved. But Miss Weldon refused to be detached from the group. They had come to show Cedric paintings of the Royal Academy and that was what they must do!

The great canvases, four or five high on the walls, soon palled on Masters Roddy and Hugh, and their papa, who was enjoying their company hugely, was perfectly willing to take them away to look at other exhibits.

Since few examples of classic painting had survived to the nineteenth century, naturally that great classicist, Lord Dooly, took little interest in the battery of paintings. Bronzes, he said positively, were The Thing.

"Well, I don't know about that," said James irrepressibly. His tutor had visited Greece and had imbued him with a preference for marble sculpture. He and his lordship embarked on a heated discussion and finally went away to look for sculpture that they could dissect on the spot.

By this time Cedric and Miss Lessenover had dropped behind. Miss Lessenover had not quite reached her eighteenth birthday and she found Cedric considerably more comfortable than the beaux of society. They exchanged gentle comments as they strolled before the paintings, stopping sometimes by unspoken agreement, and generally enjoying each other's sympathetic company.

Deserted by the party to which she had been at pains to remain attached, Miss Weldon looked up ruefully at Mr. Haverill.

"I expect you are familiar with all the exhibits," she said. "It is all wonderful to me. Pray choose what you admire most and I promise to commend it."

"No, no," replied Mr. Haverill lightly. "Surely you have found that a gentleman must always defer to a lady's taste."

"While privately preferring cockfights and mills?" she asked with a twinkle.

"Just so. Now, if I may suggest—"

"Oh, yes—"

"Let us look at Lord Elgin's marbles. They are the topic of the moment, having been brought back from Greece at his personal expense, and you will be continually required to give your opinion of them."

Miss Weldon admitted that she had several times been embarrassed by the lack of an opinion. He offered his arm and she laid her hand very lightly upon it, feeling a bit overwhelmed in a way that was quite new.

"I must tell you, Miss Weldon," he said, as they walked along, "that you were right. Clawson's shoes were pinching."

"There was no mistaking the signs," she said.

"If one knows what to look for. Well, you will be glad to know that I have told Clawson to get new shoes and bring the bill to me."

"But that will not do at all," she objected, halting abruptly, forgetting to be embarrassed, and looking earnestly into his face. "He will ten to one get other ill-fitting shoes. You must send him to you bootmaker."

"Send my butler to my bootmaker?" said Mr. Haverill, astounded.

"Yes. You have no trouble? Your bootmaker knows how to fit shoes properly?"

"Of course he does! I would not patronize him otherwise."

"There. You see. Clawson needs a proper fit." She perceived that Mr. Haverill rejected the idea as extremely lowering. "No? You would rather not? Lady Luce says gentlemen are very jealous of their tailors, and I suppose it is the same with cobblers. Well, then, you must go with Clawson to his man and superintend the fitting."

Mr. Haverill shook his head in disbelief.

With a trifle less confidence, she added: "Servants cannot sleep until noon and sit two hours at dinner. They are on their feet constantly, you know. It pays to keep them comfortable."

"I suppose," said Mr. Haverill, "you wish me to line them up for inspection?"

She colored slightly, led by the hint of a twinkle in his eye to declare, "No, indeed. Very likely your housekeeper sees to the girls. You can ask Clawson about the men."

"Can I?"

"My papa says," she continued warmly, "that simple kindness must come before pride."

"Minx!" said the gentleman. "I never sleep 'til noon."

Fortunately for Miss Weldon's composure, James and his lordship approached them, both demanding that they come at once to see the Elgin marbles. Before devoting her attention to Lord Dooly, Miss Weldon cast a last anxious look at Mr. Haverill and devoutly hoped he would not complain to her uncle of her pertness; she detected quivers at the corners of his mouth, which seemed to indicate he was only amused. How superior he was in poise to James and Lord Dooly, though not much older!

Not a great many days remained until Carolina's ball. The house churned with activity. Lady Tufton took no part except to ensure her most sophisticated friends were invited. Knowing the Tufton diamonds would show splendidly against her white skin and brilliant blue gown, she did not (momentarily) think of rubies. Mr. Haverill had requested her first dance. She was tolerably satisfied.

Carolina soon saw that her uncle was correct. The servants rustled about like so many worker-bees, buzzing contentedly. They appeared to take much pleasure and consequence from being the manufacturers of a Social Event of the Season. Mrs. Moffett and Bigelow both came to Carolina for many small decisions concerning her tastes. She could not, of course, give them any real direction, having never attended such a large and formal event, much less having staged one, but she appreciated their consideration of her pleasure.

Lord Tufton's study was the Command Post. It was from here that his secretary issued gilt-edged invitations and catalogued responses. His lordship dabbled a hand in everything, even descending to the cellar with Bigelow to count bottles of wine. In particular, he dealt happily with decorations for the dancing room, designing scalloped swags of rope-greenery to encircle the cornice, accentuated at their high points with cascades of pink roses and pink ribbons. That way, he said, when the room became crowded the festiveness of it would remain visible.

No one noticed that Cedric was almost never home, not even his fond sister. She was absent often herself at fittings on her ball dress and at various social functions for which invitations were beginning to come her way.

One afternoon as she and Lady Tufton were walking to have tea with Lady Franklin, they encountered James Haverill on the pavement. He was looking, he explained, for Cedric.

"I have scarcely seen him since we went to Somerset House," Miss Weldon answered. "I supposed he was with you."

"Oh, no," said James. "I have stopped for him every day, but never catch him home."

"How strange," Miss Weldon murmured. "He has no other friends in London that I know about."

"Very likely you will find him skulking about the Royal Academy," said Lady Tufton. "He talks of little else." Her tone was impatient. She missed Cedric's admiring company and was feeling his defection.

"The museum! To be sure! I had not thought of that. Do you suppose I shall be obliged to tour the whole building to run him down? Best be on my way, then. Will you save your first dance for me, Miss Weldon?"

She explained her uncle was promised that.

"Then the second?" he asked cheerfully.

Miss Weldon thanked him and agreed.

James escorted them to Lady Franklin's door, providing quite unnecessary support up eight steps to the threshold. There he left them with many assurances that he anticipated a famous ball.

The lack of concern for Cedric's welfare evidenced by James and Lady Tufton was not to be matched by Cedric's sister. A lifetime of affection for her only brother and the habit of three years at the domestic helm of the vicarage, had imbued Carolina with a deep sense of responsibility for her sibling. Although Cedric might secretly enjoy dreams, he was accustomed, as was Carolina, to her thinking for him. His path was smoothed—swept—certified. How he would handle Independence could not be surmised. Carolina did not believe a lad of his sound upbringing would fall into serious temptation, but she was much more alert than he to the perils that might assail an unsuspecting and inexperienced young man. She berated herself for not keeping closer watch upon him and devoutly hoped Lady Tufton's solution to the mystery would prove correct. Her face was troubled as she followed her aunt into Lady Franklin's drawing room.

Her ladyship saw at once that Miss Weldon was out of curl, and assuming some ill-judged action or sharp word of Lady Tufton was the cause, made it a point to accord Miss Weldon a warm reception. Lady Franklin's gracious manner and positive outlook, reinforced with tea-confections of spun sugar, proved sufficient to restore Miss Weldon's spirits.

"Well, miss," said Lady Franklin, "whom will you permit to open the ball with you?"

It had not occurred to Carolina that she would open the ball. Nor had it occurred to her aunt, who said immediately: "The ball will be opened by Mr. Haverill with *me.*" As Lady Franklin looked dubious, she added: "You know there will be stragglers. Carolina will have to wait with Gilly so as to be properly presented."

"Latecomers have no claim upon their hostess," objected Lady Franklin. "The ball is Carolina's, isn't it?"

"You know it is. Or perhaps I should say the ball is Gilly's, for he has ordered everything—not that I complain, you understand. He has saved me a great deal of boredom.

But I can see that no one will want to wait until Carolina is released from receiving in order to begin dancing. I shall open the ball myself as soon as most of the guests have come."

"I am sure you will be an ornament," Lady Franklin replied smoothly. She turned to Carolina and asked who would be honored with her first set.

Carolina's eyes danced. "A most charming gentleman, my lady."

"Ah," said Lady Franklin, delighted. "Someone special?"

"Yes, indeed," Carolina replied promptly. "A titled gentleman."

Her ladyship raised her brows and exclaimed, "Not Dooly!"

Carolina shook her head, laughing. She was too kind to remind her that she had called the gentleman charming, so she said: "More charming than he. I am sure my aunt will agree."

Whereupon Lady Tufton made a moue and explained that Caro was teasing about her uncle.

Lady Franklin clapped her hands. "Very clever! You and Haverill can look to your laurels, Harriet."

But Harriet was not apprehensive. She did not think a vicar's daughter dancing with an uncle would create the merest ripple in the social pool. Carolina was very pretty, she would allow, and Gilly did very well as a husband (if he lacked the savoir faire of a Corinthian), but neither had distinction. She and Mr. Haverill would excite admiration, she thought, giving little heed to the fact that when Mr. Haverill solicited her for her first set he, like Lady Franklin, little dreamed he would be opening Caro's ball. What his demeanor would be in such a situation she did not know or even wonder.

Poor Harriet! She would have been astonished if she knew Lady Franklin felt some grudging compassion for her. She was youthful, beautiful, fully confidant, and flatteringly courted. If the court of her admirers shifted like the sands of Arabia there was a smoothness, a facility of the shifting that led her to think the gentlemen she admired were the ones who languished for her. The admirers came when attracted (she thought) and fed her vanity with slavish attentions until another lady's amiability lured them from her side, at which time she deplored their taste, decided they were not so amusing as she thought, and dismissed them unregretted from her consideration. To be sought after was so agreeable! Although her suitors were fickle, she noticed only their numbers.

At first Lady Franklin had feared the example of Lady Tufton to her niece would be detrimental. It was a relief, for she liked the girl, to find Carolina's affection and dependence were turned upon Lord Tufton. The interesting and entertaining thing was that influence was in reverse. That is, if Gilly could be believed (and of course he could) as well as Lady Franklin's coachman's gossip to Lady Franklin's dresser (a reliable source), Miss Weldon was not so much affected as affective. Her adherents now numbered Nannie, Betty, Bigelow, Mrs. Moffett, Marlene, Cook, John Coachman, Masters Roddy and Hugh, assorted footmen, and his lordship. Cook had been heard to say Miss Weldon was the Plum of the Pudding, so that the Lesser Orders had got into the habit—strictly among themselves—of calling her Miss Plum, which was more dignified than Little Puss, but said very much the same thing.

Lady Franklin inspected her guests shrewdly, and rendered the opinion that Miss Weldon would be a credit to her aunt, which was a masterly statement for it left Lady Tufton with no disagreeable rejoinder.

It was difficult for Carolina to comprehend a selfish character. The vicarage family was a loving one, not so preoccupied with one another that they lacked concern for others. Mrs. Weldon was happy to bestow upon the needy of her parish such small independent income as she possessed, income which in Lady Tufton's case was frittered away upon silver loo and Denmark Lotion and geegaws. Papa always said happiness came from within, but Lady Tufton seemed a dry well. Nor had she learned that she must lose herself in order to find herself. Carolina had the uncomfortable feeling *she,* being the only Christian soldier available, should make a push to awake Lady Tufton to her error, but a method of doing so eluded her, even as her heart pounded alarmingly at the prospect.

Meanwhile, their ladyships were discussing the latest *on dit* about a George Faulkes and a dubious Lady Hilton, neither of whom was known to Carolina. She allowed her mind to return to the puzzle of Cedric's whereabouts, no nearer solution than when James Haverill had first mentioned it. The sound of her own name, as it always does, drew her attention.

Lady Tufton was rashly asserting that Lord Dooly was very attentive to Caro and was hourly expected to come to the point.

Lady Franklin, who supposed Lord Dooly's mother had no such expectation and who strongly disapproved of such discussion in Carolina's presence, endeavored to turn her guest's thoughts by wondering if Lady Dooly would be bringing out her third daughter next year—a biddable miss with unusual charm, considering who had reared her.

But Lady Tufton was not to be deflected from her convictions. Lord Dooly would suit her aspirations, and therefore he must be wooed (if Caro would only exert herself) and even coerced into a declaration.

Flushed with shame, Carolina heard Lady Franklin impatiently and bluntly chide: "That's enough, Harriet. The chicken cannot cackle before it is hatched. Some things are better left unsaid."

Lady Tufton's mouth snapped shut. Quite clearly she would have liked to retaliate, but she stood in too much awe of her hostess to do that, knowing (resentfully) that her social position owed much to the sponsorship of Lady Franklin.

"Tell me about your ball dress, my dear," said Lady Franklin soothingly to Carolina, ignoring the conflagration on her right.

"It—it's pink, my lady," she stammered.

"Ravishing! Designed by Gilly, I collect?"

With some difficulty they pursued a conversation while the smoke from Lady Tufton's eyes rose slowly to the high ceiling of Lady Franklin's drawing room.

Presently, having put out her fire with sips of tepid tea, Lady Tufton announced they must go and, using an invisible broom, swept Caro like a scrap of paper from the house. Her temper was held in check as they retraced their steps to Tufton House, only to be unleashed upon the hapless footman who took fifteen seconds to open to her knock.

When she had dressed him down to her satisfaction, she descended on Gilly's study, spoiling for a fight. Fortunately for his lordship, he was not there. Her eyes roved the room, fastening upon a decanter that someone had left upon the desk.

While Carolina, hovering uncertainly in the doorway, watched with horror, Lady Tufton poured a glass of brandy, tossed it off, cast a quelling look at her niece, and said: "Better hope to God that woman doesn't turn on you! . . . Gilly, Gilly, Gilly. She thinks the world of Gilly, but she disapproves of *me*." She hurled herself into a chair, only to rise from it almost immediately.

"There is nothing here," she said in a singularly lost tone.

Carolina half-stretched out her hand. Now was the moment, she realized, to speak as Papa or Mama would of spiritual things, but what Lady Tufton might accept from her sister she would never tolerate from her sister's child. Although Caro felt cowardly, she believed a single adverse word would trigger more than she could handle. So she said matter-of-factly: "Let us go upstairs. Would you like me to brush your lovely hair? Mama finds it relaxing, and Papa says a woman's hair is her crowning glory."

Lady Tufton stared at her a moment and replied, "Very well," in a disinterested voice.

Neither lady had a thought to spare for Cedric until they reassembled for dinner and Cedric was found to be whole and serene, with no deficiency in his customary young-old courtliness. So very much himself did he seem that Lady Tufton forgot she had entertained anxiety about him. His truly sincere admiration blew upon her disposition like Elysian breezes.

A period of quiet reflection had brought her ladyship to the conclusion that the turbulent tea party was best left unmentioned. Lady Franklin's criticism (as indeed *any* criticism) was galling, but Lady Tufton read her character well enough to know Lady Franklin would not complain to Gilly. So she garbed herself in amber velvet which became her wonderfully, though it was somewhat formal for a dinner at home *en famille,* and was rewarded by generous admiration from the two gentlemen with whom she dined.

Miss Weldon was so delighted by her aunt's improved mood and so reassured by Cedric's wholesomeness, that she was able to consume a shocking amount of raspberry trifle, which pleased Bigelow and Cook exceedingly, each taking credit for the event.

Eight

The lack of a proper ballroom was not felt by any of Lord and Lady Tufton's guests to be a hardship, since the guest list had been limited to a suitable and select number of one hundred and fifty. Some expressed surprise at the sight of "Christmas" garlands in the spring, but all allowed them to be pretty and thought the clusters of pink flowers very striking.

Lady Tufton had been pleased to set Lord Dooly's immense arrangement of orchids upon a table on the landing where everyone might see them as they came up the stairs, and evidently this situation found favor with his lordship, for he was unusually affable when he bowed before Miss Weldon and requested her first dance.

Miss Weldon was embarrassed (though not regretful) to explain that both her first and second were engaged. His lordship was then obliged to master his indignation and request her third. His mama, who had preceded him in the receiving line, was fortunately reciting her ailments to the first acquaintance encountered and so did not hear this humiliating exchange. She did not know of Lord Dooly's floral offering and, being interested only in her own affairs, had taken no notice of the lavish display upon the landing, although considered thought might have told her no such specimens were to be found outside their own greenhouses.

The arrival of James with his cousin was heartening to Miss Weldon, who asked him to locate her brother and see that he was introduced to agreeable people, as her ladyship had not included him in the receiving line.

"To be sure, I will," James promised. "I like Cedric, you know, and am sorry not to have been able to bear-lead him around the city."

"Yes," said Miss Weldon anxiously, "It is very strange how he keeps disappearing."

"Oh, well," replied James bracingly, "There are lots of things in London to interest a man."

Carolina said that was what she understood and Cedric was not a man.

James protested Cedric was more man than she realized, which did not comfort her in the slightest, as was noticed by Mr. Haverill when he bowed and kissed her fingers.

He asked no questions, however, since the Earl of Aintree was just greeting Lady Tufton and must be presented to Miss Weldon without delay, for he was almost as rich as Golden Ball and was known to be in the market for a fourth wife to mother his seven children. He had been pointed out to Carolina on two previous occasions as a Catch, but since she was inclined to view as a Bluebeard any man who had buried three wives (although he was well-enough looking and not, it was said, disagreeable) she greeted him graciously, but without any encouraging glimmer.

If the truth were known, the Earl thought Carolina charming, but by now he had had his fill of school-room misses who bred and expired. He rather thought he would prefer a dasher like Lady Tufton, who was probably unattainable and therefore more interesting. Nevertheless, being willing to do his bit toward the success of Harriet's niece, he solicited a dance from Miss Weldon and was rewarded with the promise of a quadrille later in the evening. Her ladyship supplied an approving smile.

Soon after this Lady Tufton abandoned her husband and niece to dance with Mr. Haverill.

"Well, Caro," said his lordship during a small lull between arrivals, "is it all to your satisfaction?"

She smiled up at him. "It is all very wonderful and seems perfect to me. If *you* are satisfied, then I shall know it is, for it is your plan and you must know if it is proceeding as you wished."

"According to plan. According to plan," he said.

"And such a beautiful plan!" She dipped her nose into her bouquet of pink buds in a silver filigree holder. "Are not these lovely? How did he choose the perfect thing?"

Knowing "he" was James Haverill, Lord Tufton replied that he expected Lawrence had heard him talking about her dress. "Here's James's mother now. I warrant James was too eager to wait for her."

Mrs. Haverill was indeed laboring under a strong sense of ill-usage. There was nothing smiling about her face. But she was too intelligent to slight Miss Weldon. In fact, she even went so far as to say James must be waiting to dance with her.

"James must wait in line behind *me*," Lord Tufton said merrily, which mollified her somewhat, and she complimented Miss Weldon on her gown.

Miss Weldon thanked her sweetly, but Lord Tufton interrupted to say she should compliment him, as he had chosen it.

A few more latecomers could be heard on the ground floor. When they had climbed the stair and been received, Lord Tufton led his niece onto the dance floor.

Lady Tufton might have performed with exceeding grace and distinction, nobly supported by Mr. Haverill, but there were many present who thought no well-nigh professional performance could hold a candle to the picture of a pretty young lady of modest demeanor and smiling face circling the room with a very elegant gentleman whose grey hair became him as well as his impeccable coat and his fond expression.

Lady Franklin, for one, had many accolades to bestow upon the debutante. Because she was charming herself, as well as something of a social lioness, her words were heeded, repeated, and endorsed. Lord Tufton, to whom she addressed some of her comments, laughed and said she was biased about *him* because she had shared childhood escapades with him, but that she was quite right about his Caro.

For a time they congenially watched her progress around the dance floor with a succession of enthusiastic young gentlemen. In the normal run of things, a guest of honor will generally enjoy abundant attention. What particularly pleased Lord Tufton and Lady Franklin now, as well as Rob Luce who was truly Carolina's friend, was that admiration and not duty motivated the gentlemen.

"With a merely respectable dowry Caro would go off very well," Lord Tufton said regretfully.

"Do not be too sure about that," replied Lady Franklin.

He looked at her reproachfully. "Why, Laura, I thought you liked my Little Puss."

"Well, I do. You misunderstand me. I mean, do not be sure she *won't,* dowry or no."

"I had hopes of James," he admitted. "But Lawrence says it would not do, and I can see Mrs. Haverill is disenchanted with the prospect. Heaven knows I wouldn't wish a disapproving mama-in-law upon Caro."

Lady Franklin answered casually, "Oh, James will not do for Carolina. I shall not be surprised at something better."

"Not Dooly!" he protested. "Harriet is hot for that match but I tell you frankly it would not sit well with me, for all his having a title."

"Not to mention wealth. Yes, I have heard Harriet on the subject, but I agree with you. At least Carolina's season is just begun and Lochinvar may not yet have come out of the west." She watched Rob Luce partnering Carolina in a gay country dance. "I suppose young Luce wouldn't do?

Gilly said he did not suppose Sir John to have much to

settle on a younger son and the prospect of Caro's following the drum was not a pleasing one, such a homebody she was.

"Too bad. He seems devoted to her—but I suppose it is brotherly feeling like yours for me."

Lord Tufton said immediately and truthfully that he adored her, to which Lady Franklin replied, "Rubbish!" and tapped him sharply with her fan.

"Look at that scamp, Cedric!" exclaimed his lordship. "He's loading Harriet out! You would think he had been a beau for decades."

"Very well brought up," said Lady Franklin.

"Yes, but such poise for a stripling. I hope my sons turn out half so well."

Lady Franklin assured him they would—if they modelled themselves after their papa, whereupon Gilly gave her her own "Rubbish!" right back and went off to find masculine company.

Mr. Haverill did not ask Miss Weldon to dance. Although his manner was unperturbed, he was exceedingly wroth with Lady Tufton for the uncomfortable position in which she had placed him. The stares when they opened the ball! How they rankled! If he had confided his annoyance to his aunt, he might have been reassured to discover she and many others only supposed he was obliging *Lord* Tufton. Too many ladies had pursued Mr. Haverill for him not to recognize the signs; what he did not know was that the *ton* had determined him to be impervious. No one, except Lady Tufton herself, had any notion he might be dangling after her.

Disgruntled, yet unwilling to go off in a huff and cause even more talk, he took refuge behind Mrs. Haverill and listened with half an ear to her running commentary. Since what Mrs. Haverill wanted was not so much response as audience (even a half-deaf one), they managed very well until James could be seen approaching with Miss Weldon on his arm.

"Do not act another Lady Dooly," Mr. Haverill warned in a low voice.

Mrs. Haverill drew herself up but made no reply. She was spared the necessity of a reproach to her son by his saying, "Come, Mama. Lady Franklin wants you to join her across the room and has sent me to fetch you. Miss Weldon has the next dance with Aintree, and I can see him headed this way."

Carolina held out to Mrs. Haverill her bouquet, and said, "They are so lovely, ma'am. I am sure you helped Mr. Haverill to choose them."

Mrs. Haverill's eyes flew to Lawrence Haverill, but he shook his head with a slight smile.

"They are my flowers, Mama. I am Mr. Haverill too, you know," James explained with a laugh. "Lawrence did advise me, however."

"Yes," admitted Mr. Haverill. "A sort of spy in the camp. Gilly revealed to me the color of Miss Weldon's dress."

"Then I must thank all three of you," Carolina said quickly, "for nothing could be prettier or more appropriate." What Mrs. Haverill had done to deserve thanks was obscure, but the statement was tactfully made.

"So they are," agreed Mrs. Haverill without enthusiasm. She rose, took James's arm which Carolina had surrendered, and nudged him into the idle throng upon the dance floor.

"Aintree has been delayed in a corner by the Countess Lieven," Mr. Haverill pointed out. "This allows me a moment to ask about the concern you showed earlier for your brother. Is something amiss?"

"Well, I do not know," said Carolina anxiously. "He seems well enough and quite—untroubled, but he is always *missing.*"

Understanding this to mean missing all day, Mr. Haverill said he was sure there was some simple explanation. "What does Cedric say?"

"That's just it. He is very evasive."

"Do not be alarmed," soothed Mr. Haverill. "It is probably a lark with James."

"Oh, no, for James can never find him either, although he had offered to show Cedric how to go out on the Town."

With praiseworthy solemnity Mr. Haverill considered that. "Cedric is too young for—er—vice, I think. Very likely he is enjoying a spate of independence."

Miss Weldon reluctantly agreed.

"If you have any further reason to be troubled, I hope you will tell me, and I will see what I can do."

She thanked him gratefully. "I hesitate to approach my uncle. He—he has a high opinion of Cedric and is going to help with his education."

"I see," said Mr. Haverill comprehensively. "Here is Lord Aintree. Remember, you can call on me any time." He remained for a time watching Carolina dance with Lord Aintree. Miss Lessenover was in the same set, wearing a primrose gown very similar to one in which Miss Weldon had appeared a week ago, and a knowing lady might have wagered it was a direct copy. In any case, the effect was good, classic lines becoming Miss Lessenover more than the frilly garments her mama had clothed her in previously. She seemed to have added an equally becoming confidence, smiling more readily, though still having little to say.

Satisfied that all was under control, Mr. Haverill descended to the dining room where a magnificent collation was laid out which he did not desire at all but beside which he found Gilly.

"I have not enjoyed a ball so much since I was James's age," Lord Tufton told his friend. "Why are you down here? Half the ladies in my drawing room must be hoping you will ask them to dance. Forgotten how to play the gallant?"

Mr. Haverill said, no more than Gilly had.

"Try the *paté*—or the lobster salad," Gilly responded encouragingly.

"No need to hawk your wares," Lawrence said. "Ah. Here comes the champagne. I will sample that."

"Do. Do." Gilly helped himself to a gaudy little cake with nut topping. "Have all you like. I'm well-stocked. . . . I say, are you not eating now? Be a knight in armour and take Harriet some champagne. She was asking for some and this may be my only chance to eat."

"What about Miss Weldon?" asked Mr. Haverill.

"Yes, take her some too. Not a debut without champagne, is it?"

Having no intention of carrying three wine glasses through a crowded house, Mr. Haverill finished his own and went off with two. Both Bigelow and a footman stopped him *en route,* offering to be of service, but he said firmly that he had been commissioned for the task.

Miss Weldon was standing beside her aunt when Mr. Haverill reached the ballroom, a set having just ended.

"Oh, splendid!" exclaimed her ladyship, accepting the wine gracefully and sipping it as she regarded Mr. Haverill over the rim of the glass. "I am parched."

Mr. Haverill missed the challenge of widened eyes, for he was offering the second glass to Miss Weldon.

"No, thank you," declined that redoubtable miss. "Papa says a lady mustn't—" She broke off abruptly, turned scarlet.

"Mustn't mix wine with country dances?" suggested Mr. Haverill.

"Yes," said Miss Weldon thankfully. She darted an apprehensive glance at her aunt, but Lady Tufton took so little interest in anything her brother-in-law might say that she entirely missed Carolina's slip.

Her ladyship was much more alert to the fact that Lord Dooly was making his way across the room toward them. He permitted himself a lingering look at Miss Weldon, but surprised all by inviting his hostess onto the dance floor.

Lady Tufton stood immediately. "How charming," she cooed. "I know your waltz, sir, and am delighted to join you."

It sounded excessive to Carolina, although she had to admit to herself that her aunt had been a reigning belle long enough to know what a gentleman might swallow. Involuntarily she glanced up at Mr. Haverill and found him regarding her with amusement.

"Miss Weldon, I believe I can read your mind," he said.

"But that," she objected with greater ease than she felt, "would be an invasion of privacy."

"I like to think of it as empathy, ma'am." His face was solemn, while his eyes twinkled. "Are you engaged for this dance?"

Her eyes scanned the room. "Yes, but I don't see . . . oh, there he is. Mr. Howard, I thought you had forgotten me."

"Never!" declared Mr. Howard passionately. He drew Carolina into the first opening among the dancers, and Mr. Haverill was left holding an undrunk glass of champagne.

He listened to its bubbles as though it had a comment of its own, then bestowed it on a passing footman, and went off to invite Lady Franklin to dance, which won him the approval of Lord Franklin, who detested "mincing and mumming" and was glad to surrender his post.

"I was never what you would call a zephyr on the dance floor," she admitted. "But I cannot spurn an offer from a nonpareil."

"Doing it too brown, my lady," Mr. Haverill reproved. "Very little more and I would think I were Lord Dooly partnering Lady Tufton."

Lady Franklin chuckled. "Heard some palaver, eh?"

"Yes. It was interesting to see Miss Weldon's expression as she listened. I thought she might lose her composure, but she did not."

"Poor Harriet," sighed Lady Franklin speciously. "Apparently Caro simply will *not* exert herself."

"And her ladyship has appointed herself proxy?"

"Something like that. Well, I do not think I can allow Caro to throw herself away on Dooly!'"

Mr. Haverill raised a brow. "What will you do?"

"Something drastic," Lady Franklin assured him. "The simplest thing, of course, would be to poison his mama's mind. Not at all difficult, you understand, for she is not ready to relinquish him and will be enchanted to hear the most detrimental things."

"Detrimental? To Miss Weldon?"

"Well, shocking, which is just as satisfactory for my purposes. Will you believe it—Miss Weldon came into her aunt's boudoir with mussed skirts and tumbled hair? Lady Dooly would be horrified." Lady Franklin's eyes sparkled and she abandoned herself to the waltz.

After a few graceful turns, Mr. Haverill asked if Miss Weldon were especially disposed toward Lord Dooly. "I hope," he said carefully, "you would not interfere if she has her heart set on him."

"You know Caro is too sensible for that," she replied. "No, no. She should do considerably better."

"Better than a title and a fortune?"

"Better than a crashing bore. Gilly and I have quite decided Dooly will not suit."

"No," agreed Mr. Haverill. "Gilly, I fear, has his heart set on James, and *that* will not suit James's mama. I have told Gilly to put it out of his mind, and you would do well to remind him the same."

"I shall do my bit for Carolina," replied Lady Franklin, which was vague enough to make her partner uneasy.

"Now, my lady," expostulated Mr. Haverill, "you would do well to keep out of the affair and leave Miss Weldon's future to her family."

"But you have just persuaded me I cannot count on Gilly's attitude," she objected. "Shall I abandon the child to Harriet?"

"Good God, no!" he exclaimed.

"You see. I shall have to take a hand."

"She has parents, has she not?" he asked.

"Babes in the woods," Lady Franklin answered with tolerant scorn. "Carolina is taking very well because she is pretty and amiable, but she cannot survive the social jungle without help. I shall have to find her a gentleman who appreciates her nature."

"Miss Weldon resembles her aunt," Mr. Haverill ventured, and was advised by Lady Franklin to look again.

He was silent a few moments. Then he said he supposed that Miss Weldon might have hidden depths. Lady Franklin agreed, adding sharply that she hoped he did not confuse strength of character with willfulness.

It was well that the music ended then, for Lady Franklin was beginning to nourish resentments toward Mr. Haverill, who had always been a favorite of hers among the young beaux.

"Well, Edward, I am glad you have reached a sensible age," she said to her husband when Mr. Haverill had returned her to his aegis and gone away. "Young men are the devil."

Lord Franklin looked at her in surprise. "Not Haverill?"

"Yes, abominable," she declared. "It's time somebody broke his heart."

"So long as it isn't you, m'love," her spouse replied. "I may—or may not, for that matter—have reached what you call a sensible age, but I am very possessive, ma'am."

"It's well you are, for I would not give a rap for you if you weren't. These matrimonial truces are not in my style." She stared across the room where Mr. Haverill was just leading out a handsome redhead. "Nor in *his* either, unless I miss my guess."

"Gently now, old girl. Better not interfere with Haverill, for he won't thank you. He knows what doesn't suit him."

Lady Franklin agreed, but asked if he thought Haverill knew what he *wanted*.

His lordship couldn't say, except he was fairly certain Haverill was not pining for Harriet.

"Certainly not! That is obvious," she said with conviction. "Poor Gilly. Still, I expect he knows Haverill well enough to trust him. She might be casting out lures to some unprincipled bounder."

To which Lord Franklin added nothing, having already spoken more than usual. He and her ladyship were very well attuned. Nothing more required saying.

Lord Dooly managed to secure Miss Weldon for supper, although Rob Luce and James Haverill had intended the same, but unfortunately fell into an engrossing debate with several other young gentlemen about the merits of perch-phaetons versus high-perch ones and their relative speeds and maneuverability. Since none of the debaters owned wheels, their opinions rested solely upon envy of certain well-known whips—James having a slight edge by virtue of his kinship to Lawrence Haverill. So while they let the crucial moment escape, the Earl of Aintree pleased himself and his hostess by carrying *her* off to the lower floor, and Miss Weldon accepted Lord Dooly and endeavored to be grateful.

Indeed, she was not ungrateful, for she knew his attentions, lugubrious though they might be, stamped her with success. Even Lady Dooly, who was generally known to be disapproving, could not in Lord Tufton's house cut Lord Tufton's niece.

Intercepting one frosty look in the course of the evening, Carolina had some thought of telling the countess she had nothing to worry about, Miss Weldon disdained her son. Of course Papa's daughter could never do such a thing, and she rather thought Papa would have a particular name for her entertaining such a thought. Besides, she might do Lord Dooly a real favor by encouraging him in a fleeting courtship during which he might learn to defy the dominance of his mama.

She went down happily enough with his lordship who did

not know, after all, he was a bore, and who had decided it was a monstrous fine ball. And in this case virtue was rewarded, for James brought Miss Lessenover to join them and the supper-time passed very pleasantly.

It is an established fact that any lady about whom gentlemen stand several at a time and whose hand is solicited more times than there are sets is indefatigable. Lady Tufton was one of such, and her niece likewise. On the other hand, success did not make Lord Tufton lighter on his feet and he began to wish the final number would arrive more quickly.

Mr. Haverill danced no more. When he finally presented himself before Miss Weldon, her program was full. Being too innocent to suppose he had waited late in the evening for that very reason, as touchier females might have done, she thanked him sincerely when she declined. Perhaps he wished to watch over James, for he did not leave, but passed the rest of the evening in a card room with no significant damage to his purse.

Miss Weldon was as radiant at the last note as at the first. When the guests had gone she thanked Bigelow and the footmen for their perfect service and sent messages to Cook and Mrs. Moffett. On the second floor as she went up to bed after fond good nights to her aunt and uncle, she encountered a maidservant and thanked her too.

The maidservant came close to saying, "Oh, Miss Plum!" but caught herself in the nick of time and gasped, "Oh, mum! It was a beautiful eggsperience. Thank *you*."

And the little maid was right. Tufton House had blossomed in more ways than one.

Cedric, who was both sensitive and gentlemanly, lingered with his uncle, who, now that the ball had ended, had gained a second wind. His lordship was pleased to be assured by the boy (who knew nothing more of Society than an evening at the Manor in Dolden Overhill) that the ball was perfect in every detail. He sipped a bit of old brandy while Cedric told him what he already knew.

"It has been a pleasure to have you here, lad," Lord Tufton said finally, interrupting the gracious flow.

"Oh, sir, your—kindness—generosity," said Cedric, stumbling a little now. "I cannot thank you—"

"But you can," Lord Tufton corrected kindly. "You can study hard at Oxford and vindicate your upbringing."

Cedric replied staunchly that he would never, if humanly possible, fail his papa and his mama and his sisters.

"Very lofty," approved Lord Tufton. "And not an impossible ambition. But it would be regrettable to turn a beau— eh? eh?—into a mere grind." At which Cedric colored slightly and laughed.

"Going home tomorrow?"

"Yes sir."

"Well, you are welcome any time, boy. In fact, you need not go at all. Would you like to stay? You can, you know. I wish you would. Need another man in this houseful of females."

And Cedric, who lived with five, whereas Lord Tufton had only two (if you counted Caro), understood perfectly.

"I would like to," he said wistfully, "but Papa expects me, but if you would be so kind as to write a letter, I can take it to him and come back in a very few days."

Pleased with both the sentiment and the expression of it, Lord Tufton went at once to his desk. He penned a brief request for the return of Cedric, cannily adding that he thought a bit more Town Bronze would help prepare Cedric for the independence of college.

The missive was handed over and the two gentlemen went contentedly to bed.

Nine

Carolina had intended to speed her brother on his way the next day, but Cedric, having the loan of one of the viscount's hacks and the assurance of a welcome as soon as he could return, set out at daybreak and had covered half the distance home when his sister at last stirred.

"Well, missy," said Nannie in benevolent disapproval, "have you slept long enough? You were a grasshopper sure enough last night, frittering the hours away."

"I was and I did," she admitted, rubbing her eyes. "Papa would be shocked if he knew how frivolous I have become. But, oh, Nannie, it was so delightful!"

Nannie, having won her point without a skirmish, promptly shifted ground and demanded: "And why not? A pretty little creature like you should be dancing to her heart's content and setting the gentlemen all topsy-turvy. I wish I could have seen you spinning about the ballroom, I do. Bigelow says it was something beautiful. Yes, and remembering to send thanks to Mrs. Moffett and Cook. We had a different sort of Belle in Tufton House last night, I warrant!"

Since Nannie's meaning was quite clear, and Carolina thought best not to understand, she asked for her dressing gown and fumbled for her slippers.

"I've overslept," she cried, seeing the clock. "Is Cedric gone?"

Nannie answered from the depths of the wardrobe that Cedric was long gone and might be halfway back.

"What do you mean? Halfway back?"

"Well, miss, his Lordship's groom says he was ordered to saddle a horse for Master Cedric *because he was to hurry back.* I dare say his Lordship wants him to make a longer visit."

"Yes, and Papa will want to oblige my uncle. Oh, how splendid."

Clad in a new dressing gown, Carolina sat down at her mirror while Nannie brushed and tidied her hair.

"How can I have slept so late?" she wondered aloud. "My uncle must think I am a lazy-bones."

But Nannie did not agree. His lordship, she opined, would not expect to see her before noon any more than he would her ladyship. For that matter, he had only just taken a cup of tea in his bedchamber himself.

"Well, I hope the servants got some extra winks," Carolina said. "It is all very well to dance all night. Those who worked to make our beautiful party are the ones entitled to rest."

"Who would brush my lady's hair?" demanded Nannie.

Carolina looked up at her contritely. "Oh, Nannie, are you tired? I can do that! Do you suppose I have anyone to wait upon me in Dolden Overhill?"

Nannie plied the brush more vigorously than ever. "I am *not* tired. No one is going to do *my* work. And when you go back home I may go along."

Carolina reached to squeeze her hand. "You can be sure I would take you if I could, dearest Nannie. How my Mama would like that! But we do not live so grandly in Dolden, you know. My papa says we are meant to serve, not be served. He would be very troubled to see me sitting indolently like this."

A footman tapped then and came in with bouquets from Mr. Howard and Lieutenant Luce. While Nannie directed the positioning of the vases, her mistress perused the accompanying notes. Mr. Howard's was a flowery message that made her shake her head. Rob was less formal: "Off to the Manor for a few days per Father's request. I shall tell everyone that you have taken the town by storm, *just as we expected.*"

Smiling, she observed to Nannie that the gala had not ended with the last chord. James's pink rosebuds on her dresser, now removed from their silver holder and set in water by Nannie, were drooping a bit, but they gave off a sweet fragrance that would always remind her of a glorious evening.

When Carolina had donned her mama's blue muslin and wrapped her mama's pearls about her wrist as a bracelet, she went down to the drawing room—still hung with garlands but its furniture restored—and was amazed to discover her aunt, ensconced before the grate, sipping chocolate. Lady Tufton was ravishing in a coral twill morning dress.

"Why, Aunt," she exclaimed. "I thought you would be sleeping!"

"There are sure to be callers," her aunt replied. "It would not be proper for you to receive them alone." She did not add that she rather expected a visit from Lord Aintree to herself, and very likely Haverill also, since he was punctilious in social matters.

Lady Tufton had scarcely finished speaking when Mrs. Lessenover and Miss Lessenover were announced, and close on their heels came Lord Aintree. While Miss Lessenover endeavored to tell Miss Weldon how much she had enjoyed her ball, the Earl made civil conversation with the older ladies. If his lordship was bored, he did not reveal it. Nevertheless, Lady Tufton was relieved when Lord Gilly joined them and engaged Mrs. Lessenover in a discussion of her daughter's musical training, so that his wife was able to flirt agreeably with Lord Aintree.

The younger ladies were enlivened, presently, by the appearance of several gentlemen of the highest fashion. Another lady arrived with her budding daughter, and finally there came a simpering fool of a woman who toad-ate Lady Tufton faithfully and therefore was one of her bosom-bows.

Servants replaced the chocolate pot with an imposing urn of tea, and sherry appeared. It was like a party all over again.

Lady Tufton was correct about Mr. Haverill's courtesy, although his sense of timing was better than hers. He and Mr. James Haverill called during the afternoon when the crowd had gone. Neither hostess found fault with this, even when Lord Dooly was added to the group.

The moment of test came when Mr. Haverill went off to visit with Lord Tufton and James was monopolizing Miss Weldon, so that Lady Tufton was compelled to entertain Lord Dooly. Eligible suitor he might be (for someone else), but even Harriet's enthusiasm (and uncertain temper) was strained by his measured clauses.

Her ladyship would never admit Lord Dooly to be a dolt. He was too wealthy and too well-connected for that! But she only with difficulty restrained an urge to shake him— and clap a lid on him, like a pot that threatened to overflow. Her boredom did not impel her to abandon her matrimonial plans. Husbands, from her point of view, were not a matter of entertainment, although if they were amiable, like Gilly, it was certainly very convenient. A lady's *first* thought must be to establish herself well. To waste her time and talents on insignificant gentlemen was extremely foolish of Caro. James Haverill might be a handsome blade, but he was not of age (which meant he had no control of his funds) and even when he did come into them would remain forever a mere Mister.

Miss Weldon's upbringing had not given her material ambitions. It had, however, taught her the proper concern for every guest, so that presently she was drawing James Haverill into general conversation with Lord Dooly and her aunt. It was easy and natural for her mama's daughter to point out to his lordship how his orchids, now distributed in smaller containers about the drawing room, had withstood the fatigue of a crowded ball. All four then civilly embarked upon a discussion of the cultivation of orchids, about which none of them knew anything.

"I had plants sent from South America and my gardener has done very well with them," Lord Dooly told them. "Strange flowers. Exotic, don't you know? Grow on tall trees."

"In a greenhouse!" protested Caro.

"Oh, mine aren't so big. May have to build a taller greenhouse. Can't be sure. That is to say, not all are trees. Must wait and see, wait and see."

Caro asked, "But how long?"

"Can't say. My gardener might be able to tell you. He says," Dooly wound up triumphantly, "the whole matter is excessively complex."

His auditors assumed expressions of amazement and awe, so as to appear suitably impressed.

Miss Weldon then found an opportunity to tell James Haverill that Cedric would be soon restored to their society.

"What is this?" exclaimed Lady Tufton, overhearing. "Cedric coming back? This is good news."

"Famous!" cried James. "There is going to be a balloon ascension and I know he will enjoy that."

"Go up in a balloon?" objected Miss Weldon. "Oh, no!"

James laughed merrily. "Of course not! It is something to *see*. Perhaps we could make up a party."

"Rather a nonsensical idea—rising in the air," said Lady Tufton depressingly.

Lord Dooly offered heavily that he believed some scholars thought there might be interesting possibilities in flight. "I prefer Terra Firma, myself, but there has been some talk of harnessing balloons in some fashion."

"Well, if *you* say so," amended her ladyship immediately.

"Oh, I do not say it can be done," Lord Dooly responded. "Just that there is speculation about air travel."

Lady Tufton declared air travel—what an imaginative

idea!—could never be so comfortable as a well-sprung chaise, but if his lordship thought they should view the balloon ascension, then by all means they must go.

Before they could debate which gentleman should escort them in which carriage, Lord Tufton and Mr. Haverill joined them and were asked for an opinion on the merits of ballooning.

Mr. Haverill looked amused, but let Gilly speak for them both.

"It is all rather nonsense, I expect, though it might be exciting—especially for young gentlemen. I fear, Harriet, you would find it a sad crush of vehicles and people."

Lady Tufton, who did not like crushes unless the "people" were *ton* beaux clustering around her begging for a dance, a rose from her corsage, her attention, said that it all sounded a hum to her and something only boys would enjoy.

James did not miss her meaning. He wilted and looked anxiously to his cousin, whereupon Mr. Haverill said lazily that gentlemen were always more interested in scientific things than ladies. "Why not wait until Cedric returns? If he wants to see the ascension then we can plan an outing for all who wish to go."

Since no one, not even Miss Weldon, could assert Mr. Weldon's desires with conviction, the project was tabled and instead they entered into a discussion of when Cedric might return.

"I know you enjoy the lad, my dear," Lord Tufton told his wife, "so I lent Cedric a hack to speed his trip. Unless Charles has something for him to do I expect him back with us in a day or two."

Miss Weldon chuckled, which drew a frown from her aunt, and said only Mama was indispensable to Papa. He would be sure to send Cedric as soon as the girls had approved his wardrobe.

"I hope it may be soon," said Lady Tufton. "He dances

divinely. We must take him with us to evening parties, Carolina."

"Now, don't make a dandy of the boy," warned his lordship. "He is young for that, I think."

Cedric's sister ventured the opinion that Cedric would never be a dandy because his interests were scholarly.

"Excellent. Excellent," said Lord Dooly, entering the conversation with some clout. "Good to know some young gentlemen have serious minds. He will like my library, Miss Weldon. I will lend him books. Yes, yes. Lend him all he wants."

Lord Tufton, whose library was known for its depth, exchanged glances with Haverill, while his wife oozed appreciation of Dooly's generosity.

"For heaven's sake!" exploded James. "He won't come to London to *read*. I daresay he will save that for Oxford." Which sentiment did not raise James in Lady Tufton's opinion and which had the effect of making his cousin, who agreed with him, decide it was time to leave.

Lord Dooly also rose to depart. He might not know the best way to charm a lady, but he did know the niceties of society, and he succeeded in kissing the ladies' hands with aplomb.

"Lord Dooly is such a polished gentleman," said Lady Tufton when the door had closed upon their guests.

"Oh, he is a gentleman, right enough," agreed the viscount, "but then so is James, and I must say James has a great deal more—well, he is more taking. Don't you think so, Caro?"

In her usual uncritical manner Carolina replied that all the gentlemen her aunt and uncle had introduced to her seemed gentlemanly.

"Naturally," drawled Lady Tufton. "They would not be presented to you otherwise. I hope I don't have to keep reminding you that you must not look upon James as an eligible *parti*. His mother would never approve the match."

"And what of Dooly's mama?" demanded Lord Tufton before Carolina could reply. "I have the impression that she disapproves. In fact, I strongly suspect *no* lady will ever meet with Lady Dooly's approbation."

"Yes, but Lord Dooly commands a fortune and can do as he pleases."

"If he dares!"

Seeing that her aunt and uncle were close to a quarrel (if ever Gilly could be said to quarrel), Carolina hastily interposed to say she did not wish to attach his lordship, and this, while not pouring oil on troubled waters, served to redirect Lady Tufton's ire.

"You are just as unreasonable as your mother! I suppose if I leave you to settle matters you will make up a match with some half-pay subaltern or a penniless clergyman. Let me tell you, young lady, there will be no nonsense under *my* chaperonage. It is your duty to marry as well as you can."

"Now, Harriet," interposed Lord Tufton, "take a damper. It is not so heaven-or-hell. Surely in England there must be any number of gentlemen who would be acceptable to you and equally pleasing to Caro. After last night, I do not think we have to worry about her attaching anyone who strikes her fancy."

Carolina thought her uncle's fondness made him over-complacent, but she appreciated his defense.

Lady Tufton's wrath had begun to subside, when her husband ruined everything by adding, "I don't see why you won't acknowledge James's interest in Caro. Look how often he and Lawrence come."

Enraged, but not wanting to say Mr. Haverill came to call upon herself, Harriet said tightly and noncommitally that the Misters Haverill were certainly very attentive, and Carolina decided it was the moment for her to expatiate again on the enjoyment of a season at London and the kindness of her aunt in sponsoring her into the *ton*.

"Harriet enjoys it," said her uncle, sincerely, if fallaciously.

At this point Lady Tufton must have been struck dumb, for she said nothing at all.

Bigelow's announcement of Lady Franklin was heralded by all with relief.

Carolina must be pleased when Cedric rejoined her in London, for she loved him dearly, and took comfort from his company. When so much was done for her pleasure, she was ashamed to admit to the homesickness that her wise parents suspected. They knew Cedric's presence would allay this, and it was so. At the same time, Carolina took upon her shoulders the responsibility for her brother and was anxious lest the egocentric life of the *ton* harm him. She held high opinions of his moral values yet knew him to be too unworldly—too trusting—to escape all temptations that came in the guise of friendship. Her own mistake, as she afterwards discovered, was in underestimating the seriousness of his nature. Frivolous affairs did not interest him and therefore could not seduce him.

Cedric cared very little about balloons. He soon realized, however, that James cared a great deal, so he agreed to go, and he joined James in urging Carolina to be one of the group. His parents had dropped enough hints to give him an inkling that James might be seriously interested, and James's constant attentions to Caro supported the idea. Cedric had seen many country swains making cakes of themselves over his sister. He himself thought Caro was just about perfect. So it seemed only reasonable to foster what romance there might be. Cedric was too young to question the likelihood of Caro's being attracted to a charming rattle. He saw James as a smashing fellow who *might* deserve his sister.

So Cedric returned and accompanied the ladies to balls

and routs, and Lady Tufton entered into a period of unusual amiability.

Many invitations came for Miss Weldon. Her papa was right: fortune hunters did not hang about her. Nevertheless, many gentlemen admired the sweetness of her face and nature, and the friends of her aunt and uncle were pleased to stamp her unexceptionable.

But Miss Weldon received no offers.

Lady Tufton fretted about this and her husband said she was expecting too much too soon. Caro was only beginning to be known. Lady Franklin, to whom Lady Tufton voiced her doubts, said roundly that offers made on a few days' acquaintance were apt to be dubious ones. The sort of parti Lady Tufton would wish for her niece would not act hastily. He would take the trouble to *know* Carolina, and then of course he would be unable to resist her.

Although in London there were as yet no offers for Miss Weldon, in Dolden Overhill the air was matrimonial.

Rob Luce had known Caro from childhood and had always held her in affection. When he saw her surrounded by admiring Town Beaux he began to think that it might be necessary to make their relationship more permanent. His father's summons presented him with an occasion to lay the matter before him, but poor Rob did not meet with success.

For a long time Sir John had recognized the beauty and sweet composure of the vicar's daughters. As a father of sons, he had suffered some anxiety lest one of his offspring become entangled, and now he was faced with the fact.

"Well, Rob," he said with a troubled face, "I cannot like it."

"But, sir," his son interrupted, "the Weldons are your friends!"

"Yes, but they haven't two pennies to rub together, and I can do so little for you. First of all, there is your mother's jointure. After that, most of what I have is entailed upon your brother, you know. You can hardly expect him to make you an allowance."

"No, of course not. I have my pay, though."

Sir John shook his head. "Hardly keeps you now."

Since his father had already helped him over several tight spots, he could not argue this point.

"A lady cannot be asked to live without all the small fineries of life," his father continued. "Even if she were willing, could you bring yourself to ask it?"

Rob bit his lip.

"I would not like to—to—deny Caro's needs. Needs aren't the same as wants! She is not accustomed to *plenty*, you know, Father. The Weldons are very frugal, but they are happy!"

Sir John shot him a level look. "Can you promise her equal happiness?"

Rob said miserably that he did not know. Then he asked: "Are you forbidding me, sir?"

"No, I am not. Carolina is a charming girl—the very sort I would wish you to choose. Your mother would be delighted." His voice dropped. "It is not your choice that pains me, but my own inability to underwrite it."

"Thank you, sir," said Rob gruffly.

Sir John was silent a long moment. "If you will be guided by me, you will not address Mr. Weldon at this time. Has Caro a *tendre* for you?"

Rob said he did not know.

"If she is the belle you tell us, your suit may be hopeless, in which case the less said the better. I recommend you spend more time with her. When you have reason to think her affections may be directed toward you, then is the time to speak to Mr. Weldon. I would not want to be the one to break two hearts! The final decision will have to be his."

"Yes, sir. I expect you are right," said Rob, dashed but—being young—not unhopeful.

"One more thing," said his father.

"Sir?"

"I suppose it is useless to tell you not to court her. Tread lightly, son. There must be no assault to her emotions."

Rob said he understood, and had he permission to return to London?

"That I *can* approve," replied Sir John, "but keep a steady head, son." He studied his offspring, seeing a clean and earnest young man, the sort a father may take pride in, but he did not see a desperate lover. With an inward sigh of relief, he added: "I expect you can spare your mother a few days, eh, now that you are here."

"Certainly, sir," said Rob with a half-smile.

They parted not ill-pleased with each other.

Sir John did not repeat the interview to his wife. Although he held her in deep affection, he had some doubts of her emotional stability—at least where the boys were concerned. He also had the usual male misapprehension that women *always* looked upon romance with a tolerant eye, yes, even with a partisan one. It was a natural view for a man to take. Lady Luce, however, was not a man and did not think like one. She adored her sons, but would have perceived instantly that Rob had not formed a lasting attachment, her wishes for his happiness not blinding her in the least to the symptoms of infatuation.

After two days pleasantly spent with his mother, Rob set off again for London, where he was welcomed warmly by Miss Weldon, though without any of the particular interest he had hoped to inspire. Miss Weldon was glad to see him, but she had not been languishing. His brother officers received him into their midst with more enthusiasm, and took him off to a cosy taproom to witness a cockroach race which drove from his mind all plans of wedlock.

Ten

Whenever Lord Tufton was unable to resist remarking upon James's attentiveness to Carolina, his wife was quick to point out that Mr. Haverill watched over his cousin like a hawk. "Give over, Gilly," she would say. "Haverill never lets James out of his sight. If you will listen to me, you will look elsewhere for a husband for the girl."

As many of these exchanges took place in the privacy of my lord's and lady's apartments, Carolina was spared some of the embarrassment attached thereto. But she heard enough to realize speculation about her prospects was rife at Tufton House. It was humiliating for a young lady, admittedly in the marriage mart, to feel herself the subject of both doubts and ambitions, and if Cedric and the girls were not depending upon her, she would have taken the first stage home.

The prospect of life with Lord Dooly was dismal. Title and wealth could not outweigh with *her* a lack of honor and affection. If pressed, she might have admitted Lord Dooly was entitled to respect for his scholarly inclinations, punctilious courtesy, and firm (if rigid) principles, but the respect which counted with Carolina was wholly bound to love. The mutual devotion of Charles and Lydia Weldon was thus both blessing and trial to their daughter. She had had the comfort and joy of a happy home; she could not be satisfied with less.

Since the viscount so clearly favored a match with James

Haverill, and since James was obviously enamored of Miss Weldon, Miss Weldon must (with sighs) consider him. She liked James. Who could not—handsome, amiable, and attentive as he was? But she felt a century older than he and was not inclined to mothering a husband. A husband, she felt, should—like Papa!—command his household with benevolent authority. It was true that the influence of Mr. Haverill upon James could only be good; perhaps in ten years James might become an admirable man such as his cousin was. Meanwhile, she could not bring herself to commit her affection and future to a light-hearted lad.

About Rob Luce's *tendre* she had no suspicion. He was her old friend and she had for him a real fondness, but like Lady Luce, would have thought his matrimonial ambitions a bit ridiculous, rather sweet, and quite definitely a phase to be outgrown.

The truth was, Caro thought less about her own situation than about Cedric's.

A dearer, more obliging young man could not exist. He dutifully escorted his aunt and sister to a round of entertainments, danced, made himself useful, never complained of long hours or insipid conversation, and restrained his yawns until safely ensconced in the homeward-bound carriage. He showed no evidence of dissipation, or even inclination to it.

But he continued to disappear every day.

That is, he had always breakfasted and gone out before the ladies or his lordship reached the breakfast table, and he generally returned shortly before time for tea.

Young gentlemen do not like to be questioned about their affairs (Mama had explained this to Caro some years ago when Rob—even dear Rob—took exception to her questions), so Carolina was reluctant to badger her brother, and, being anxious, spilled out her worries the next time Mr. Haverill asked about her troubled demeanor.

By this time Mr. Haverill, who knew the pitfalls for green young men but who had formed some opinion of Cedric's reliability, was able to say with comforting assurance, "He has found something to interest him. I do not think it can be dangerous or damaging. If you permit, I will make some discreet inquiries."

Miss Weldon was able to breathe a thankful assent before Lady Tufton claimed Mr. Haverill's attention.

Mr. Haverill's inquiries bore no relation to badgering. Knowing any butler worth his wage kept a firm finger on the household pulse, he addressed Bigelow at their next encounter with his customary "Good morning, Bigelow," and added casually, "Mr. Cedric in?"

Bigelow replied that Cedric had gone out.

James was already mounting the stairs in anticipation of finding Miss Weldon in the drawing room when Mr. Haverill, handing over his gloves and hat, said, "Dear me. I never seem to come at the right time to catch Mr. Cedric."

"An early riser, sir," offered Bigelow. "Out every morning by nine."

"Ah, these young people!" Mr. Haverill murmured, and Bigelow indicated his agreement with a slight nod.

After that it was a simple matter to set a groom (divested of Haverill livery) to watch in Grosvenor Square. Two days later, Mr. Haverill mounted to the garret of a made-over house and presented his impeccable self in the studio of a portrait painter.

The portraitist, who had shown little interest in James or his friends, recognized a gentleman of distinction and affluence. He put down his brush and came forward wondering what fee he might ask for a portrait of the gentleman—or his current ladybird—or even (possibly) his wife.

Mr. Haverill explained smoothly that he was the cousin of young Master David Haverill and that, being in the area, had thought to visit the studio to acquaint himself with the painter's style.

"May I look about quietly?" he asked. "I do not want to keep you from your work."

Perceiving the gentleman was a new sort of customer with some understanding of the muse's demands, the painter assented and returned to his easel.

Mr. Haverill surveyed the attic with interest. In his home were many fine paintings, but until now he had taken little interest in the circumstances of their creation. The light, the colors, the odors here intrigued him. Several students labored at cruder paintings of their own. He walked slowly among them, stopping at last beside a blond head, familiar, but bent in desperate engrossment over a nearly finished still-life.

"Very nice," approved Mr. Haverill.

Cedric looked up apprehensively, but appeared unable to speak.

"Is it for sale?" asked Mr. Haverill.

"Oh, no, sir," gasped Cedric, focusing anxious eyes upon him.

"If you change your mind, come to me. Don't look so alarmed, lad. I'll keep your secret."

Cedric stammered thanks and colored hotly, but Mr. Haverill had already moved to another student with a civil comment. None could suppose he took a special interest in any one of them.

The mystery had been solved, but what to tell Miss Weldon remained a problem. Her confidence in Cedric's character and Mr. Haverill's estimate of him had been vindicated. Where most young blades would be chasing after light-skirts or risking their father's credit at cards and dice, Cedric had been *studying.* Not scholarly subjects, to be sure, or even finance or politics, but at least he was at work, creative work, which Mr. Haverill could only endorse, although he suspected it might find little favor with the vicar. That Miss Weldon's views in many ways resembled her father's he had begun to suspect. Would she be shocked by Cedric's dabbling in art? He rather thought she might, though she would excuse him out of sisterly fondness.

So he told Miss Weldon that he had found Cedric to be wholesomely engaged. "He is making the most of his visit to London by pursuing a study of cultural things. This is intelligent of him, you know."

"Oh, yes," agreed Caro eagerly. "Cedric is very intelligent!"

"Yes, so I would judge. Give him his head, Miss Weldon. He will not disgrace you."

Caro cried she was not afraid of *that*. Mr. Haverill smiled encouragingly. "Of course not. Let me say instead, he will not come to harm. I shall pledge myself to see that he does not."

Feeling she had the best possible advisor and Cedric a guardian angel, Carolina thanked Mr. Haverill warmly, and if she did not abandon all worry, at least formed an optimistic view of the outcome of Cedric's activities.

Lord Dooly was becoming so marked in his attentions to Miss Weldon that it was rumored there were bets recorded at White's on his coming up to scratch. Although Miss Weldon had not heard of them, Lady Dooly had, and the honeyed venom which issued from her mouth had the dual effect of encouraging many to wager his lordship Would Not Dare while others thought her ladyship exceedingly unladylike and therefore backed Miss Weldon out of defense for the underdog.

Lady Tufton was enchanted. This sort of rumor did not dismay her, for it meant, she was convinced, that Dooly was almost snared.

Two suitors and a brother held somewhat different views, however, each having Miss Weldon's welfare at heart, and each believing he knew best what should benefit her. Mr. James Haverill and Lt. Luce of course each thought Miss Weldon would be happiest with *him,* and Cedric, when each in youthful fashion had confided his hopes and opinions, was ready to welcome either as his brother. An odd confederacy grew among the three. They claimed as much of Caro's time as possible, watched Lord Dooly and reported his progress to each other, planned and rejected strategy.

"My governor says if Caro doesn't favor me, I mustn't offer," Rob admitted glumly.

"Of course she favors you," declared Cedric. "She always said you were best of the Luces, even though she knows John is my special friend."

"That doesn't mean she'd marry me," objected Rob.

"Can't let Dooly carry her off," objected James.

"Well," said Cedric, "then you offer."

James said he would like to, indeed he would, just the wife he would like, only he wasn't sure he was ready yet to get leg-shackled. "The mater wouldn't take it well," he explained. "No offense meant, Cedric, but she wouldn't like it."

"What's that got to say to anything?" demanded Rob. "Better you than Dooly!"

"You don't know m'mother. Would cut up rough."

"Not for long," insisted Rob. "Caro's a gem. Your mother'd be bound to come around sooner or later. All the old tabbies of Dolden think Caro's perfection." When James looked doubtful, he added belligerently, "And she is!"

"You needn't shout at me," objected James. "I think she's perfection, too. If you want me to offer—"

"I want to offer *myself*," Rob interrupted, "but Dooly— good God! He has a title and a fortune!"

"At least James has plenty of the Ready," Cedric pointed out. "It had better be James."

Rob sunk his head in his hand and seemed unconsoled by James's saying, well, he would do it. "Have to shake Lawrence, somehow," James muttered.

"Would *he* object?" asked Cedric, who had some certain anxieties of his own concerning Mr. Haverill.

"Oh," said James, "he likes Miss Weldon well enough.

Stands to reason. Wouldn't stand up with her at balls if he didn't—doesn't 'oblige' people, you know. Besides, he can't care whom I marry! But a fellow doesn't make an offer when his cousin is along!"

Rob was then heard to groan, and the three gentlemen regarded each other with a singular lack of enthusiasm.

A few mornings later, as Mr. Haverill was experimenting with a new design of neckcloths under the watchful and admiring eye of his valet, a knock fell upon the street door and an over-zealous footman opened widely enough for a stranger to insinuate himself into the hall. Clawson stepped forward promptly to defend his territory. He was an experienced butler who generally could gauge exactly any visitor's importance, but for once he hesitated. The youth carried a large flat parcel, like any tradesman's flunky, yet he had a singularly beautiful and gentlemanly face and a coat of respectable cut.

The visitor smiled sweetly and asked if Mr. Haverill were at home.

While Clawson was wondering what reception would be proper, the pleasant voice added: "I wonder if you would ask him to see Cedric Weldon."

Clawson, upon whom the name of Weldon acted powerfully, said, "Certainly, sir. Please follow me." He deposited Cedric in a parlor and went off (on comfortable feet) to summon his employer.

Having finally arranged his neckcloth, Mr. Haverill was being assisted into his coat by his valet when Clawson announced the guest. Mr. Haverill eyed him shrewdly. The fact that Clawson had come himself instead of sending a footman clearly indicated Clawson would require his employer to see Mr. Weldon. Mr. Haverill bit his twitching lip and said that he would join Mr. Weldon presently.

"Very good, sir." Clawson then opened the door and

waited implacably until Mr. Haverill preceded him down the stairs.

"Well, Cedric, good morning," said Mr. Haverill, going into the parlor and firmly closing the door.

"Good morning, sir," replied Cedric calmly, for though he found Mr. Haverill somewhat imposing, he liked him and therefore did not fear him.

"Have you come to sell me the still life after all?"

"Yes, sir—that is, no, sir." He cast his host a rueful half-smile. "My instructor had some rather unflattering things to say about the still-life, sir—"

"But the one who buys is the one to pass judgment," interrupted Mr. Haverill.

"Well, sir, I could not let you—not after what he said—so I have brought this." He had been drawing the wrapping from his canvas and now set it upon the mantel and stood back.

Mr. Haverill studied the painting in silence. It was a smallish square, the near-view of a chair-arm, heavy and carved, and lolling on it, like a leopard in a tree, was a handsome, spotted cat. Two legs dangled in easy abandon, and upon the creature's face was an expression of sensuous satisfaction.

"Full of fresh mouse!" exclaimed Mr. Haverill.

"No," corrected Cedric gently, "fish heads."

Mr. Haverill chuckled. "I like it. Is it the painter's cat?"

"No sir, ours."

"Good God. Never say you did this from memory!"

Cedric admitted that he had.

"Well, that is talent indeed." He was about to buy it on the spot when his natural astuteness nudged him to ask questions. "I should think you might want to keep it," he suggested slowly.

"Oh," said Cedric, "of course I *would*. M'sisters would make a noise about it, I expect, but—you see, sir—well, I need the money."

Mr. Haverill examined him thoughtfully. "In dun territory, lad?"

Cedric shook his head. "Oh, no, sir," he replied, unoffended. "I'm taking lessons, you see, and I cannot be a charge on my father or my uncle for *that.*"

"Perhaps not. Does your father know you paint?"

A sudden flush in Cedric's cheeks told Mr. Haverill a great deal.

"No, sir. I have been making little sketches for a long time, but this is my first opportunity to work with oils. I'm afraid my father would be shocked. He—he is inclined to think art a waste of time."

"What about Leonardo da Vinci? Reubens? Velasquez? Surely he admires them!"

Cedric exclaimed, "But, sir, they are *great!*"

"Yes, and greatness begins with aptitude." He was about to offer to frank Cedric for his lessons, when it occurred to him that it might, in the long run, lead astray a scholarly mind (the vicar ought to know his son better than he), interfere in family relationships, and cause problems of unanticipated sorts.

He asked if Cedric wished to pursue a career in art.

"No, sir," declared the youth firmly. "My uncle is most generous and kind—I am to go to Oxford. There is so much I want to study! I shall only paint for pleasure, sir, although I hope to learn to do it as well as I can." His eyes danced then. "Do you think my father would like a Madonna for his church?"

"I can't say about him, but I will buy your cat. He is a handsome beast."

Cedric felt obliged, even if it queered the sale, to explain apologetically that the cat was female and the mother of eighty-two children.

"Good God!" exclaimed Mr. Haverill. "How can she look so pleased?"

"They are singularly beautiful children," Cedric assured him with a grin.

"Very well. I will buy *her*. How much?"

"Two pounds?" asked Cedric tentatively.

"Five," said Mr. Haverill. Cedric protested it was too much, but Mr. Haverill said never fear, he'd turn it to good account. "There is one stipulation, however. You will not mention our arrangement—or the picture—to anyone."

"Not even Caro?"

"Especially not Miss Weldon. I will tell her myself when the time seems right. I think, though, that if you do not want her to write something alarming to your parents you will make some effort to be more—er—visible, for she tells me you are often missing and she is growing troubled."

"Caro is? I thought she was too busy to notice my coming and going!"

Mr. Haverill said he believed Miss Weldon was devoted to her brother and extremely anxious about him.

"Yes," admitted Cedric. "Caro is eldest, you know. She is accustomed to watching over all of us."

"If you go about some with James I think she will cease to worry or count your hours. You like James, don't you?"

"Oh, I do! He's a great one. So much more knowledgeable than I."

"Only in some ways," said Mr. Haverill. "Only in some ways. I fancy your History and Latin are stronger than his."

"Yes, but I like History and Latin," Cedric said. "James is mad for sporting things. Wants to ape you, you know."

Mr. Haverill's calm was shaken. "Ape me!"

"That's what he says. Thinks you are top of the trees."

"What a hum! I've already agreed to buy your cat. No need to turn me up brown!"

Cedric was too much a Weldon to dispense empty flattery. It did occur to him, however, that perhaps he had been too familiar with the gentleman who was his benefactor.

"I am grateful, sir, and I thank you," he said earnestly.

"When I look about your home and see magnificent paintings—well, I wonder if mine will be only an embarrassment to you. I am not so blind that I cannot see it is crudely done."

Mr. Haverill said he thought Cedric's problem was that he saw only *five pounds* instead of a painting. "Now, I see something different altogether."

"A cat?" asked Cedric doubtfully.

"A way of life," replied Mr. Haverill.

Eleven

The morning of the balloon ascension came in with a torrent of rain. Concerned for his balloon, if not for his person, the balloonist cancelled his flight. There was no way to publish the information across London, but no one of any wit would venture out in such a downpour. Even among the witless, few enjoy being drenched.

The ladies sat a while by the grate in the morning room, and Carolina soon found the light too poor for needlework. She knew no gossip with which to amuse Lady Tufton. Very likely her ladyship thought her dull company, especially after Caro failed to be suitably shocked or impressed when several choice *on dits* were advanced by her aunt.

"Perhaps someone will call," said Lady Tufton, finally.

Caro looked doubtful. "Ladies won't want to put their feet down outside."

"No," agreed her aunt, "and what beau will risk wilting his neckcloth? Well, let us go up to the drawing room where there is at least a view of the square."

Rose draperies and a larger fire made the drawing room more cheerful without dispelling the ladies' boredom. Nothing showed of the square, due to sheets of water upon the windows. A couple of times Lord Gilbert looked in on them and evidently found their company less interesting than his books, for he soon went away. Of Cedric nothing was seen.

Carolina could have amused herself by immersing herself in a book, or even reading aloud. Lady Tufton, however, showed no interest or inclination toward reading, and Carolina felt it would be ill-mannered to withdraw her company by taking up a book. Her aunt changed chairs restlessly and cast about for entertainment. "I declare, I don't know when I have been so bored," she complained.

"Let us have the boys in to play," Caro suggested. "They might enjoy tiddlywinks or cutouts."

The boys' mama protested that nothing made children more perverse than bad weather. "I do not feel equal to chatter and constant motion."

They ate an early nuncheon to pass time, and when they rose from the table were pleased to discover the cloudburst had ended, and water was draining from the pavements. By mid-afternoon a weak sun promised better things. Lady Tufton brightened also and ordered her barouche brought around by four.

"The streets may be muddy," Caro warned.

"Well, the horses won't mind," her aunt replied. "Let us change our clothes." She did not care at all if the horses and carriage were dirtied, making more work in the stable.

After passing the barrier at Hyde Park Corner they advanced placidly along the carriageway, nodding to acquaintances. The crowd was sparse, but growing as the sky became clearer. Since the same winds that were blowing away the rain clouds were also buffeting the park, there was a livelier breeze than generally comfortable for ladies in picture hats.

Presently they saw ahead a curricle drawn to one side and a gentleman on horseback speaking with its occupants.

"That is Haverill's rig," Lady Tufton pointed out. "I do believe it's James driving." Then the lady with him turned her head and they saw it was Mrs. Haverill.

Lady Tufton ordered John Coachman to pull up alongside. And the horseman obligingly guided his horse out of their way, turning to be revealed as Gilly's friend, Lawrence Haverill.

Polite greetings were exchanged and general approbation of the change in weather. The stamping of Mr. Haverill's team and their gentle pulling at their bits kept James attentive to his responsibilities, so that he could contribute little to the conversation. The burden of talk fell mainly upon Haverill and Lady Tufton, the latter animated, her doldrums forgotten. Mrs. Haverill was only a shade better than civil; fortunately she did not notice several admiring glances cast by her son at Miss Weldon.

By this time the wind had become riotous, and all three ladies clutched their hats with tendrils of hair blowing across their faces.

"This is too windy for you," Mr. Haverill declared. "My house is nearest. Let us go there for tea. I have a new painting of which I would like your opinion."

Nothing could have met with more enthusiastic approval. Lady Tufton took the compliment to herself. Mrs. Haverill was equally pleased, liking nothing better than to act as hostess for her husband's nephew; it was also an excellent opportunity to study James's attitude toward the chit. And that chit, having no designs on anyone, was not intimidated by the dragon mother.

"If you will excuse me," Mr. Haverill said, "I will ride ahead to prepare for your comfort." He clapped his heels to his hack and went off at a brisk gait.

The carriages were then turned toward Park Lane, from which they went east into Mount Street. Followed by James, the ladies entered Mr. Haverill's house to be received by Clawson in descending order: "My lady, ma'am, *Miss Weldon.*" He had clarified Caro's connection with his new shoes, and was sure it was wonderfully beneficent.

They were escorted to a room on the ground floor where Haverill awaited them. He had chosen this parlor for its western exposure which let in the pale late sunlight. If Mrs. Haverill expected to serve their tea, she was disappointed, for Clawson dispensed it from a buhl table against the wall, presenting a cup first to the viscountess, next to Mrs. Haverill, and finally to Miss Weldon, for whom he reserved his deepest bow. The gentlemen elected to have tea also, and conversation was desultory as they sipped. Small cakes and thin bread spread with fresh butter were passed by a pleasant-faced woman of middle years.

"What is this about a new picture, Lawrence?" Mrs. Haverill asked.

"I've bought one. Something quite different from my usual."

"Where have you put it?"

"In my study. Will you come there?"

James would have preferred to remain flirting with Miss Weldon. When it appeared the ladies were moving to another room and intended to be polite about whatever they saw, he trailed after them, very conscious of his promise to Cedric and Rob Luce.

Mr. Haverill led them to the wall where Tabby Four Toes was hung.

"Good God!" cried Mrs. Haverill. "Why ever do you want an old tomcat on your wall?"

"What makes you think the beast is male?" he asked.

"Because he looks so self-satisfied," she replied tartly.

Caro exclaimed, "Why it looks like—"

"—an amiable creature?" finished Mr. Haverill quickly. "So the artist says it is. A fond mother of many offspring. Do you like the artist's style, Miss Weldon?"

"Y-yes."

"So do I. There's real talent, although the artist says he only paints for enjoyment. He is a scholar, you see."

Miss Weldon's eyes flew to meet Haverill's, but she said nothing. Understanding flowed between them.

"When did you take to cats?" James asked. "Never had a live one that I remember. I think you must be bamming us."

"No, no. I admire talent when I meet it. Lady Tufton, what is your opinion?"

Like James, she suspected Haverill might be teasing them, and so responded noncommitally, "Most interesting."

"Very skillful, I think," persisted Haverill. "Note the detail of the chair arm, Miss Weldon. Isn't it realistic?"

"Oh, very!" Miss Weldon recognized it.

The older ladies having no noticeable interest in cats, their host now suggested another cup of tea, but Mrs. Haverill said she must be going home. She rather thought her son was hanging a bit much to Caro's side.

Lady Tufton promptly concurred it was time to leave. Although she was enjoying the intimate visit to Haverill's home, to linger without the chaperonage of the other matron might expose her (and Caro) to charges of being fast. "Come along, niece," she commanded.

As the older ladies moved toward the door and James sprang to open it, Caro said softly to her host:

"It is Cedric's work, isn't it?"

"Yes. And *very* good," he replied. "Be easy, Miss Weldon. Cedric's commitments are unchanged. Say nothing to your father. Let the boy express himself this way; you can see only good comes from it."

The ladies and James had moved into the hall. Haverill added hurriedly: "He will tell his father himself—before long. It is best that way."

They followed the others.

James was saying to his mother: "Our house is close, Mama, so let us walk. The flagway has dried. No need to call out Lawrence's team." And she assented.

Farewells were said. Lord Gilly's ladies entered their barouche and rolled away.

"I would have thought," said her ladyship, "that Haverill would have served something more lavish than buttered bread. He can certainly afford it!"

"Mr. Haverill never overdoes, does he," responded Caro.

Lady Tufton allowed she might be right. "His clothes are impeccable but never the excess of fashion. And his jewelry—now that you make me think of it—he wears the best, although only a piece or two at one time. A Corinthian, not a fribble."

Caro made no reply, and presently her aunt began to comment on Haverill's house, which, though smaller than her own, met her standards of elegance.

Meanwhile, James and his mother were walking home, James silent because of the turbulence of his emotions. Unaware of her son's inner turmoil, Mrs. Haverill observed in pleased accents that Lady Tufton would catch cold by casting out lures to Haverill. James scarcely heard her. He was thinking his offer could not be put off any longer.

When the door had closed upon his guests, Mr. Haverill stood lost in thought a few moments until, looking up, he found both Clawson and a footman watching him closely.

"Weather looking better."

"Yes, sir," Clawson agreed.

"Think it will hold tomorrow?"

The servants conferred with a glance. "Yes, sir."

"Better get out to see my tenant at Kole, then. Tell Finchley I'll want him and my curricle at eight A.M. And send Weems up."

Clawson said, "Yes, sir," a third time, but Mr. Haverill was already climbing the stairs. "If Mr. James stops by tell him where I've gone."

Kole was only a few miles beyond Dolden Overhill.

Two days later Bigelow might have been surprised when James Haverill presented himself alone at Tufton House, had he not been summoned to arbitrate an armistice between Cook and the fishmonger's impertinent boy. It fell to a footman to admit James, and although he aspired to domestic heights he had none of the deeper insight into gentry ways that was enjoyed by a very proper butler.

Accordingly, James's hat and gloves were received, Lord Tufton was acknowledged to be In, and James was promptly delivered to his lordship's study with no flicker of interest on the footman's part.

"James, my boy! Come in. Come in!" was all the footman heard before the door closed, and there was nothing exceptional in that. Who could have guessed an Offer was imminent when Mr. James was in and out of the house constantly until one (less sharp than Bigelow) might suppose he was a near relation of some sort?

Although Lord Tufton cherished hopes, he had not as yet succumbed to expectations, so he did not immediately perceive that James was arrayed in the most fashionable of waistcoats, that his shirt-points were higher than usual, and his manner agitated.

"Good to see you," declared his lordship convivially. "Came to visit the ladies, I'll be bound. What? Aren't they home? I had not heard them leave."

To which James responded that he was glad to see his lordship and that the ladies had not gone out, at least, the footman hadn't said so—although, for that matter, he hadn't *asked,* as it was his lordship he wanted to see. He then robbed his words of all veracity by looking fixedly at the hearth and seeing nothing.

"Well, sit down, James," said Lord Tufton, resuming his own seat and anticipating a pleasant coze with a young man he liked. "You won't think me antisocial, I hope, when I admit to preferring a call like this to the finest Crush of the Season."

"Oh, no, sir," said James, groping his way to a nearby chair.

"Why did you want to see me?" asked the viscount.

"I—wanted to talk to you, sir," said James, at which point his conversation failed, and for the first time Lord Tufton received some inkling of James's intentions. Could this be an offer? And must he broach the subject himself?

To give James a moment to assemble his wits, Lord Tufton rose, took a hearth broom, and casually swept the immaculate hearth which James had scrutinized with such avid disinterest. Avoiding James's eye, he asked gently: "About Caro, my boy?"

James let out his breath. "Well, yes, your Lordship. I would like your permission—that is, I admire Miss Weldon—and—well, I've never made an offer before, but if you are willing, sir, I would *like* to."

His hopes realized, Lord Tufton abandoned the hearth broom and beamed upon the confused suitor.

"Of course I am willing. Like nothing better," he said heartily. "And I will confess to you that I hoped you and Caro would make a match. The only thing is, though—I really feel I must point this out—you are somewhat young for matrimony."

"Past twenty," responded James, "and I don't care much for raking—although, of course I enjoy sports. But Cedric seems to think—well, sir, we can't let Dooly snap her up. It doesn't bear thinking of!"

"No, no!" agreed his lordship with feeling. He had little interest in the opinions of James's mother, but did ask what Haverill thought about the matter.

"Lawrence?" repeated James, surprised. With no knowledge of Mr. Haverill's sentiments, he said he was sure Lawrence admired Miss Weldon, and anyway had nothing to do with the case.

"Your trustee, is he not?"

"Yes, sir, but very obliging. I mean, he watches my agent closely, and all that sort of thing, but he would never interfere with—with my happiness."

It was true Haverill had gone from town, leaving James to pursue his inclinations. Lord Tufton, determined to see the matter favorably, observed that Haverill was very fond of James. "Well, my boy, you have my blessing. Permission will have to come from Mr. Weldon, but before you go haring off to Dolden you should reach some agreement with Caro. Like to see her now?"

"Y-yes, sir," replied James gamely. Having never read any novels, he wondered what one *said* to a young lady when one invited her to share the rest of one's life.

A footman was summoned and replied to inquiry that Lady Tufton had gone out, but that Miss Weldon was in the drawing room.

The gentlemen exchanged relieved glances.

"Show Mr. Haverill upstairs, please," said his lordship.

Miss Weldon, looking fetching in Susan's white frock with the new green ribbons, was seated on a loveseat with needlework in her lap. When James was announced she laid her sewing beside her and looked up with a welcoming smile.

James thought if one must be a tenant-for-life, one could not ask for a more agreeable partner. He took her hand, kissed it, but did not let go.

Despite the fact that she had received no previous offers, Miss Weldon knew as much about them as any other young lady who had graduated from the nursery, and she recognized more quickly than her uncle what lay in store. An awful moment of decision was upon her.

Kneeling appeared beyond him. James clasped her hand in both of his. Best to get it over at once, he thought.

"Miss Weldon—Caro—Cedric says—your uncle says—" He swallowed hard. "Will you marry me?"

She tugged her hand gently but James held fast.

"Because Cedric says? Because my uncle says?"

"No, no," cried James, jarred. "You must know I admire you excessively! I should have said that first, shouldn't I? But dash it, Caro, you must know by now I admire—and— honor you. Say yes, so we can all be comfortable again."

It was not like any proposal she had read.

"So who can be comfortable?" she demanded.

"Cedric and Rob—and me, of course—and your uncle, too, I expect." James swept her embroidery to the floor and sat down beside her abruptly. "You must not marry Dooly! It won't do at all!"

"Why not?" she asked, agreeing with him but wanting to get to the bottom of things.

"Stuffed shirt," he asserted. "Sure to make you stiff-necked sooner or later—and that would be sinful."

Miss Weldon's eyes began to dance, although she said soberly, "Do you think it likely?"

"He will try," James declared. "I could not bear it!" He had always thought Caro's eyes beautiful, and now with them so near, so sparkling, he had a sudden urge to kiss her, but not knowing if he should—or could—or mustn't—mastered himself and again squeezed her hand and begged her to say yes.

Miss Weldon replied with a question of her own. "Mr. Haverill, are you proposing with some quixotic notion of saving me from—from being turned into a snob?"

"Well, not exactly," said James. "It does look, you know, like Dooly is getting serious. Such a stick. Oh, I know he is gentlemanly and all that, but not jolly at all, and we thought—"

"We?" interrupted Miss Weldon.

"Rob and Ced and I. We thought you deserve better. Not that I'm puffing myself up, of course. He's richer than I and has a title, which I haven't, if you care for that—though I can't think you do because you've always been so gracious to me. We thought," he concluded, "you might like me better."

Miss Weldon, who had noted without distress that James said nothing of *loving* her, was willing to believe he liked her, so she said readily and honestly: "I do like you, Mr. Haverill." Since it would hardly be proper to discuss Lord Dooly, she embarked upon no comparisons.

In tones of great relief, James said, "There then! That's

something to build upon!" He wondered if now was the time to kiss her.

"No," said Miss Weldon firmly, as if she had read his thoughts. "Not to build a marriage. I am deeply sensible of the honor you have done me, but I think what you and I have built is a *friendship*. I do so value your—"

"Caro!" cried James. "Are you rejecting me?"

Miss Weldon nodded.

"But you can't!" he objected, dumbfounded. The triumvirate had not considered the possibility of this.

"Well, I have." Amusement saved her from being cross. "You know," she added reasonably, "your mother would not like it."

"Maybe not at first," he admitted. "But sooner or later she'd come around. Cedric says all the old tabbies—well, never mind about that. My mother thinks I'm a catch because that's the way mothers think, I expect."

"She does not think I am one, however," Miss Weldon pointed out.

"But it's my marriage and you suit me very well. Never met another female I could face being shackled to." A sort of defensive indignation began to assail him, and when Miss Weldon observed that viewing matrimony as shackles was not conducive to happiness, he shouted that she was twisting his words, and he stood up and began to stamp back and forth in frustration.

Amused, vexed, not precisely flattered, and more sure than ever that she did not wish to wed James Haverill, Miss Weldon was casting about for a means of ending the interview, when sounds of a carriage arriving before the house brought matters to a head. She could not let Lady Tufton come upon them!

Miss Weldon rose, held out her hand, and said briskly, "Mr. Haverill, my answer is no. Put the thought of marriage away from your mind. I thank you, but—no. Come! Do not let us quarrel, for I am too fond of you for that."

Remembering his manners, James flushed, bowed over her hand. "I shall not despair," he murmured.

"You must go. Lady Tufton has returned."

"Oh my God. Yes, of course." He went rapidly toward the door. Hand upon the knob, he whispered, "Your eternal servant, ma'am." Then he went out and Miss Weldon collapsed in a spasm of giggles which she managed to stifle with one of her aunt's velvet cushions.

Mercifully, her ladyship greeted James in the hall without suspicion and passed to her own chamber before discovering the depravity of her niece.

Twelve

The most lighthearted laughter will not endure when there is no one to share it. Carolina had just brought her merriment under control when the door opened and Lord Tufton's beaming face appeared around the edge of it.

"May I be the first to wish you—"

He broke off, the smile changing to concern as he discovered the room held only one abashed occupant. He came inside and closed the door, saying doubtfully, "Caro?"

The awfulness of what she must relate struck her then. Her heart plummeted.

"Oh, my lord, I am so sorry!" She went toward him in a little rush, hands outstretched. "I do thank you—you will think me ungrateful—and indeed I feel a *wretch*—but I cannot—cannot—"

Her eyes swam with tears.

"You rejected James!"

"Yes, sir. Please, please forgive me! I know you hoped—and you have been so good—"

But his lordship was seeing again the young Harriet, the Harriet who had repulsed a splendid suitor for *him*.

"There, love. There," he said, folding her in his arms. "I thought you liked James. If he doesn't please you, it was quite right to toss him aside."

Whereupon Caro wept, and apologized, and defended in somewhat incoherent fashion. The plunge from hilarity to abysmal remorse racked her spirits, and the kindness and fortitude with which her uncle bore his disappointment was almost more than she could sustain.

"You haven't whistled James down the wind for a title, have you?" he asked anxiously, which Carolina denied with such vehemence that her tears dried up.

Lord Tufton offered his handkerchief.

"Now," he said, as she mopped her face and blew her nose, "put out of your mind all idea of ingratitude. Nothing would please me less than for you to enter into a loveless union out of some sense of obligation." He smiled encouragingly. "Until Roddy doubles in size and quadruples in years and presents me with a daughter-in-law you are the only daughter I have. Your happiness is what matters to me. I was a wishful old man thinking James might provide it."

Carolina smiled back at him. James was sweet, she admitted, but such a *boy*. Papa and her uncle had spoiled her for that sort of husband.

"Naughty Puss!" cried his lordship.

Although neither said so, both wondered what was to become of her. Matches such as James Haverill did not bloom on bushes! And both their minds turned simultaneously to Lady Tufton. She would say young ladies—especially poor ones—could not expect to please themselves in matrimony. The fortunate ones achieved respectable unions and thanked those who made them possible. Lady Tufton, despite her ambitions as regarded Lord Dooly, would be both angry and vitriolic. Neither her husband nor her niece fully understood her desire to rid herself of the burden of a beautiful young competitor, but they knew she would be furious.

"I think," said Lord Tufton wisely and courageously, "you must leave it to me to tell your aunt about this."

"Oh, yes, sir," Caro breathed thankfully.

"I believe there is a ball tonight," he went on.

"Yes, Lady Millbank's. We are invited for dinner, too."

Lord Tufton examined his watch.

"Ah, time for a rest. Run off to your room for a nap,

Puss, so you can be beautiful tonight. There should be a
duke or two present at Lady Millbank's for you to try your
charms upon for a change."

Carolina denied any interest in dukes, but allowed she
would be glad of a quiet time upstairs. She kissed his cheek
and went from the room.

Not being eager to confront his wife, Lord Tufton descended to his study in hopes of organizing his thoughts and
preparing his ammunition. As he reached the lower hall the
front door opened to Mr. Lawrence Haverill's groom.

"Afternoon, Finchley," said his lordship, who being a true
gentleman always spoke to those he knew, regardless of their
status.

"Afternoon, my lord. Mr. Haverill brought back a letter
for Miss Weldon."

He proffered an envelope, and Lord Tufton recognized Mrs.
Weldon's hand. A mother's letter needed no censoring. His
lordship signaled for a footman to deliver it to Miss Weldon.

What Carolina needed was not so much Rest as Escape.
Thankful to leave her uncle to his shattered hopes and the
onus of placating Lady Tufton, she climbed to the second
story in a rather mouselike demeanor and gently shut herself
into the quiet of her chamber, where her mama's letter presently was delivered. Never could a message from Mama be
more thankfully received (assuring her of mama's love) even
though it sang James's name enthusiastically:

Dearest—
Mr. Haverill has been at Kole and has called on his way
to London and has kindly offered to carry a note to you. He
is visiting with your Papa while I write, but I shall not write
long for I wish to become acquainted with him myself. After
all, he is James's cousin, and James (from your letters) has
become a suitor? Well, perhaps not yet. Susan says he is a
beautiful young man. As a mother, however, I must feel there
are more important qualities than physical ones—though

Papa is admittedly handsome—and I hope, by conversing with Mr. Haverill, to form some opinion of James's family. All are well here. Tabby Four Toes appears to be increasing again. How shall we find homes for the children? God bless you, child. I wonder why Mr. Haverill has come?

> *Fondly—*
> *Mama*

When Nannie came in a bit later to help her dress for Lady Millbank's dinner, she found her lying listless but awake upon a chaise longue near the window. Their eyes met, and the unhappy heroine knew she must unburden herself, however disapproving Nannie might be.

"I refused Mr. James," said Miss Weldon with a slight quaver which would have won Nannie, if she were not already enslaved.

"Yes, missy, I knew," said Nannie.

"You *knew?*" exclaimed Miss Weldon, sitting upright.

"Well, yes, Miss Caro. It was generally known Mr. James came alone and was private with his lordship."

Since the vicarage kept no secrets from Annie or Jem (or the whole of Dolden, for that matter), Miss Weldon should not be surprised that the staff of Tufton House was privy to her affairs!

"Then Mr. James had an interview with our young lady and went away looking like a wet partridge," continued Nannie, "not to mention your red eyes as was seen by several. Bound to mean an offer and a turn-down."

As Carolina braced herself for Nannie's disapproval, Nannie added roundly: "And very proper too. Mr. James won't do for *you.*"

Carolina burst into tears and flung herself onto the comforting cushion of Nannie's breast.

"There, love," soothed Nannie, patting and hugging in the most reassuring manner, so that Carolina felt four years old again. "There! He's a very bright young gentleman, I'm sure, and must think the world of you or he wouldn't be making offers. The thing is, does he know what he's doing? I mean, does he understand what matrimony is? Does he appreciate you?"

Evidently Nannie did not expect Carolina to supply the necessary answers, which was fortunate, because she was unable to do so.

"Mustn't grieve, love. We'll find the right husband for you in a winking, I promise you!"

Consoled by Nannie's warmth and affection, but too distressed to heed her pronouns, Carolina quite missed the implication that Nannie, along with Lord Tufton and his wife, had her own aspirations for the girl. Nannie's ambitions would have dismayed Carolina, although any maiden lady who has spent a lifetime raising other people's children might be held to judge character astutely.

"What we need is a nice young dook," had been suggested in the servants' dining hall, but Nannie had sniffed and observed darkly that dukes were seldom nice or young.

None of this did Nannie repeat to her charge, merely cuddling and encouraging, and bit by bit transforming Caro into a poised young lady about to dine out with a hostess of the first stare.

What, meanwhile, his lordship said to his wife was not learned. Her manner was glacial when they met in the lower hall before driving to Lady Millbank's, but flow with angry words she did not. In fact, she did not speak to her niece at all and very little to his lordship, so whatever Lord Gilbert had said to her resulted in a mixed blessing. At Lady Millbank's, she was exceptionally gay, collecting a court of admirers and ignoring the two with whom she was displeased. It made Lord Gilbert and Caro very uncomfortable but did not punish them to the extent which she intended.

Lady Millbank's dinner was served to an elite group of

twenty-six which included the Prime Minister. Conversation was expected to be lofty, and may have been so, although Caro, seated between two lesser lights, found her partners more interested in mild flirtation. She and her aunt and uncle had been included by virtue of Lord Gilly's being a favorite cousin of the hostess; Cedric, at seventeen, was beneath her notice, and no one named Haverill appeared.

After dinner, when other guests arrived for the dancing, Caro looked anxiously for James Haverill, wondering if things would be awkward between them, but he did not come. Mr. Haverill was late and remained distant in Lady Millbank's large ballroom.

The punitive attitude of Lady Tufton did not escape the sapient eye of Lady Franklin. "On a high horse," she muttered to herself, and beckoned Caro with a smile. "Sit here, child. How delightful you look."

Grateful to be swept under Lady Franklin's wing, Caro took the neighboring seat. There were fewer young blades present, more important men from government circles with whom she was not acquainted. Fewer partners sought her out, yet enough to keep her spirits lively, even when every dance was not claimed. It was nearly twelve when Mr. Haverill presented himself before Miss Weldon and requested the honor of the next dance. She looked up quickly with a welcoming smile, which faded before the coolness of his demeanor. It was clear James had confided in him. Why had he asked her to dance when clearly he was so disapproving of her?

It was unjust.

Miss Weldon had not expected praise for allowing James to escape her impecunious toils. Since the Haverills held themselves so very high (or so Aunt Harriet said), very likely they dismissed such a misalliance for James as impossible. But James saw otherwise. *He* was vulnerable. And Miss Weldon's generosity in turning him off might surely be acknowledged by James's family.

She would have liked to have declined the dance, but her few ebullient young swains were examining the punch bowl and she had no other solicitation to fall back upon gracefully. She accepted Mr. Haverill as a partner and allowed him to lead her into a waltz.

The musical selection was unfortunate, for it brought her into close proximity to her partner with his arm about her waist. She could not fail to note the rigidity of his form and face. He was angry. *She* was hurt.

When they had circled the floor once in silence Mr. Haverill asked stiffly when he might wish her well.

Miss Weldon said promptly that she hoped he would *always* wish her well. What he meant she did not know. To quarrel on the dance floor was unthinkable.

There was a pause. Then Mr. Haverill asked if she enjoyed smashing James's hopes.

"No," she answered soberly. "That is, he seemed disappointed, of course, but I cannot believe he has formed any—any lasting sentiment for me. I do not think my refusing his offer will cause him any real grief."

"So little grief, in fact," said Mr. Haverill scathingly, "that he could not face tonight's ball."

It was strange. James's family who rejected her as unsuitable appeared ready to assume she snubbed *them*. The color rose to her cheekbones as she managed to say steadily, "I cannot understand, Mr. Haverill, why you are so displeased. Your cousin's offer was honorable and sweet. I admire him and hope for his happiness as much as you. I cannot, however, suppose his happiness lies with one who is rejected by his family. The unwillingness of the Haverills to receive me has been made very plain to me by both your aunt and mine."

"Harriet?" he cried.

She ignored this outburst. "My papa," she said, "would never wish me to accept a gentleman whose relatives look upon me with disdain."

"Disdain? What nonsense is this? Would I ask you to dance if I disdained you?"

Miss Weldon said she believed he might since he was obviously willing to combine dancing with a critical attitude.

Momentarily silenced, Mr. Haverill clenched his jaw and steered her through the dance with abrupt and automatic turns. By this time Miss Weldon's good nature had been severely buffeted. She raised her eyes to his face.

"Mr. Haverill, we have met as friends. Let us speak openly as friends so there is no misunderstanding. You have guarded your cousin constantly. Perhaps to leave him alone for two days was a mistake, but—"

"You do not understand," he interrupted.

"No, I do not. James is safe from me and you cannot seem to understand that."

The expression in his eyes was inscrutable.

"So," he said harshly. "My aunt was wrong. You are determined to have a title."

Tears of vexation and hurt rose in her eyes. "Sir," she responded, her voice breaking a little, "my parents have taught me that loving kindness can be neither bought nor commanded. I shall marry no man unless I find in him abiding pleasure. In a moment I will appear to have ripped my hem and then you can return me to Lady Franklin."

Unconvinced, but wrung with guilt, Mr. Haverill inclined his head. Presently onlookers saw Miss Weldon trip, exclaim, and catch up her skirt. Then Mr. Haverill led her from the floor to Lady Franklin, who, seeing the stony face of the one and the deep flush of the other, immediately lamented the fictitious tear and took Miss Weldon from the room.

They found a vacant parlor. Lady Franklin closed the door and received a weeping girl into her arms.

"Hateful!" stormed Caro. "Cruel. To think—to think—oh, I hate this city!" She gasped and sobbed while Lady Franklin made cooing sounds but otherwise made no effort to stem the flow. "This wretched *ton!* No one has any *feeling.* It is no place for me. I want to go home."

Her ladyship listened with much sympathy and greater insight. "It is Haverill who is hateful, I collect?" she suggested, producing a handkerchief. While Caro mopped her face, she took the precaution of locking the door.

"Yes. Haverill," said Caro with loathing. "I refused his precious cousin, you see, and he had the nerve to accuse me of title-hunting."

"What an ass," observed Lady Franklin laconically.

Arrested, Caro looked up from the handkerchief. "Ass" was not a noun she could associate with Mr. Haverill. "Oh, no. Not that exactly," she corrected. "He was not himself at all. Not suave. He has been so k-kind, so helpful. I thought he *liked* me. What can have set him off?" She dabbed her nose violently. "Beastly!"

"Never mind," consoled Lady Franklin. "He will learn his error when you marry a lieutenant of the Life Guards."

"Rob? Do you mean Rob? Why, he is my *friend.* I cannot marry him!"

"Well, then, another. Or a nice, doting young clergyman. He will see!"

The ghost of a wry smile rippled across Caro's face. "Aunt Harriet has forbidden soldiers and preachers, my lady."

Perceiving the tempest had ended, Lady Franklin took the risk of asking if she regretted her refusal of James. "I would not want you to pass up happiness because of silly pride," she said.

"If I had pride, there is none left. Mr. Haverill did demolish *that.* Perhaps," Caro said bleakly, "it is just as well. Papa says pride is the worst sin. No. James is dear, but I do not wish to marry him. Very likely, I shall not marry anybody."

Lady Franklin accepted this improbable prophecy matter-of-factly. She produced cologne from her reticule and dabbed Caro's face. After hair-smoothing and a period of calming conversation, they were able to return to the ballroom with Caro's hem miraculously repaired. Mr. Haverill had retired to a card room. Mr. Howard appeared to claim Miss Weldon, who went again onto the dance floor with every evidence of pleasure and no sign that her heart was broken.

When Lord Dooly claimed her afterwards she was so very cordial to him that Lady Dooly was obliged to watch her usually dutiful son sitting in Miss Weldon's pocket for the remainder of the evening. There were many titillated by the sight of Dooly's mama fuming on the sidelines.

Miss Weldon smiled a lot with her mouth and talked animatedly, but her thoughts were not busy with Mr. Howard, or Lord Dooly, or Rob, or any of numerous young gentlemen who wished to dance with her.

She hoped Mr. Haverill was losing a great many pounds in the card room! He was *not,* but only because he did not think punishing his purse was a suitable way to mend his spirits. *Had* he misjudged the girl?

Thirteen

Lord Dooly had received more encouragement than Miss Weldon intended.

The morning after the Millbank ball, having eluded his mother, he knocked at Tufton House and enquired politely for Lady Tufton. His luck was in.

Bigelow explained that her ladyship had gone out on morning calls. To snub and punish Caro, Lady Tufton had left her behind, but Bigelow neither understood nor reported this.

"I see," said Lord Dooly, concealing his satisfaction. He did not, of course, ask to visit an unchaperoned young lady. "Will Lord Tufton receive me, in that case?"

"I believe so, my lord."

Bigelow then conducted the earl to Lord Tufton's study and announced him to the viscount, who greeted him civilly, if without enthusiasm.

"Good day, Lord Dooly. Happy to see you." A polite lie. "Will you sit here?"

Lord Dooly accepted the offered chair, and making the most of evading both his mother and Lady Tufton, proceeded to make an offer in form for Miss Weldon.

The fond uncle's heart sank. How was he to repulse a dullard who, beside being rich, was of higher rank than himself? Would Caro feel obliged to accept such a suitor?

Fortunately, Dooly flowed with flowery phrases in admiration of the lady, which gave Lord Tufton time to arrange his thoughts.

"I am thirty-two years of age, Lord Tufton," Dooly said. "I have been on the town thirteen years and have seen young ladies come and go. You will agree that is no slight experience? Miss Weldon quite outshines all the rest. A lovely lady, what? She has a classic beauty that appeals to one of my intellectual interest. You will notice the present fashions with their Greek lines quite become her. I long to see her in a chiton—white, of course, with perhaps a border of green leaves. Her nose is not Greek, but I must not count that a flaw in an *English* lady."

He laughed lightly. "And when charm is added to beauty a lady becomes exceptional. I'm quite thankful I waited until now to choose a wife. Miss Weldon has natural dignity that must always be admired," he said, concluding that she would be an ornament to his coronet. Polite society considered him "a catch." He knew it. Lord Tufton knew it. Caro would know it.

A lull having finally been reached, the viscount replied heavily that he honored the earl for his sentiments and thanked him for his compliments to Miss Weldon. "I am sure Carolina admires and respects you, Lord Dooly," he said. "But I cannot presume to know a lady's—ah—tenderest emotions."

Dooly was nodding complacently. "Yes, very true. We gentlemen can only *guess*. Miss Weldon has been very gracious to me—so interested in my studies! I hope—in fact, I *believe* she returns my regard."

Lord Tufton devoutly hoped the opposite.

"Mr. Weldon will have the final word in this matter," he pointed out. "I will certainly give my approval, for what it's worth. You would like to address her now?"

"I would, sir.

Still hesitating, Lord Tufton mentioned the necessity of tactfully separating Miss Weldon from her aunt, and Dooly eliminated this last impediment by reporting that Lady Tufton was away making calls.

"Oh. Well. In that case, we can proceed. If you will let me place you in the library while I send for Caro."

He shut Dooly into the library and went upstairs himself to find and prepare his niece.

She was in the drawing room, staring from a window. Lord Dooly's tiger could be seen waiting patiently with his lordship's curricle in the square. As soon as her uncle entered, his face sober, she realized what had happened. Visions of Lady Tufton's exultation, critical in-laws, Cedric's need, parental anxiety, and her own gentle dreams jostled each other in her head.

"Well, dear Caro," said her uncle, "you have a choice to make. Dooly is waiting."

"Must I see him?" she asked.

He nodded. "Yes. You must. He has made an honorable offer and desires your personal reply." As he spoke, he laid an encouraging arm about her and she pressed her forehead against his shoulder briefly, before drawing back.

"It's all so difficult," she protested.

"Not really, you know. It's your life—your whole life. Other people's random wants should not take precedence over your happiness. Lord Dooly is a worthy man; only you can say if you could—adjust to—accept and be satisfied with him."

She smiled wryly. "Where do I go?"

"The library, dear. If your aunt should return she won't notice you there. I'll be in my study if you need me."

She went with lagging steps down the staircase and entered the library where Lord Dooly was found pacing restlessly in apparent agitation.

"Miss Weldon!"

"My lord."

They stared at one another. Then Dooly took her hand and implored: "Say you will!"

"Will what?" demanded Caro, whether from perversity or confusion she did not, herself, know.

He jerked his chin back abruptly as though jolted. "Miss Weldon! Surely Lord Gilbert told you what we settled!" Was she playing games with him? She looked utterly desirable and he could scarcely wait to embrace her.

Caro took her hand away and, avoiding couches, sank hastily into the embrace of the nearest arm chair. With no conscious thought of kneeling, Lord Dooly found himself on his knees on the carpet before her, looking up into her face, whereas before he had been comfortably looking *down*.

"Lord Gilbert gave his approval—you and I—us—make a match—" Dooly's voice rambled, fell away.

Was this a *proposal?* She hardly knew what to say, for to draw him out and preserve his self-esteem without laying herself open to further entreaties seemed impossible.

He looked miserable, a film of moisture on his brow, his girth straining against his coat.

"Oh, pray get up, my lord," she exclaimed. "To grovel is beneath one of your—stature."

He liked that, and staggered to his feet. "So kind, so considerate!" He said nothing of love, but began to offer her three homes, jewels, and an elevated position as his countess.

None of this had any appeal for Carolina. It sounded as if he were intending to purchase her, and she was sorely tried to obey Papa's teaching to deal kindly with all manner of men. But when he said urgently, "I can promise you every comfort, Miss Weldon—Caro," she suddenly realized poor Dooly was offering not himself, fond if dull, but his financial resources which he saw as his greatest attraction.

She rose then and impulsively held out her hand, which was a mistake for he seized it and kept it.

"Say no more, dear sir. If you are suggesting what I think, I must halt you now, for farther I cannot go."

By this time he was sensing rejection. "Lord Gilbert encouraged me—" he began.

"But I do not. Release my hand, sir! I thank you for honoring me. I admire your gentlemanly ways, your—your scholarship, but I cannot give you the affection you deserve. We can be no more than friends."

"I would be more," he protested, resentment creeping into his voice as she moved toward the door and he followed.

"I am sorry, but you cannot," she said. "I wish you well. Friendship is all I can offer. Good day, my lord."

She opened the door and Lord Dooly found himself going into the hall. Although he had not finished with Miss Weldon, she had finished with him. An upstart country girl from a vicarage!

A footman was coming toward him with his hat and gloves. He seized them, storm clouds crossing his face, and went angrily from the house.

Behind he left a wilting lady, troubled, unsure, anxious, guilty, filled with remorse.

The same morning found Mr. Haverill troubled in conscience and nursing a headache, which conditions may have been related, although he did not realize it. In search of fresh air, he rode into the park, running over in his thoughts the recent encounter with Miss Weldon. Had his own behavior been less than gentlemanly? Surely he was civil! Was she unfeeling toward poor James's disappointment (about which he had heard a tirade)? What had he said to console his cousin except the old saw about ladies acting reluctant to first offers while angling for second or third avowals of passion? Was James more mortified than heartbroken? Was Miss Weldon—in preferring Dooly—set more on title than affection?

Without deliberate plans, he left the park and rode east.

As Mr. Haverill turned his mount into Grosvenor Square, he could see a tiger tending two horses before Lord Tufton's house. The blue and red livery was familiar. Dooly's colors?

He rather thought so. And what did it mean . . . or did it mean anything?

While he was thus meditating, his horse, left to his own inclinations, took matters in his own hooves, ambled to Lord Tufton's hitching post, and halted. The post was familiar to him. Perhaps he felt some equine fondness for it. He waited as though tied. Mr. Haverill nodded absently to Dooly's tiger.

At this point the front door opened and Lord Dooly appeared, a furious scowl not improving his countenance. When his eye fell upon Mr. Haverill he drew back abruptly, gritted, "You, too?", hurled himself into his curricle, and clattered off, leaving his tiger to go home as best he might.

Lord Dooly's manner betrayed immense indignation. Clearly, something was very wrong!

"On the other hand," muttered Mr. Haverill, "something may be *right.*" He dropped to the ground, hastily looped his reins about the friendly post, and sprang up Lord Tufton's steps.

Bigelow admitted him and accepted the hat and gloves which Mr. Haverill thrust sideways as he advanced into the hall, his attention fixed upon the agitated young lady just climbing the stair.

"Miss Weldon!" he said commandingly.

She hesitated and turned her head halfway toward him.

"I wish to speak with you, if you please."

It was evident that Miss Weldon did *not* please. However, she did not know how to refuse him. The monumental refusal of Lord Dooly had quite sapped her strength. She nodded slightly and descended.

Mr. Haverill then fixed his eye on Bigelow. Guessing, correctly, that the lady had passed a difficult half hour in the library, he asked, "What room is vacant?"

Bigelow responded with great sensitivity, "The dining parlor, sir."

"We will go there," said Mr. Haverill.

If Bigelow entertained any thought of the impropriety of

a *tête-à-tête* between Miss Weldon and Mr. Haverill, he repressed it manfully. He inclined his head, led them across the hall, and closed them into the dimness of the dining parlor with a sigh no one heard, but which relieved Bigelow immensely.

Miss Weldon, staring blindly at the flowers of the carpet, counted madly, waiting for tranquility to overtake her. Instead, Mr. Haverill's hands seized her shoulders and a tremor shot through her. He turned her gently toward him.

"Miss Weldon—Carolina—"

Finding himself deserted by the English language, he did what he had been wanting to do for a long time. He bent his head and kissed her.

It was very strange. The ormolu clock on the mantel ceased its noisy count and somehow (incredibly!) the room filled with light. When Mr. Haverill raised his head, Miss Weldon made no attempt to draw away, but stood gazing up at him, her mouth parted in astonishment, her face suffused with pink.

Mr. Haverill was not made of iron. He dropped his hands to her waist, drew her close, and kissed her with increased warmth—not so much passion as to alarm an innocent young lady, but enough, at the same time, to exhilarate a gentleman. When this kiss ended Miss Weldon hid her face against his chest and Mr. Haverill laid his cheek agreeably against her hair.

"Do you find this pleasant?" he asked in tender, if ragged, tones.

"Yes," said Miss Weldon baldly to Mr. Haverill's waistcoat.

The corners of his mouth quivered.

"Have I permission to speak to your uncle?"

The answer was more low, but unmistakably affirmative.

"Adorable," whispered Mr. Haverill. His arms tightened a bit. "Is Lord Tufton at home now?"

"Yes," she said.

"I see," observed Mr. Haverill, "that you indulge me with only one word. However, as it is a very satisfactory word, this does not matter. Now, I have one further question for you to which your word will be the proper answer. Do you love me?"

"Y-yes," admitted Miss Weldon, nodding against the obliging waistcoat.

The gentleman laughed, kissed the top of her head, and went rapidly from the room.

Miss Weldon waited, swaying, her hands clapped to her scorching cheeks, until he had time to reach her uncle's study at the back of the house. Then she fled through the hall, two flights up the staircase to the sanctuary of her room, quite unheeding of the interest with which her agitation was observed by Bigelow, two footmen, the second floor maid, Lord Tufton's valet, and a boy who was gathering ashes.

Mr. Haverill tapped at Lord Tufton's study and being borne on the wings of exhilaration passed at once within.

"Well, Lawrence, come in," exclaimed his lordship unnecessarily. "You are the very one to console me. Caro refused James."

"I know," replied Mr. Haverill.

"But that is not all," continued Lord Tufton. "Do sit down. Why are you pacing the carpet?"

Mr. Haverill, who had been prowling the room, cast himself into a chair with no appearance of relaxation, but Gilly was satisfied.

"It is all very unsettling, First Harriet was complaining that Caro had received no offers, and now the minx has turned James down! Yes, yes, I know you said James's mama wouldn't like it, but it seemed perfect to me. . . . Well, I expect Caro knows best. An antagonistic mother-in-law would be painful for such a soft-hearted girl. But wait till you hear! She has refused Dooly also. At least, he asked permission to address her—and I couldn't very well refuse, could I? Even though I would not half like the match. Bigelow says Dooly left in a dudgeon, so it looks as if Caro told him no."

"Yes," agreed Mr. Haverill authoritatively from a vantage point Lord Tufton did not suspect. He crossed and recrossed his legs.

Lord Tufton went on: "What Harriet will have to say I do not know. She is sure to fly up in the boughs."

Mr. Haverill said very likely.

"I tell you, Lawrence, it's the devil being father to a pretty miss!" Lord Tufton chuckled. "They say everything happens in threes. I don't suppose you would care to make Caro an offer?"

"Yes," replied his friend, "I would."

Still thinking it was all a huge joke, Lord Tufton pointed out that his little puss was in a negative mood, to which Mr. Haverill replied that he had had some words with Miss Weldon himself and did not find her negative at all.

Gilly stared at him in astonishment. "I believe you are serious."

"Of course I am serious," exclaimed Mr. Haverill impatiently. He sprang up and began to roam about the study, disturbing objects on the mantel and interfering with Gilly's pens and papers. "I suppose you will laugh at my folly. The impossible has happened. I have discovered a female I cannot—*cannot,* you understand—live without. Well! Well! Why are you silent? Can I have her? Speak up, Gilly!"

It was not to be supposed that Lord Tufton would deny Mr. Haverill's suit. He was surprised, yes indeed, but most vocal in his approval. His dearest friend? His almost-daughter? Nothing could have been more felicitous!

"She hasn't a sixpence, you know," he said apologetically, being scrupulously honest.

Mr. Haverill replied, hang all sixpences. After which the

gentlemen congratulated each other for their various and sundry accomplishments, many rather nebulous, and Lord Tufton sent for brandy.

It was some time before Mr. Haverill could settle peacefully in a chair. When he did so, he was laughing at himself.

"What a joke," he said ruefully. "I thought I was impervious."

"So did we all," agreed his lordship, "but I am glad to see we were wrong. I am happy for you, Lawrence. Caro is very dear. Of course I am delighted for her also, since I believe you will make the best of husbands—now that your heart is engaged. Besides—" with a twinkle—"you can be very useful to Caro's sisters."

"I shall certainly hope to be," replied Mr. Haverill. "They are smashing girls. In fact, do not be surprised in a couple of years if James finds Miss Susan irresistible. She will look up to him, I think, and he will like that."

"Excellent!" declared his lordship. "All joking aside, you have my best wishes. . . . I will be certain to assure Charles Weldon of my complete approval."

"Thank you, Gilly," said Mr. Haverill fervently, forgetting he had been a matchmaker's target for many years. "I will send off a note tonight asking leave to wait upon him as soon as convenient to him."

His lordship, believing any time would be convenient to receive a wealthy and distinguished suitor, replied mildly that he rather thought Haverill would find Mr. Weldon pleasantly disposed. He then pledged himself to writing a letter of recommendation, and Mr. Haverill seized upon the suggestion with enthusiasm, commanding Gilly to prepare it at once so that the letter might be conveyed by the groom carrying his own.

When Gilly had complied, penning a brief but affirmative note, Mr. Haverill departed with a spring in his step, and his lordship settled to another glass of brandy and the enjoyment of good news.

* * *

Unfortunately, Lord Tufton's pleasure did not last very long. A carriage was heard to stop outside as Harriet returned to her home, ill-humored because a shower had spoiled her morning, and not disposed to visit Gilly in his study, where he promptly called her.

"Must I?" she asked crossly.

"Yes, you must. Good news!" he said with a hurried kiss to her cheek. "So much has happened. You missed all the excitement. Dooly offered for Caro and she refused him."

"She did what?" shrieked Lady Tufton, arrested in untying her bonnet. "Refused *Dooly?* Oh, the ninny—the fool—the idiot. You must call him back! I will deal with Caro. She must not be allowed to refuse him!"

"Wait," interrupted his lordship. "You haven't heard the best. Of course she can refuse Dooly. Haverill has offered, too."

Lady Tufton threw down her bonnet to a sofa. "James? Pressing his suit again? Never say she has accepted him after all. His mama will put a stop to that."

"No, no," said her husband, still delighted with the news he had to tell. "Not James. Lawrence. Lawrence offered for her himself. Is it not splendid?"

Before his eyes, Lady Tufton swelled with wrath. *"Lawrence?* Impossible! There can be no doubt you misunderstood him. Depend upon it, some quirk—some ironic joke upon his aunt—has made him push James's suit. Oh, how outrageous of him to taunt you!"

"No such thing," said Gilly firmly, feeling in his bones a distinct chill. "He asked for Caro and I gave my consent. How could I not? He is everything admirable."

"Impossible," Harriet reiterated, adding decisively, "It won't do. He must have been disguised!" Her eye fell upon the brandy bottle, and she caught it up and held it to the light. "To be sure! Nearly empty. Oh, you will both have sore heads, I warrant. He will have forgotten this folly by tomorrow."

"*I* shall not," Gilly protested.

"Scandalous! She has thrown herself at him. You must forbid him to address her."

Shaken by his wife's rage, and perilously close to disliking her, his lordship said, "Too late, Harriet. It appears to have been settled between them before I knew."

"Worse and worse!" cried her ladyship. "She has thrown herself at him and he is too much the gentleman to draw back."

Gilly shook his head. "Haverill gives every evidence of a man in love."

"Love?" Lady Tufton's lip curled, and it was not becoming. "With a green goose? What rubbish! You are being foolishly sentimental, Gilly! Haverill is a sophisticated man. Anyone can see he prefers mature women. Heaven knows how many seasons ambitious mamas have tried to force simpering damsels on him. Oh, I daresay Caro is as dazzled as the rest and made a bid for his attention—behind our backs, of course, in a sneaky fashion one despises—but what is there in *her* to attract him?"

She flung back and forth in the room, her skirts hissing at each angry turn. "What would he see in *her?*" she repeated scornfully.

By this time Lord Gilbert was wrestling with monumental shock. He answered painfully: "Haverill sees what you do not: genuine sweetness—"

"It will bore him in a fortnight!"

"*—and* strength of character."

She laughed shrilly. "Strength of character? Oh, I will allow she is enterprising enough to pursue her ambitions! We have certainly been deceived! A meek little mouse—*so* obliging, *so* agreeable. Haverill is your friend, is he not? You can't allow him to be victimized by a schemer! You should have said no at once."

"Well, I didn't," Gilly replied shortly. "The match has my blessing, although of course Charles Weldon will have the final word."

"Then write to him immediately. He is too much a dreamer to want Caro in a wretched union, and too little a realist to snap up a rich *parti* at any sacrifice. That chit can never hold Haverill's interest! You will have to put a stop to the affair at once."

Lord Tufton said stoutly that he did not intend to do so. "They love one another." He looked at his wife beseechingly and added, "Do you not remember, Harriet?"

"Love is expensive," she retorted.

"So is everything worth having. I do not think Haverill regards the cost."

"Oh!" she cried impatiently, "there is no reasoning with you. I can see you are determined to be mawkish. Well, *I* shall not stand idly by. Do you hear me? I will settle matters without you!"

She ran from the room, slamming the door to punctuate her intention, and Gilly sank into a chair, shaking with disillusionment.

Meanwhile, upstairs, Carolina had been ricocheting about her boudoir. She was too elated to settle in one spot, giddy with emotion. She both longed to feel Mr. Haverill's arms about her again, and dreaded to face him after her own abandoned behavior. Mama and Papa, she feared, would condemn such conduct, but Lawrence Haverill had not! He had called her "adorable," hadn't he?

With tumultuous spirits she awaited a summons from her uncle; and when the passing of time caused her to realize a summons was not to be forthcoming, she fell into greater agitation, wondering if Mr. Haverill regretted—if his lordship denied his sanction. About her aunt's attitude she had some misgivings, not wanting to put a name to Lady Tufton's sentiment. Lord Gilbert, on the other hand, she knew to be fond of her. The question was: would his fondness extend to bestowing her on his *friend?* Would he think her unworthy of the splendid Mr. Haverill?

Floating, as she was, in euphoria, it was doubly shocking to have the door hurled open by a blast from Hell.

"So!" cried Lady Tufton, advancing upon her with burning eyes. "You are not the milk-and-water miss we thought, but a—viper!"

Caro, rising to her feet, stumbled slightly. The color receded from her face, but she had presence of mind to close the door and keep her aunt's tantrum from the household. Although she had not expected approval, the vitriol poured upon her was terrifying.

Her ladyship spewed forth the same statements that had stunned her husband, embellishing them now with the most ugly and devastating adjectives. Poor Caro shrank before her strange attack. She could not understand it and consequently could not defend herself. She know she was not avaricious or scheming or forward, and to be called so was more nonsensical than alarming, but her aunt's passion frightened her.

"I can only suppose you tricked Haverill into an offer," Lady Tufton said.

Stung, Caro replied that Mr. Haverill had not made her an offer. He had only requested leave to approach Lord Tufton.

Lady Tufton stared at her in surprise. "No offer? He hasn't offered? Well, that puts matters in another light! Gilly can tell him 'no'—or he could have—but he very foolishly gave his consent—so you will have to be guided by me and reject Haverill. If, that is, tomorrow he still feels obliged to offer. You can never hold the interest of a man of his caliber. A most unfortunate match. You must refuse him!"

"No," said Carolina, very white, but raising her chin slightly. "If he asks me, I shall accept. I l-love him."

"In a pig's ear," retorted her ladyship in a manner more suited to Billingsgate than Grosvenor Square. "You cannot suppose him in love with *you?*"

Caro gazed at her in horror. Only now, at her aunt's scathing words, did she remember that Mr. Haverill (just as James and Lord Dooly) had not said anything of loving her. Had she read into his embrace affection that was not there? Shaken and humiliated, she could say nothing.

Her eyes narrowed, Harriet detected some vague advantage. "You have tried to snare him," she accused.

"No!" gasped Caro faintly.

"Do not contradict me, miss. It is obvious your behavior has not been what it should. A poor return, indeed, for my kindness to you! Well, you need not think I will overlook such outrageous action and insubordinate talk. Hear this: your ambitious fling is at an end!"

The grey specter of Cedric's blasted future swam before Caro's eyes. "I am sorry, Aunt," she began, "but—"

"No more!" interrupted the viscountess. "I have heard enough. You will remain in this room until your father comes. I am through with you!"

Fourteen

The triumph of vituperation over both Lord Tufton and Miss Weldon in no way satisfied Lady Tufton's ill temper. They were pulverized. *She* was unsated. She sped down a flight to her own chamber where, with one desolate victim below her feet and an apprehensive one above her head, she set about scorching paper. Ink splattered on the first sheet. She hurled it to the floor. This was one letter that would not be delegated to his lordship's secretary! In bold strokes she acquainted Mr. Weldon with the abominable behavior of his eldest daughter and commanded him to come immediately to remove the ingrate from the shelter of her uncle's roof.

At this point Lady Tufton recalled Cedric, who was somewhere about the city and should be returning shortly. *He* could escort his sister home. This would, however, require the use of her ladyship's coach, besides depriving her of speaking her mind in person to Charles Weldon.

She signed her name to the letter, secured it with a wafer, and rang her bell. When Mrs. Gibbs answered the summons Lady Tufton directed her to fetch her groom.

In the ordinary course of duty, Mrs. Gibbs would have scorned to fetch anybody anywhere and would have relayed the message indignantly to a footman. But her ladyship's air was alarmingly militant. Disgruntled, and privately thinking my lady's boudoir was no place for a groom, she threw a shawl about her shoulders and hurried to the stables.

"Well, lass," said the groom, who was ten years Gibbs's

senior and who had been born on Tufton property, "what's the nip? Devil after ye with his fork?"

"Same as," panted Gibbs. "My lady's in a proper pelter. She says you are to come at once."

"Then I'll do it," he said, grinning at her. He buttoned his coat, brushed his sleeves and knees, and started up the garden path, while Mrs. Gibbs, allowing her curiosity to overcome her caution, followed close behind him.

Lady Tufton desired her groom to carry a letter to Mr. Weldon in Dolden Overhill.

"Now?, m'lady?"

"Yes," she said curtly. "Take any horse in the stable, only go at once."

He cast a dubious eye at the window. "It wants only two hours to dark and I do na know the route, m'lady."

"You can ask, can't you? Ride for two hours, then, and rack up somewhere till dawn. There won't be a moon, I suppose, with the drizzle we're having," she conceded. "Go as far as you can." She held out the letter and a purse.

The poor fellow worshipped his mistress in spite of herself, and the details of Caro's imprisonment had not percolated to the lower floors, much less to the stables. So he said, "Aye, m'lady," and went off with the items she offered. The purse, he could tell by its weight, would buy him a good dinner, a comfortable bed, and maybe even a warm bedfellow. He liked to ride. He had authority to appropriate Lord Tufton's best hack, and it was no burden to carry a missive to the one man Lady Tufton (and Miss Weldon) desired most to see (although for different reasons). He trotted from the mews, happily unaware of Miss Plum's incarceration or his idol's cruelty.

It was not long after the messenger's departure that Nannie discovered her young lady had been locked into her chamber.

Nannie was always beforehand in laying out her charge's clothes, but this evening the most enchanting rumors of an

Accepted Suitor had reached her, so she went up early, hoping and expecting to be told all.

But the door would not open and she was obliged to knock sharply.

Caro's voice said thickly, "W-who is it?"

"Nannie, miss. Can I come in to see about your clothes?"

Caro scrambled from the rumpled bed.

"Oh, Nannie." She twisted the knob but the door did not move.

"You will have to turn the key, missy," said Nannie in her best nursery voice.

"Oh, yes. Of course."

But there wasn't a key.

"The key's gone, Nannie," she said.

Both of them then rattled the knob.

"I'm locked in," Caro croaked. The tears sprang to her eyes and she leaned her head against the dark panel.

Putting two and two together and arriving correctly at thirty-four, Nannie said bracingly, "Half a minute, love. *I'll* see to this." She went down the steps to Lady Tufton's apartment and with a piercing look upon her employer announced that Miss Caro's door was Fastened Shut.

Lady Tufton replied that Miss Weldon was resting.

"No, mum," contradicted Nannie. "She spoke with me. She was wishful for me to come in, but the key is missing."

"I think that your hearing is beginning to fail," replied her ladyship coldly. "Miss Weldon is resting. She has had a difficult day. She will not be going down to dinner. You may assist Nurse with the children this evening."

"I see," said Nannie disapprovingly.

"I thought you would," said her ladyship.

Outside my lady's door Nannie muttered "Difficult day!" and cast about in her mind for an ally. Bigelow? Mrs. Moffett? One or the other might have a duplicate key but would not dare to risk his employment by yielding to her demand for it. No, they were as powerless as herself. She went in search of Lord Tufton.

But the viscount, in distress, had left his home and, while Nannie sought him, was himself seeking Mr. Haverill.

God help him! He still loved Harriet, but the naked exposure of her character grieved him almost more than he could bear. Because he deplored Caro's situation he, like his wife, determined that the girl must be delivered from his house as soon as possible. But it was a rainy night and Dolden was miles distant. His brain could not wrestle with the problem. It seemed to him that Haverill, as Caro's betrothed, was the one to take matters in hand.

Clawson was glad to see his lordship but was obliged to say Mr. Haverill had gone out without acquainting his household with his destination.

"Did he send off a letter, do you know?" asked Lord Tufton.

"I believe so, my lord. At least, his groom rode off some hours ago. I heard Mr. Haverill say, 'Bring a fast answer!'"

"Excellent! Excellent! Well, I shall try to find Haverill. If he comes in early you might tell him I wish to see him." He thought of adding, "As late as midnight," but feared to start gossip.

So he went off in a hackney, cheering the driver's heart and lining his pockets by crisscrossing London in vain pursuit of Mr. Haverill.

Because he dreaded the spread of scandal he failed to look the one place Haverill might logically be found—two doors from his own house, at Lady Franklin's, where Haverill and my lord and my lady were sharing the delights of Haverill's romance. As Lady Franklin was gratifyingly enthusiastic, her husband (as always) amiable, and both willing to go over the same ground repeatedly, the discussion took considerable time.

"I told Gilly," said Lady Franklin triumphantly, "that Caro would do better than James or Dooly!"

Afterwards Mr. Haverill wandered into Brook's, where Lord Tufton had looked earlier, and lightheartedly tossed away the blunt he carried. He never did make contact with Gilly.

At two A.M. he had returned to his house and addressed an observation to the painting of Tabby Four Toes: "Well, you will be a bit of home for her." Which Tabby Four Toes appeared to understand very well. And if she did not actually purr, her expression was benign.

When Finchley returned at midmorning the next day Mr. Haverill was dressed and had broken his fast early enough to jolt the household. Something was in the wind, though no one knew what.

The note which Mr. Haverill entrusted to his butler, to be delivered by a footman, said plainly, "Miss Carolina Weldon, Tufton House." Clawson, with accelerated pulse, realized that he held a clue. But he only said, "Very good, sir," planning to take the note himself and thereby protect his master's secret a bit longer.

The bays were brought round. Mr. Haverill donned a natty driving coat. The groom was sent below to a nuncheon. Mr. Haverill mounted into his curricle, followed by his valet and a valise, gave his team the office to start, and set forth for Dolden Overhill.

The horses were fresh and mettlesome. The valet blanched at every rapid turn, but would have died rather than admit his fear. It was obvious they would make a fast trip, and Weems had little confidence in light, sporting vehicles. By now, however, he had some suspicion of their errand and would have been irreparably offended to have been left behind on such a momentous occasion.

Midway they passed Charles Weldon on his way to town, but as both gentlemen were traveling *ventre-à-terre* and as neither carriage bore distinguishing arms, neither gentleman recognized the other.

The pike experienced a new sort of busyness. Only that

morning Lady Tufton's groom had breakfasted, all unknowing, at the same inn as Finchley as they pursued their opposite directions. Mr. Weldon received Lady Tufton's poison
about the time Finchley reported to his master in London.
Both gentlemen set out in a fever, one of wrath (counting
vehemently), one of joy. Thus it was that not long after Mr.
Haverill had presented himself at the vicarage, Mr. Weldon
reached Grosvenor Square.

Matters in London, during this time, were at a standstill.
Lady Tufton and Cedric dined together at the long table.

"Caro is resting," she told him. "No, no, not ill. Just tired
from so much gaiety! I advised her to cosset herself this
evening."

Cedric accepted this without suspicion. Harriet was as
beautiful as ever, although he thought her manner somewhat
distrait. Perhaps she was tired too.

They did not talk a great deal.

When one's thoughts are active one does not notice a quiet
room. Cedric knew that Caro had rejected Lord Dooly, the
information having been relayed by Dooly himself whom
he had met in Hookham's Library. Lord Dooly was fully
conscious of his own condescension in offering for a vicar's
daughter. He assured Cedric that Miss Weldon was being
coy, or else she was stunned by her unexpected good fortune.
In either case, he had recovered from his irritation and said
he was optimistic of a "yes" within a week or so.

Cedric hoped not.

With James and Dooly both rejected, did that mean Rob
stood a chance? Having no knowledge (for all his History
and Latin!) of the finances of matrimony, Cedric could see
no objection to Rob. He was partial to Rob. They had been
next thing to brothers for twelve years already.

By the greatest misfortune, Lady Tufton was in the hallway next day when Clawson presented Mr. Haverill's note.

"I will take it, Bigelow," she said firmly.

Although Bigelow looked reluctant, both he and Clawson knew young females did not receive letters without their guardians' permission. The note was handed to her ladyship, who went into the morning room and lost not five seconds in tearing it open.

It was brief: *"Sweet Caro—Do not, I pray, think I have deserted you. I leave at once for Dolden and hope to return to you with your father's blessing in twenty-four hours. Haverill."*

Not especially loverlike. Nevertheless it infuriated Lady Tufton. She made an angry noise and cast the paper into the fire, little guessing that Mr. Haverill had wisely kept his message unimpassioned in case she should read it.

Poor Miss Weldon, for whom it was intended, never saw it at all and did indeed begin to think herself deserted.

Meanwhile Nannie had cast off all inhibitions. Balked at releasing her darling, she could talk, and talk she did. Belowstairs seethed Cook, who was very vocal, leading the outcry of response. Poor dear Miss Plum! It was scandalous, that's what it was! Mrs. Moffett wrung her hands and avowed she had no key. The storerooms, yes, but not chamber ones. Bigelow was similarly situated. He showed his cellar key and the ones to the silver presses. He had no keys to occupied rooms.

Normally Mrs. Gibbs supported the wishes of her mistress and was jealous for her reign as belle and queen, yet she held no resentment toward the sweet young lady and could *not* countenance locking her up like a felon.

"What's to be done?" asked Mrs. Gibbs, suddenly democratic and hobnobbing with her inferiors—after they had got over being doubtful of her loyalties because she was Lady Tufton's dresser.

"She needs food, she does," said Cook.

"Yes," said Nannie, "but she'll be too upset to eat."

"The idea of jailing Miss Plum like that!" protested a

footman. "Frightening, you know. Send her into the dismals."

Bigelow reminded them at this point that any young lady who could look on Blood was not going to be overset by Adversity, and they nodded agreement.

"I best tell Mr. Colefence," said Nurse Betty.

They stared at her, uncomprehending, until Bigelow remembered Colefence was John Coachman's real name, bestowed on him by a legal, if worthless, father.

"Oh, yes," he agreed, "John Coachman."

"He'll know what to do," said Betty confidently. "I mean about getting word to Lady Franklin."

They regarded her with awe.

"Very good thinking, Miss Betty," commanded Bigelow generously, and Betty turned scarlet.

"Shall I go now?" she asked.

"Do!" urged Mrs. Moffett.

Betty hurried out.

"If his lordship's man weren't off visiting his mother what is sick, *he* could have a word with his lordship," suggested a little maid who admired the valet quite openly and always kept track of his whereabouts.

"Well, don't look at me," objected the footman, who was filling the valet's shoes temporarily. "His lordship and I aren't on such terms as I'd want to be the one to give him bad news!"

"*I* will do it," said Nannie pugnaciously. "Just tell me when he's home *and* awake *and* decent to receive females. I'll tell him what a midden her ladyship has made of this house!"

It was past noon, and Lord Tufton was both at home and awake. He lay in his bed wishing there were some way to undo the past twenty-four hours. Knowing only that Caro was keeping to her room (not that she was locked in), he assumed she wished to be alone. Perhaps she had turned against him along with Harriet.

He must reach Haverill today and make some plan. He rang his bell.

As matters fell out, neither Nannie nor any other of the household was obliged to inflict more pain on their master. Within thirty minutes of Betty's reaching John Coachman the facts had infiltrated every stratum of the Franklin establishment and Lady Franklin was throwing on her clothes. To Bigelow's delight she swept furiously into Tufton House. He took her to Lady Tufton in the morning room.

"Ask his lordship to come down at once," she commanded.

"Certainly, my lady!" replied Bigelow enthusiastically. He want upstairs himself.

"Why, Laura, how nice to see you," said Lady Tufton, being the charming hostess.

"You won't think so when you hear what I have to say," Lady Franklin retorted.

With the caution born of a guilty conscience, Harriet made another try: "What has put you out of sorts?"

"Shrewishness," said her guest.

"Not yours, Lady Franklin. Never that!"

Lady Franklin replied that she rather thought she could make a capital scene if matters required it. "It wasn't *my* shrewishness I meant, however," she said, "but yours."

"Mine!" cried Harriet recoiling.

"Perhaps vindictiveness would be a better word. Come in, Gilly, and tell me why you have Caro locked in her room."

"Locked in her—" His eyes flew to his wife.

"Without food," continued Lady Franklin.

"Oh, my God!" he cried. "Harriet, you wouldn't—you haven't—"

She objected angrily, "No one has a right to interfere in

my discipline of *my* niece. She is a wanton jade. She has humiliated us!"

"She has not humiliated me," Gilly said. "Give me the key."

"No! She has cast herself at Haverill like a wanton."

He was very white by now. "Give me the key or I will take it from you by force."

Lady Franklin, who had long thought a good spanking would improve Lady Tufton's temperament immensely, but who had no wish to be a witness to mayhem, interposed a calming voice. "Give over, Harriet. You never wanted Caro here. I'll take her off your hands at once."

Key obtained, his face grim, Lord Tufton mounted the stairs under the watchful eye of Bigelow and several lurking footmen and maids. What had transpired in the morning room could not be known by the servants, but his lordship's purpose was plain.

He put the key into Caro's lock and opened the door.

"My dear, dear child," he said.

She went into his arms dry-eyed, but weak with relief.

"I can never—never—I did not know—I am so sorry—" he whispered. And Carolina discovered she was obliged to comfort *him*. With soft kisses to his cheek and assurances of her affection and absolution of all blame, she revived *his* spirits, which activity had serendipitous effect upon her own. Bigelow had read her character truly; Papa's daughter was not overset by harsh words. Shocked, wounded, but not slain.

"Lady Franklin is here," he said finally, pulling himself together. "I will send her to you while I try to decide what is best to do. I have been unable to locate Haverill. Well. We shall see. . . ." He handed her the key with a slight, crooked smile and went away.

Caro sagged against the nearest piece of furniture, which happened to be a stalwart bureau. Lord Gilly had not forsaken her. *He had not known.*

When Lady Franklin appeared in a veritable cloud of indignation, victory, and affection, she was able to greet her with some prepossession, and no rancor at all.

After kisses and hugs, Lady Franklin announced with satisfaction that Harriet's nose was certainly out of joint. "Gone her length," she asserted. "Gilly has reached the limit of his tolerance."

"Oh," said Caro anxiously, "I would not want to cause trouble between them."

"Fiddlesticks," replied her ladyship heartily. "Any trouble *she* made. High time Gilly took the reins of that unbroken filly! Never you mind. He has spoiled her rotten and has to pay for it, but I shouldn't be surprised if this did them both good." She drew Caro to a seat beside her on the chaise. "Now, love, I have been thinking. It was my plan at first to remove you to my house. However, that would be certain to set tongues wagging, and gossip we do not want. If you are willing, I think it best to leave you in your room until your father comes. Lady Toplofty has sent for him, you see, and from what I know of Charles Weldon he will not be slow in coming."

"Papa? Papa? Oh, how glad I am!" cried Caro, her face taking on a happier expression. "He will come very fast, if he knows—" Her voice faltered.

"Yes," agreed Lady Franklin, "he will come. Today, I expect. But what I want to know is where is Cedric? Gone? Or only blind and deaf?"

Caro was obliged to smile at Lady Franklin's indignation. She said hesitatingly, "If my uncle did not know—my—situation, I daresay Cedric does not. My aunt may have told him something, made some excuse for me. He is very trusting, you see."

"Yes, but where is he *now?*" objected her ladyship.

"Somewhere about the City. He goes out early every morning. You must not think Cedric would desert me." It was difficult to exonerate her brother without revealing his secret.

Fortunately Nannie came in then with a tempting nuncheon tray embellished by Cook with a fan of orange wedges and ivy leaves. Lady Franklin flowed with trivial gossip about the Duke of York and the Duchess's dogs until Nannie had settled the tray before her missy, seen her begin to eat, and gone away satisfied.

When they were alone again Lady Franklin said, "I had thought to take you home with me, but it would be difficult to account for such a removal without stirring up unpleasant speculations."

"Papa will take me home, I expect," said Caro.

"Perhaps," agreed her ladyship, with no tone of agreement. "He will want to consult with Haverill, of course, and no one seems to know where he is just at the moment." To her surprise the troubled look returned to Caro's eyes. "I know about your betrothal, child. Don't worry. Your Papa is sure to approve. Once they have settled things between them, Haverill will want to send a notice to the newspapers." She smiled teasingly. "I cannot think Haverill will want you to go off at such an interesting time."

"I am afraid Mr. Haverill offered because—because—out of some sense of *obligation,* and I cannot—"

"Obligation!" squawked her ladyship. "What sort of ninnyhammer idea is that? Didn't I have to listen to him rave in the most besotted fashion? He *loves* you!"

"He didn't say so," objected Caro, mortified, but determined to be honest.

Lady Franklin was more scandalized than ever. "Didn't say so? Well, of course he did! That is, of course he must have. A gentleman doesn't reach the age of two and thirty with all the females of London ready to swoon at his feet without knowing what he wants and how to ask for it. I warrant he can make love superbly. Why, just his smile would be enough to set my heart thumping—if I weren't already wrapped up in my own dear Franklin, that is. You aren't going to tell me you aren't head over heels in love with him?"

"No," Caro admitted in a small voice. She did not doubt the sincerity of Lady Franklin's views. Nevertheless, she knew she had nothing to offer Mr. Haverill, and she was abysmally sure he had said nothing of love. "Papa will take me home if I ask him. And I shall!" she concluded on rising notes.

Thereupon she choked up, and Lady Franklin, reflecting how very *trying* Romeo and Juliet could be, asked rather unfeelingly if she was going to turn into a watering-pot.

It clearly was not a moment for rational debate. Lady Franklin offered her handkerchief and waited until Caro had regained control of her emotions. Then she said calmly that there was no hurry, they would await the coming of Charles.

It would be excessive to say Lady Tufton felt remorse—or even shame. When she and her spouse passed on the stairs later in the day, however, with only the merest nod of recognition on his lordship's part, she became uneasy enough to think it might be well to absent herself from Tufton House for a while. She knew she had him under her thumb, but there are times to *press* and times not. So she chose her newest and smartest gown and her most fetching bonnet of blond straw with primroses under the brim, directed John Coachman to the residence of a sycophantic lady, and prepared to spend an afternoon being flattered (by the lady) and ogled (by the beaux of London). There were several delightful, unnecessary, and expensive little purchases her ladyship could make and which Mrs. Kenton could enjoy vicariously. They could visit a mantua maker and reject everything in the shop. After this they could drive in Hyde Park, bowing and being bowed to in a revitalizing manner.

Fifteen

Any other lady except Lydia Weldon would have quaked in her shoes to be deserted by her husband when a promising caller was due at their home. Until Mr. Weldon had driven off in a passion of defense for his daughter, however, and she had called after him, "Bring Caro home!" which he did not hear but intended to do, only then did Mrs. Weldon remember the expected visitor.

"Oh dear," she said to Susan, "there's Papa gone. Suppose Mr. Haverill should take it into his head to come now?"

Susan was enraptured with James Haverill (as though *she* were his object). "If Mr. James Haverill were coming," she replied sapiently, "we might expect him to arrive any moment, but as it is only his cousin I cannot suppose he will be in any great hurry."

Her mother agreed this was reasonable. "I hope you are right, my love, for what I can say to him I do not know, and he will want to talk to your papa, anyway."

It was very perplexing. Mr. Haverill had written a civil note, Lord Tufton had endorsed what he called "an excellent match with a worthy gentleman." It had all seemed delightful! Yet neither gentleman realized that the wording of their missives was just vague enough to confuse the identity of Caro's suitor. It appeared to Mr. and Mrs. Weldon that Lawrence Haverill would present himself in Dolden Overhill to solicit Carolina for his cousin, James.

They had hardly ceased to exclaim and praise the lord for

Caro's good fortune, when Lady Tufton's outpouring of rage arrived via the hand of her unwitting groom. Something was very wrong. They could not reconcile Lady Tufton's raving with her husband's clear delight, and from Caro herself they had heard nothing. Surely Lord Tufton would have forwarded a letter from her with his own had she desired to communicate with her parents. Caro's silence was the most puzzling aspect of the matter.

Mrs. Weldon and Susan went upstairs to "turn out" Caro's room in preparation for her return.

"The more I think about it," said Mrs. Weldon, "the more I realize there is no reason for Mr. Haverill to come at all."

She could not have been more wrong. Mr. Haverill was no Suitor's Advocate, but a suitor himself, traveling as fast as prime horse-flesh could transport him. He would have preferred to ride cross-country and only an excellent sense of etiquette restrained him. To arrive sweaty and splashed, fresh clothing rumpled in a saddlebag, was not conduct proper to a gentleman on such an errand as his. Besides, it would have been impossible to persuade Weems to bestride a horse!

It was mid-afternoon when Mr. Haverill and his servant reached Dolden Overhill and entered the local inn. Leaving Weems to arrange accommodations, Haverill stayed only to cast off his driving cloak, wash dust from face and hands, drape a fresh cravat, and permit a shocked valet to slap the dust from his breeches and boots. Then he re-entered his curricle and went at a trot to the vicarage.

As it happened, he encountered Mrs. Weldon on her own doorstep, she having just come around a corner of the house with a bouquet of flowers. He sprang down, handed his vehicle to the care of Mr. Weldon's stableboy, doffed his hat, and went forward.

"My dear sir—" she began immediately, stretching out her hand.

"Ma'am!" He kissed her hand lightly.

Mrs. Weldon had not experienced that courtesy for many years, since no one in Dolden, not even Sir John, indulged in such gallantry. Glowing, she led him into her drawing room and discarded her flowers in a heap.

"I scarcely expected you," she said.

"But I wrote—"

"Oh, yes. My husband had your letter. I mean to say, I did not expect you at just this time. My sister wrote, too, you see, in a most—most *agitated* manner and requested Charles to come at once."

Mr. Haverill's brows met. The slight uncertainty natural to a prospective suitor vanished. "Is something wrong?" he asked.

She hesitated long enough to examine the gentleman with a searching look. What she saw was reassuring. He appeared both substantial and attentive, and Mrs. Weldon, who was long accustomed to following the lead of a benevolent autocrat and who therefore was thankful to lean upon masculine strength, said frankly:

"Seriously wrong, I fear. My sister demands Charles remove Caro from her house. We have had no word from Caro, and Harriet's letter is well nigh incoherent."

Mr. Haverill's frown deepened. "Would you permit me to see the letter, ma'am?" he asked.

Remembering Harriet's violent passages as well as repeated use of Mr. Haverill's name as the victim of an unprincipled schemer, Mrs. Weldon faltered, "So personal—oh, I don't know." Mr. Haverill had come, she thought, to bespeak Caro for his cousin, and it did not seem propitious to embroil him in an ugly tangle. If only Charles were home!

"You should be speaking with my husband," she temporized. "I am afraid you have had a wasted journey, for of course he went off at once. Indeed, you must have passed along the way! " She glanced at the clock upon the mantel. "He should be near to London now."

Mr. Haverill made no move, as she had hoped, to withdraw tactfully. Instead, he leaned forward, saying earnestly, "Mrs. Weldon, any problem of Miss Weldon's is of deep concern to me for I hope to wed her."

It was not the speech he had planned nor was Mrs. Weldon at all prepared to fill her husband's office.

"You—wed—Caro?" she cried in open astonishment.

He nodded with a slight smile. "She and I have reached an understanding. Lord Gilbert approves. I hope you will give us your blessing."

"Well, of course—that is, you must ask Charles. We did not know—we thought it was *James* Haverill who had offered."

Mr. Haverill's eyes twinkled. "I believe he *did,* ma'am, and was refused."

"Oh," she cried. "I *see.* That is, perhaps I will when my head stops spinning. Of course you must read Harriet's letter! Maybe you can explain—" She vanished from the room.

At the top of the stairs, Susan and Charlotte pounced upon their mother and followed her into her chamber, whispering feverishly, "What does he say? What does he say? Such a splendid gentleman!"

"He wants Caro for himself!" whispered Mrs. Weldon, beginning to ransack her husband's bureau. The girls breathed ecstatic "oohs" and hugged each other.

"Not there," mumbled Mrs. Weldon. "Not there."

"What are you searching for, Mama?" asked Charlotte.

"Harriet's frightful letter. Where *can* Papa have put it?"

"In his desk, Mama?" Charlotte suggested sensibly.

"Oh, dear me! The very place! How perfectly hen-witted I am. The desk!"

She hurried downstairs again, making her way to the vicar's study, where his large desk waited with its accoutrements in precise array. The vicar *did* like Order in his home. The letter was reposing docilely in a top drawer.

"There you are, you dirty creature," she said aloud. "Come with me and do your worst!"

Another moment and the letter had passed to Mr. Haverill's hand and Mrs. Weldon was able to sit down and wait
for him to solve her problems.

Mr. Haverill did not fail her. Harriet's diatribe was perfectly transparent to him. His mouth tightened as he read.
How to explain the lady's outrageous jealousy without
wounding the sister whose approval he sought posed something of a dilemma. He folded the paper and looked up.

Mrs. Weldon was watching him closely. "You may say
what you please," she said unexpectedly. "I have never been
able to do so, you know, being a clergyman's wife—and
practically a *nun*—except for five children, of course. For-
bearance is all very well, but when one's precious daughter
is involved, matters are less simple."

"I, on the other hand," declared Mr. Haverill inaccurately,
"am never forbearing. Your sister—"

"Yes?" prompted Mrs. Weldon bravely.

Mr. Haverill looked down into her anxious face. So like
Harriet's—and so unlike. It was Caro's green eyes he saw.
And Caro's soft mouth.

"Your sister," he continued in a milder tone, "has been a
reigning belle for ten years. She cannot—er—tolerate competition. I must tell you, dear Mrs. Weldon, that you did a
cruel thing when you sent a little beauty into her household."
And he smiled beguilingly as he spoke.

Fascinated by the enchantment that smile added to the
gentleman, Mrs. Weldon beamed back. She could recognize,
if Susan could not, the superiority of Mr. Haverill over his
handsome young cousin. There was something of *age* in it,
poise, serenity, humor, and good sense. If Caro loved this
man, she should be happy with him.

"Say no more," she advised. "I understand perfectly."
And Mr. Haverill was relieved that he need not describe
Harriet's stalking of himself. "Well, Charles will bring Caro
home, for it's the very last thing I said to him, and you will
want to see her, I expect—" She broke off, realizing her

words had almost led to inviting Mr. Haverill to be a guest of the vicarage. A clergyman's wife, one might think, would be above suspicion, but Mrs. Weldon had the uneasy feeling that country morals would question the propriety of her entertaining a single gentleman in her husband's absence.

He guessed the difficulty. "Indeed, I await both Miss Weldon and her father," he said, rising. "You must be wishing me at Jericho! With your permission I will call tomorrow. Meanwhile if you need assistance in any way, you can reach me at the inn."

"The Feather and Thistle?" she said, unbelievingly.

"I understand that is its name. My valet is engaging rooms there."

Mrs. Weldon protested that she would be very much surprised if Bounce kept more than one or two even passably neat.

"If there are two, Weems will have them," he replied calmly. "He is more particular than I, so I can expect some comforts will have been discovered. Do not be anxious about your daughter, ma'am. Gilly—Lord Tufton—cherishes her. Between him and Mr. Weldon all will be arranged satisfactorily."

During the course of this speech, he had moved into the hall. At the outer door he bowed, said, "Y'servant, ma'am." He stepped into his curricle, tossed Jem a coin, and inspired his team to trot.

"Bless my soul!" said Mrs. Weldon. She had leisure for about two breaths before her three younger daughters descended on her with chirps and squeals and demands to hear All. Over their heads she could see Annie had come into the hall, wiping her hands upon her apron.

"Not a word to anyone, Annie!" she said.

Annie sniffed indignantly.

"No one," repeated Mrs. Weldon sternly.

"No, mum," agreed Annie. Her tone was plaintive, but her face revealed quite clearly her delight in sharing a family secret. Miss Weldon had received a flattering Offer; that much was plain. Perhaps it was just as well Annie had not discovered *which* gentleman was the hero of the drama, for while her heart was gold, her intentions pure, and her fondness for every Weldon abiding, at the same time her tongue was fastened in her head by the merest tags of root, and there was not a shadow of doubt her brother would be arriving any moment to see if he could make it flap about the Swell at the inn.

Meanwhile, at the Feather and Thistle, Bounce had had a go at Weems with singular lack of success. Disgruntled, he went into the kitchen to complain to his wife that he did not see how such a slow-top could keep a post as a gentleman's gentleman.

"Slow-top he may be," retorted Mrs. Bounce. "You may think as you please about that. What *I* notices is Mr. Weems has your best parlor and chamber, your best tablecloth, your best claret, and fires in both rooms."

"Arr-r-r," growled Bounce and retreated into the taproom whence he could watch for the return of Mr. Haverill.

No one, of a dozen persons, saw the day end as its beginning had promised—least of all Mr. Haverill. Although he held no exalted opinions of himself he did not expect Mr. Weldon to refuse his suit. He had envisioned sharing a convivial cup (of tea, if nothing else) with the vicar by this hour and being urged to partake of the vicarage dinner. Instead, he was met in the inn yard by Bounce, whose communications about *Mister* Weems's arrangements for the gentleman's pleasure made it quite plain that Weems had all well in hand, including a neat pigeon pie which was Mrs. Bounce's specialty.

But Bounce at his best (that is to say, at his most obsequious) was more than Mr. Haverill could stomach. He had

scarcely descended from his curricle before he was entering
it again and asking directions to Sir John Luce's residence.

"You'll find it easy enough, sir," said the innkeeper.
"Shortest route by the lane at the church, a quarter mile
past the vicarage. Look for one gatepost, sir, the other being
blasted some years back by a bit of lightning, and her ladyship, holding Sir John, doesn't tamper with the works of
God."

When Mr. Haverill had thanked him and driven off,
Bounce went indoors to tell his wife that the gentleman was
acquainted with Sir John, which fact elevated the stature of
Mr. Haverill, but in no way explained his visit to the vicarage or his racking up at the Feather and Thistle.

Something of this was in Mr. Haverill's mind as he proceeded up the lane. He had every intention of announcing
his betrothal as soon as Mr. Weldon agreed to it; meanwhile,
it seemed best to protect Carolina and her parents from local
gossip. A call upon Sir John Luce, of whom he had no
knowledge at all and only a nodding acquaintance with his
son Rob, should confuse everyone, besides filling an empty
evening.

Bounce's directions led Mr. Haverill to the home-farm
entrance of Sir John's tidy manor, which may have explained
the lack of interest in gateposts. A farmer's boy guided him
into a proper carriageway, and as Mr. Haverill drew up before a charming Tudor manor house Sir John himself appeared on the doorstep.

"Knew I heard wheels," Sir John said with satisfaction.
"Good day, sir." Being the largest landholder in easy radius
of Dolden Overhill, he was accustomed to visits from all
who had business in the parish.

Mr. Haverill surrendered his team to a groom and introduced himself. A few courteous words about Rob Luce did
wonders. Sir John was ready, metaphorically speaking, to
clasp Mr. Haverill to his bosom. He led his guest upstairs

to a long, chintz-hung apartment where Lady Luce was sewing in a window embrasure.

"I say, m'love. Company." Sir John led Mr. Haverill forward and presented him as a friend of Rob.

"Oh, splendid," exclaimed her ladyship, tossing aside her work. "Enough of that dull mending. How do you do, Mr. Haverill? Pray tell me all about Robert."

It was not a subject on which he could be particularly fluent. However, by the exercise of moderate ingenuity and common sense he was able to reassure his hostess that Rob had not contracted any putrid sore throats or fallen victim to card sharps, and that military life seemed to agree with him so thoroughly that he had the endurance to dance all night.

She then asked if Mr. Haverill had met her dear young friend, Miss Weldon.

"Yes," he answered solemnly, having anticipated the question. His manner would have done credit to Edmund Kean, being a masterpiece of polite disinterest as he added: "A very pleasant young lady."

Lady Luce immediately (if erroneously) perceived her dear Caro held no allure for a gentleman of Mr. Haverill's sophistication and she changed the subject by inviting him to dine with them.

"Of course he will stay," Sir John answered for him warmly. "I have some fine old shotguns that will interest you, Haverill."

Lady Luce said one could view firearms any hour and Mr. Haverill must come out at once while the light held to see Desdemona's litter; whereupon she propelled the gentlemen willy-nilly to the kennels, leading Mr. Haverill to wonder whether he had stumbled upon a second Oatlands.

But he found Sir John and his lady to be kind and genuine. They had sufficient pride to exhibit flawless manners and not enough to be condescending. If Sir John several times mentioned his good neighbors, the Weldons, and Lady

Luce had occasion to praise the sweet vicarage daughters, Mr. Haverill did not object.

That Mr. Haverill was Rob's friend was all that was required to recommend *him* to their approval, and had they suspected Mr. Haverill held the most exquisite Designs upon Miss Carolina Weldon, they would have loved him on the spot.

Poor dear Mrs. Weldon spent a less comfortable evening. Although her conscience had not permitted her to entertain Mr. Haverill, even for dinner, that same relentless conscience now smote her for not giving him a more cordial reception.

"Papa should return tomorrow," she told her daughters, "and we will be obliged to invite Mr. Haverill to dine *then*. It will be so difficult to provide an adequate—"

"Oh, no, Mama," objected Charlotte, confidently assuming the reins for which Caro had prepared her. "Susan can fix lovely flowers everywhere and we can call Molly or Katie up from the village—both serve very nicely, you know— and it will be quite delightful."

"I would not want to give Mr. Haverill a false impression of us with serving maids left and right," murmured Mrs. Weldon, whose sweet composure was devoid of vanity. To impress anyone was never her design. "I simply meant we cannot supply the niceties to which I am sure Mr. Haverill is accustomed, and he would think a lot of servants ridiculous in a vicarage!"

"Fustion!" declared Charlotte. "Molly or Katie aren't a 'lot' of servants!"

Susan smiled and agreed with her sister, adding that serving girls always looked alike and that she could not suppose Mr. Haverill would count them.

Charlotte nodded vigorously. "I daresay he doesn't even know how many his own housekeeper employs." In this she wronged Mr. Haverill, for he knew both numbers and names of all his employees. "We will give him a good dinner," she continued, "and make him just as welcome as the Dean or Bishop Holt, which will not be difficult at all, for you know Papa treats *everyone* the same!"

"Very true, my love," admitted Mrs. Weldon, relaxing. "And unless Papa denies his suit—"

"He wouldn't!" shrieked Charlotte.

"—Mr. Haverill will soon be a member of the family."

"Soon" was not quite speedy enough for Mr. Haverill. A lusty cock in the inn yard roused him early and the recollection of Harriet's iniquities, of which he knew only the least, drove any vestiges of sleep from him. Hunching under Mrs. Bounce's best blue and white comforter, he arranged the forthcoming day in his mind and resolved to stay away from the vicarage until tea time.

As soon as noises rose from the kitchen, he sent down for breakfast, and would not have been surprised to see the pigeon pie come up. Luckily, *Mister* Weems, whose instincts were as splendid as a duke's, had graciously shared the promised pie with Mr. and Mrs. Bounce, and Bounce had stood him genially to a buttered ale in an evening the Feather and Thistle would not soon forget.

There were, instead, berries, and rich cream, ham, and toast, and very respectable coffee. Weems was allowed to dress Haverill with greater care and persuade him to wear a garnet ring of great antiquity and family significance. Like all his clothes, these were of excellent style, yet easy in cut so that once donned they could be forgotten. No exaggerated shirt points to stab his cheeks or coats so snug they might split if he bent an arm! When Weems stood back with a satisfied smirk, Haverill knew he passed muster. He clapped a hat on his head and went out in the balmy spring air to examine the village.

Ten minutes were sufficient for circling the green. He was pleased by a general air of modest prosperity for which he rightly gave Sir John some credit. Windows sparkled, doorsteps were scrubbed, no litter was visible. Even two roaming dogs did not seem unduly shaggy or ill-behaved. He did not see the lumberyard on the back street, but would have believed it a jolly place for children to play. James would have thought the town quite dead, he reflected, but *he* found the tranquility refreshing.

After making the circuit and admiring great oak and elm umbrellas, he went across to the church and entered.

It was not an ancient building, perhaps only 75 or so years old, but nicely proportioned, with well-dressed stone walls and some handsome woodcarving at altar and baptismal font . . . a likely spot for Caro and him to begin their adventure into matrimony. He wondered if Mr. Weldon would escort the bride, or perform the ceremony, or even attempt both. Then he chuckled at himself, for of course he would have no say in the matter.

When Mr. Haverill retraced his steps to the inn he found that Sir John had returned his call and was waiting in his private parlor. With good will on both sides, their acquaintance advanced. Sir John was invited to stay for luncheon and was pleased to share stewed chicken and a *mélange* of vegetables fresh from Mrs. Bounce's garden. It was all very congenial, but as the hands of the parlor clock crept past one, Mr. Haverill began to wonder uneasily how he would escape his new friend in order to call again at the vicarage.

Fifteen tense minutes were passed by Mr. Haverill. Then Sir John—that good fellow!—said regretfully that there was a farmer, five miles west, who had some pigs he thought he might like to buy and whom he had promised to visit that day. After farewells and hopes of further meetings he went on his way—that *best* of fellows!—without asking the embarrassing question of why Mr. Haverill had come to Dolden Overhill.

As soon as Sir John had ridden out of sight, Mr. Haverill hurried up the slope to the vicarage.

It was nowhere near time for tea.

Sixteen

The vicar changed horses twice in order to keep fresh ones poled-up, and he was fortunate each time to get swift animals, so that he was able to give some vent to his emotions by a hot pace. His thoughts, however, were not on speed records, but on the puzzling brangle concerning his daughter. Judicious though fond, he knew Carolina was a good girl—better than that, a girl of character and intelligence. He did not think the *ton* at its worst could subvert her. Whatever was wrong could not be *Caro.*

Harriet, on the other hand, he detested. It was Sin, of course, and he had wrestled with that particular demon through the years without overcoming it. For the most part, by concentrating on the amiability of his wife, he was able to keep angry thoughts from his mind, which was not exactly what the Lord expected from him, but seemed the best he could do. Usually he was able to forget Harriet.

Only this time he could not.

Another man could have relieved his tensions by hurling profanity at the traffic of London. This the vicar was denied. Lumbering drays, curs, heedless bucks driving to an inch, and pedestrian vendors of all sorts clogged the way, so that his temper grew, instead of diminishing, and when he pulled up before Lord Tufton's residence he was still muttering, ". . . seven, eight, nine, ten, one, two . . ."

Bigelow had a footman watching and a groom waiting in the pantry. He, himself, was never more than a dozen steps from the hallway and was first to reach and welcome the esteemed parent of Miss Plum.

"Mr. Weldon, sir!"

Other servants appeared in decorous haste.

A bit surprised at the welcome, but glad to hand over horses, luggage, hat, cloak, and gloves, Mr. Weldon entered the house, shedding first one item and then another as he asked for his daughter.

"If you please, sir," said Bigelow authoritatively, "his lordship has requested to see you *first*. May I show you to his study, sir?"

The vicar said impatiently, "Yes, yes!" and began striding down the hall without waiting for the ceremony of being announced. He opened Gilly's door himself, hearing the butler behind him say hurriedly: "Mr. Weldon, your lordship."

Neither gentlemen paid Bigelow any heed except to ascertain that he had shut the door.

"My dear Charles," exclaimed Lord Gilbert, coming forward, "I owe you apologies!"

"Never mind apologies," said the vicar. "What I need is facts. Couldn't make head or tails of Harriet's diatribe other than she wants my daughter *out.*"

His lordship looked grim. "I have learned she sent off a message after mine went with Haverill's, but I do not know what she may have said."

"Said?" inserted the vicar bluntly. "Raved, more like. No round-about now! Give me the story."

"Yes. I will." Lord Gilly motioned Mr. Weldon to a seat, and poured him a cup of tea. Fresh pots had been brought up every half hour since noon so that the cup steamed cosily.

"Caro," said his lordship, "took very well." He poured sherry for himself and sat down. "Young fellows underfoot all the time—some eligible, some not—no fortune hunters, of course. James Haverill with my friend, Lawrence. Young Howard. Rob Luce. Some others who don't matter. The most notable, you might say, was Lord Dooly, since he has both title and wealth. Harriet set her heart on catching *him*."

"Never mind what Harriet wanted. What about Caro? She like him?"

"No. That is, she treated him the same as the rest—civil—well, more than that. Sweetly, do you know?"

The vicar nodded that he knew and sipped his tea.

"But Caro wouldn't have Dooly as a husband, which made Harriet very angry, especially as she had already refused James Haverill."

Mr. Weldon looked up in astonishment, almost emptying his cup upon his vest. "Refused James Haverill!"

Lord Gilly chuckled. "Disappointed me too at first, but the little Puss knew she didn't want him."

"Then why," demanded the perplexed father, "did Mr. Haverill ask to visit me?"

"To make a proper offer. Did not my endorsement reach you?"

"Proper offer? Endorsement? Yes, I had your letter along with his. But since when did a 'proper offer' change a female's sentiments? You needn't think I'll force Caro into a loveless match. Proper offers aren't worth a tuppence to me!"

"If I am any judge, it is a love match," said Lord Gilbert happily. "Who would have thought!"

"I, for one," objected the vicar, "don't know *what* to think. Doesn't sound like my Caro. Why refuse James if she loves him? Nothing against the boy, is there?"

Lord Tufton's mouth had fallen open. "B-but I wrote you and *explained*. . . ." he began.

"No, you didn't," said the vicar firmly.

His lordship began to laugh. "L-Lawrence wants her for himself! And she—it appears, wants him—and *I* think the whole arrangement is just about perfect."

"Awk!" replied Mr. Weldon eloquently.

"Haverill was rushing me. I suppose it wasn't clear what

I meant. Take it from me, Dooly is a dead bore. James is a charming boy—has some growing up to do, but ought to turn out well, you know, though not for Caro. Lawrence is a rare, fine chap. She couldn't do better."

"Then why," asked Mr. Weldon persistently, "has Harriet rung such a peal over my child?"

A cloud settled over Lord Gilbert's face. "Disappointment," he said slowly. "At least I think it has to be disappointment. She had her heart set on Dooly."

The vicar restrained himself from pointing out the folly of Harriet's setting her heart on any female's choice of spouse.

"Harriet is—it hurts to say this, but I wouldn't be honest if I didn't—Harriet is—er—accustomed to getting—"

"Spoiled," said the vicar succinctly.

His lordship admitted it. "She would have accepted James," he went on, "because she knew I favored the boy, but she wanted Dooly. Seems to have some idea Dooly's mama would be an asset to any girl wanting to cut a swath in the *ton*."

"As if Caro would!" exclaimed the vicar in tones of disgust.

"No," agreed his lordship. "Dooly offered in spite of his mother who, as I see it, is a demmed moldy cheese. Beg your pardon, Charles, but that's my view! As for Lawrence, Harriet says he'll be bored with Caro in a couple of weeks."

"He might," admitted the vicar fairly, "if he's a rake."

"Lawrence? Gammon! Very proper fellow, for all his smart looks. I get the idea he feels he's found a female he can respect."

This sounded reasonable to Charles Weldon, who knew his daughter's worth. "I better have a talk with Haverill," he said. "But first, Caro."

Lord Gilly sent a footman to summon her. Since he had left the door ajar, they could hear the rapid patter of her feet upon the stairs and along the marble of the hall. She flew

straight to her father's arms. Lord Gilly closed the door quietly and retired behind his desk, endeavoring to blend himself with it, while father and child exchanged fierce hugs.

"Not to worry, darling," said Mr. Weldon huskily.

"Oh, no," agreed Caro. Although she could see no solution to her troubles, she trusted Papa to deal with them.
"Can you take me home?"

He said he both could and would—as soon as he conferred with Mr. Haverill. "Your uncle says he has made you
a fine offer. We will have to consider his wishes in the matter." He held off Carolina to look into her face.

She colored faintly and lowered her eyes, which spoke
volumes to her parent.

At this point Lord Gilbert cleared his throat and said, "Bit
of difficulty reaching Haverill. I sent around to his house
again, a little while ago and he's away from town. They
cannot say where he may have gone."

The vicar privately thought he could guess. "In that case
we will head to Dolden as soon as the horses have been
rested and baited. Can you pack up quickly, dearest?"

Before she could answer, the door opened and Lady
Tufton entered like an ice storm.

"So," she said frigidly, fixing her eye upon her brother-
in-law, "you are here."

Mr. Weldon was more afraid of his own anger than he
was of hers. "I am," he responded sturdily.

"You owe me an apology for foisting this girl upon me."

Lord Gilbert made a protesting sound, but the vicar cut
him off. "I foisted no one on you. My daughter came at the
express invitation of yourself. We did not suppose your own
sister's child would be unwelcome to you."

"She would not, had she been a different sort. But a
mealy-mouthed sneak—"

"You will have to be specific, my lady," Mr. Weldon interrupted. "We sent you a lady born and a lady raised, as
everyone in Dolden Overhill can testify."

"Oh—*Dolden,*" said Lady Tufton dismissively. "I agree Caro can put on an act of meek and obliging nature. She's been clever, I can say that. But all the time she has used her wiles and *our* sponsorship to ensnare *our* particular friend."

"Did Caro make the offer or did Haverill?" demanded Mr. Weldon. "I understand she also received two other unexceptionable offers. *They* found her charming, without her being accused of *ensnaring* them. I think you must acquit Caro of deceiving as many as *three* gentlemen."

"Three or a dozen. The tactics have the same results anywhere she goes. Disgraceful!"

The vicar's eyes narrowed. "Perhaps you lack understanding of a warm and amiable nature, ma'am."

Lady Tufton glared from him to Caro and back again. "What has amiability to do with managing an elegant establishment or entertaining the *ton?*"

"With entertaining the *ton,* very little. As far as a household is concerned, surely you know a mistress is better served by her staff if she is beloved?"

Caro had not before heard her papa indulge in sarcasm. His face had become white with anger, and his nose had sharpened, yet he was still restraining his temper.

"You're wrong there," Lady Tufton snapped. "Servants obey when they know they must."

The distress on Lord Gilly's face was shocking to behold, although only Caro had looked, for the two antagonists saw only each other. His lordship had emerged from behind his desk, nearing his wife, yet holding back, horrified and helpless.

"I did not come to quarrel about servants," Mr. Weldon said.

"You came, I trust, to remove your offspring from my house."

"Yes. That. As soon as you have explained the violent letter with which you favored me," he replied.

Lady Tufton had not mowed down her kinsman's defenses

as she had expected to do, but the fight was not over, and she enjoyed fights. Over Gilly (and servants) she always won.

"Your so-called 'lady' is an ungrateful chit. Where is the gratitude one should expect from a clergyman's daughter? I received her into my home, I gave her beautiful clothes, I introduced her to elevated circles, and I presented her at a costly ball—do not interrupt, Gilly!—I have done a great deal for your country mouse, more than you and Lydia expected, I daresay! And this ingrate has used her relationship to us to insinuate herself into Mr. Haverill's company—to seize every advantage to entrap him—a gentleman far above her, *our* particular friend. What has she to attract such a superior man?—no money, no *savoir faire,* no social connections except us. Even her looks are but a copy of mine! She may do all right in the country; London is another matter, Haverill is accustomed to ladies of sophistication—mature ladies—ornaments—"

Mr. Weldon was trembling now with rage, yet unshaken in purpose. "Madam," he said awfully, "look to your own behavior before condemning others. Caro is Haverill's choice. Thou shalt not covet!"

Lady Tufton gasped, and reached out blindly toward her husband, who came quickly to place a supportive arm about her.

"All right, Harriet," he said in a dead voice. "Let that be the end of it. Come. I'll take you to your room." He led her out the door, saying over his shoulder to Mr. Weldon: "Wait for me."

The door closed on them.

"Oh, Papa," cried Caro, "was it all jealousy? Was that it?"

"Yes. Clearly. There was a desire for dalliance, too, I fear. Much folly."

Tears blurred Carolina's eyes. "You were hard on her, Papa."

"Was I? I think it needful. I did not, you realize, accuse her of anything. For your sake, for Gilly's sake, for her own sake she needed a clear look at Self. Perhaps life will be better for Gilly from now on, although it seems unlikely. I hope you will forgive me for sending you to such a house."

"It was not all bad," she said. "My uncle is an excellent man. The children are dears—do you think we can have them to visit us this summer? They would enjoy the country."

Bigelow and a footman came in with tea and a message that Nannie was packing for Miss Weldon. His lordship would join them shortly.

When Lord Gilbert returned, the interview with him was brief, as he felt his presence was required upstairs. His shame and his apologies were equally great.

"I feel much of the blame must be mine, for I have spoiled Harriet badly."

Mr. Weldon disagreed. "Do not take her behavior upon your conscience, I beg. You may have indulged her too often, but the choice of words and actions was the result of *her* will. A kind nature, such as yours, cannot readily understand the willfulness of another. Things should be better now this is out in the open."

Lord Gilbert shook his head, but said he hoped so. He then returned to his wife's chamber.

Father and daughter sat down to talk quietly of home and springtime, and to await their horses' pleasure. It was decided, after some debate, to attempt the first stage of their journey, then seek a light supper and early bedtime at a convenient inn.

Lady Tufton was not seen again by the Weldons. They did, however, receive a proper send-off, for his lordship was there, not able to say much, and suspiciously gruff, with a last hug for Caro and a handclasp (warmly returned) for Mr. Weldon.

John Coachman and the grooms had polished Mr. Weldon's curricle until it glistened. Cook had packed a hamper large enough for a half-dozen travelers. Mrs. Moffett offered a veil to "protect the sweet young lady from the nasty dust," Mrs. Gibbs gave a handkerchief drenched with scent, and Bigelow a bunch of violets from the vendor on the corner. The whole staff tumbled into the hall to say farewell.

Touched and grateful, Miss Weldon thanked them gently, mentioning kind services from each in a way that enchanted them, and if her voice quavered a little they thought that eminently satisfactory, too.

When Mr. Weldon had presented a purse for Bigelow to distribute—a modest largesse, but greater than his means could well afford because his heart was full—they said goodbye a last time and went out to the square, and Mr. Weldon assisted his daughter to her seat.

"Let us go quickly, Papa," she whispered, close to tears.

"Certainly, love," he replied. He took his place, signalled the groom to release his horses, and set the team in motion. As they swung out of Grosvenor Square, he said, "Better a kind heart than the riches of Croesus."

"Oh, yes!" she agreed fervently. She did not look back, although Lord Gilly was watching from his doorstep.

They were almost on the outskirts of town when Carolina gave a horrified little gasp and laid her hand upon her father's arm.

"Cedric!" she said. "How could I forget Cedric? We did not see him."

"Never mind," Mr. Weldon replied. "I had an interview with that young gentleman last evening. He has gone to stay with James Haverill until he has wound up the affairs that took his mind so disgracefully from his duty. I gave him two days to present himself in Dolden. Oxford indeed! When I can't rely upon him to protect his sister?"

Carolina protested urgently that he must not blame Cedric, because he had been deceived. "He doesn't realize everyone isn't as *good* as he is, Papa."

"Well, he knows now, and very shocked he is, I will say, though that in no way mitigates his failing to look after you."

"But, Papa, I have always looked after *him*."

"So you have. Time for a change. Oh, I do *feel* for Gilly!" Then he pursed his lips tightly to prevent his tongue from leading him into deeper Sin.

That night, sleep refreshed both.

As they wheeled through the spring countryside next morning, Carolina recovered her spirits enough to observe unfolding vistas and to remark upon them, only once mentioning wistfully that the way home must always seem pleasant. As a true man of the cloth, Mr. Weldon concerned himself with souls and took little note of vegetation. In this case, however, he made an effort to admire undulating downs and greening spinneys as she called attention to them, for he recognized her effort to recover herself. She did not mention Mr. Haverill's name, and neither did he, judging it wisest to leave matters of the heart to the discretion of her mother. He would have thought a splendid suitor would offset any unpleasantness an aunt could devise, but since the suitor apparently did not do so, he could only conclude he understood young females even less than he did wives—however much he might love them.

The pace homeward was less swift than when he had come. Sir John's horses were retrieved at Cowling. When they left the turnpike at Dunn Cross, Carolina fell silent and the troubled expression returned to her eyes.

"Not much longer, love," he said.

"Oh, I will be so glad to see Mama," she replied.

"And she you. She is expecting me to bring you, I fancy."

"Do you think I am being punished for enjoying a London Season so much?" Caro asked in a small voice.

"Certainly not! 'God is not the author of confusion.' I am

glad you enjoyed your Season. Gilly certainly did so—as much as he was allowed to, I mean."

"I am thankful you chose Mama," she said, the rest of her thought unspoken although thoroughly understood.

He replied that a gentleman invited trouble if he paid court before using his head.

"Yet my uncle is intelligent."

"Yes, but he was snared before he thought."

Carolina smiled a little. "Now, Papa, you and Mama have both always told us you fell in love on sight!"

"Very true," he agreed, "at least on my part. I did not, however, dangle after her until I had satisfied myself concerning her character."

"But suppose it had been bad?"

"Then I should have rusticated, or something, until I recovered. From what I understand, Haverill hasn't dangled after you at all."

"No. And—Papa!—I cannot think he feels any attachment for me. He has gone off in the most mysterious manner—almost as if he were *escaping*—"

The vicar, who held some expectations of discovering Mr. Haverill in Dolden Overhill, which they were now approaching, reassured her hastily by saying he assumed there must be a reasonable explanation.

They passed into the village, forked up the vicarage lane and turned into the drive. Jem came running around the side of the house as Mr. Weldon reined his horses. Carolina sprang down lightly.

When she plunged into the hall of the house Mrs. Weldon was coming from the drawing room.

"Oh, Mama, Mama!" she cried, and hurled herself weeping into her mother's embrace. She did not see Mr. Haverill standing shocked in the doorway of the drawing room.

With great presence of mind, he withdrew out of sight, conscious of an almost overmastering passion to *kill* Lady Tufton, as Mrs. Weldon led her sobbing daughter up the stairs.

Mr. Weldon entered the front door, stripping off his gloves. He stuck his head into the drawing room.

"You're here," he said.

"Yes," said Mr. Haverill. "Was it bad?"

"Horrible," replied Mr. Weldon. He shed his travelling cloak onto a chair and set his hat upon the nearest table, thereby imperilling Mrs. Weldon's best china cherub.

"Well, sir," he said, weary yet cordial, "come into my study and we'll put our feet upon the fender."

It was, of course, a figure of speech, for the fireplace had no fender, only black andirons wrought by a smithy grateful for the vicar's intercession at the Throne of Grace. But it was an easy room, a comfortable room—for all the tears, repentance, supplication, joy, remorse, and desperation it had witnessed. Since a fire generally smouldered on the hearth year-round (this time of year too small to heat but keeping out the damp), a gentle aroma of wood-smoke hung over all. There were many books, and comfortable seats.

Like all visitors to the vicar's study, Mr. Haverill found himself relaxing.

Mr. Weldon liked the room himself; he had met and conquered many problems there. Perhaps long hours spent upon his knees in conversation with his Maker added to his appreciation of the place.

The vicar's own chair, however, was presently occupied.

"Might have known," he rumbled, lifting a handsome, large, *enceinte* cat from the seat. He did not deposit the creature upon the floor, Haverill noted with amusement, but sat down and settled Tabby Four Toes on his lap, motioning Mr. Haverill to another chair.

"Cedric gone," he explained ruefully. "Surrounded by females, you see."

Mr. Haverill smiled and said immediately that he hoped this would make Mr. Weldon receptive to a son-in-law.

"You," said the vicar, since he had been enlightened by Lord Tufton.

"Only with your blessing, sir," replied Mr. Haverill.

Mr. Weldon stroked the cat.

"If it's only that," he said slowly, "there's no problem. But you see, Harriet caused a—rare dust-up, and Caro's in a taking."

"I wish I had been there," Haverill averred.

The vicar shook his head. "No, you don't. Fearful thing. Tufton humiliated. Servants about to rebel like the Colonies. Caro cut up to mincemeat." He shook his head as though to reject unpleasant thoughts. "Poor child—all unsettled. Not, I fear, in the mood for matrimony."

Mr. Haverill looked taken aback. His own recollection was of tenderest moments. "I wasn't there when she needed me! Mrs. Weldon let me read Lady Tufton's letter, and I could guess what transpired, but of course no one could know."

Whereupon the vicar favored him with an explicit report, including Lady Franklin's intervention.

"Bless Lady Franklin!" Mr. Haverill exclaimed. "Let me see Caro, sir. I believe she returns my sentiments. You were wise to bring her home. Now let me see what I can do to set things right."

Having encountered every vice and virtue, the vicar was very quick to read character. Haverill's, he felt instinctively, was good. Besides, it would be a goosecap who could resist the elegant gentleman sitting opposite him.

"Yes," he said. "I think I'll put her in your hands now. . . . After she's had a bit of time with her mother and a rest." Overcome by some mysterious parental emotion which Haverill could appreciate without understanding it, Mr. Weldon took out his handkerchief and blew his nose.

Mr. Haverill, deeming the proper time had come, set forth his personal credentials. Many ambitious fathers would have heard him with satisfaction, but Mr. Weldon scarcely noted pound or acre, for he was thinking about the importance of Character and Disposition to the happiness of his daughter.

Seventeen

While the gentlemen were talking, Mrs. Weldon shut Susan and the younger girls out into the upper hall, and Miss Weldon was allowed some privacy in which to calm her spirits. Although Mrs. Weldon's emotions were a tangle of anger and curiosity, she asked no questions.

"There, love, there!" was about all Mrs. Weldon ventured to say, caressing her daughter. To think one's *sister* could provoke such floods! The most shocking wrath assailed her.

But Caro was becoming conscious of dear, familiar surroundings and a very special, if anxious, face.

"Oh, Mama," she said, "I expect I've disgraced you."

"In what way?" asked her mother.

Since Caro really did not know, and only partially understood Lady Tufton's rage, she was not able to answer this.

"My aunt was very angry at me."

"Always had a horrid temper," Mrs. Weldon explained, not appearing to suffer any shame for the behavior of her daughter.

"But, Mama, you don't understand. She talked dreadfully to me—said I had thrown myself at Mr. Haverill—and *trapped* him—"

Mrs. Weldon's eyes flashed dangerously, but there was no perceptible change in her tone as she said: "Well, that is very odd. When a gentleman is 'trapped' he is sure to drag his feet. I can't think he would go pelting into the country to present his suit to the lady's father!"

"Oh!" said Caro, sitting down suddenly. "Did Mr. Haverill do that?"

"Yes, he did. Indeed, he is with your Papa this very moment."

"Now?" Torn between elation and alarm, Caro mangled her handkerchief and avoided meeting her mother's eye. "But I don't—he doesn't—oh, I'm sure we would not suit. It is so humiliating. I am sure his sentiments are not—he is only being civil. Oh, it is all a terrible mistake!"

Never having known civility to be carried to such lengths, Mrs. Weldon with greatest difficulty preserved a solemn countenance. She had had ample time to estimate Mr. Haverill's sentiments and was rapidly assessing Caro's. She said mildly, "Not 'terrible,' dear one. The matter is simply resolved. If you do not love him, you can refuse his offer."

"Can I?" said Caro in a failing voice.

"To be sure you can. Your Papa and I would never force you into a distasteful match."

"No, Mama. I did not suppose you would. But it is not *that,* exactly. Mr. Haverill is very handsome, kind and so easy to talk to—and of course very rich. But Mama! I could never marry a gentleman for benefits to Susan and Charlotte and Melissa—oh, and to Cedric, too, because he bought his picture—although Uncle Tufton has promised help for him. I *couldn't,* Mama."

Groping her way through scrambled clauses, Mrs. Weldon said certainly not and waited for further revelations.

"I couldn't marry a Plump Purse, Mama! Maybe it's vain of me, but what I want is a husband who l-loves me."

"And you don't think Mr. Haverill does?"

The answer was a bleak "no."

Mrs. Weldon considered her searchingly. "I see. Then of course you must say no to him. Regretfully, of course, but firmly. And promptly, dearest."

Caro paled. "Must I? Cannot you tell him—or Papa? Cannot Papa tell him we would not suit?"

Her mother shook her head.

"It's gone a bit further than that," she said, steeling herself to meet Caro's pleading gaze. "It is my understanding that you led Mr. Haverill to believe his suit would be acceptable. He has a natural pride, child. You owe it to him to explain your change of heart."

"But how can I," cried Caro, "when I—"

She broke off, remembering vividly the depravity with which she had received his caresses. The color flooded back into Caro's face, and Mrs. Weldon turned aside to hide a smile.

"It is very simple. He will comprehend quickly. You need not say much. Just that you have had second thoughts—that you appreciate the honor—that sort of thing. But at once, Caro! You cannot keep him kicking his heels in Dolden."

As she spoke she poured water into a basin and handed Caro a cloth. "Wash your face, love, while I shake out another dress."

Wondering why one should array oneself for the end of the world, Carolina did as bid and allowed her mother to button her into the white frock Susan had lent. Her hair was brushed into soft curls about her shoulders, and powder lightly dusted upon her nose to subdue its pink.

"Go down to the drawing room, child, and I'll send Mr. Haverill there," said Mrs. Weldon in the most casual and *unfeeling* manner.

Caro gnawed her lip, and went.

When she had seen her daughter enter the drawing room, Mrs. Weldon sought Mr. Haverill in the study. He sprang up at her entrance and, hearing that Miss Weldon waited to see him, exited with alacrity.

Mrs. Weldon closed the door and leaned against it. "She intends to reject him," she said.

Mr. Weldon snorted. "Only a ninny would do so!"

"But Caro's not a ninny," she objected.

"I didn't say she was," he replied.

His wife chuckled. "And I didn't say she *would* reject him. I only said she *intended* to."

Mr. Weldon drew her into his arms. "You think what I think?"

Mrs. Weldon said she did.

He kissed her warmly.

"Three more girls," he said. "I don't know if I can live through it."

"Cedric will be worse," she warned. "He loves everybody—has no discernment at all."

"Do not worry. I can always cut off his funds and that will discourage all, but truly devoted females."

"But suppose Gilly franks him?"

"Gilly would not fund a bad connection. He has sons, remember. I am confident he will think exactly as I do."

They sat down close together and were silent for a time.

"A chick leaving the nest," the vicar sighed at last.

"It's only natural," she defended.

"Ordained by God," he agreed. "But I don't have to enjoy it, do I?"

Having no intimation that he would receive his *congé,* Mr. Haverill strode rapidly down the hall and entered the drawing room without knocking.

"At last!" he cried, coming purposefully toward her.

Miss Weldon retreated behind a chair.

"Oh, please! Let me speak first."

He halted, smiling. "Speak away—so long as it is your one beautiful word."

"One word?" she faltered.

"The word 'yes.' Have you forgotten?"

"Y-yes," she stammered. "I mean, no. That is, I *cannot*— I have been thinking about us, you see. I do admire and honor you, Mr. Haverill, but—'"

"Honor me? Good God, Caro, you sound as if you are about to cry off. You? A jilt?"

She echoed, "Jilt?", horror-struck to realize that was exactly what she could be called. She began tentatively to explain that they should not suit, but Mr. Haverill paid no heed, for he was colorfully damning Lady Tufton, saying she had poisoned Caro's mind. Then he sent the defensive chair skidding across the floor and swept Caro into his arms. With a devastating drop in tone he said, "I love you. I want to marry you."

Poor Caro, driven by her own desires, while resisting his (although they were the same), capitulated in the most craven fashion and was spun away in a passionate kiss. It was so successful a ploy that Mr. Haverill repeated it.

"What is more," he continued, resuming his belligerent attitude, "I intend to do so."

She had no trouble with continuity.

"Yes," she said, smiling.

Mr. Haverill laughed, and drawing her to sit on a sofa, tucked her in the curve of his arm.

"Now, what," he asked, "was all that rot about crying off?"

"I did not want a loveless marriage," she admitted, "and you said nothing about loving me."

"Didn't I?" He was stunned. "Good God, I've had my eye on you since I first met you."

"But you disapproved of me—"

"Disapproved!"

"I mean, didn't think me eligible for your cousin."

He drew back, staring at her in astonishment. "How could you think that?"

Finding it easier every moment to unburden her heart, Caro explained that he had always been so protective of James. "You never let him come to my uncle's house alone. You were always with him."

Mr. Haverill laughed and shook his head. "Little love,

you have it all backwards. How else was I to see you? Come to know you? Surely by now you realize the beautiful viscountess is a man-eating tiger! I came with James because he protected *me*."

The vicar and his wife looked up hopefully when Mr. Haverill entered with their daughter.

"Sir," said Mr. Haverill, "Caro and I have agreed we should suit very well."

Mr. Weldon examined his daughter's rosy face. "So you should," he agreed. His wife gave a glad little cry and sprang up to embrace her child. When the vicar had finished exchanging handclasps with Mr. Haverill, Mrs. Weldon kissed his cheek and told him they would love him and count him as one of them. He was conscious of a family warmth he had never known.

"You will be our son," she said.

"Thank you, Mama," he drawled. His eyes were dancing, for he very well realized there were fewer years between him and Lydia Weldon than between him and his intended bride.

"Oh, I am so happy!" cried Caro in a miraculous right-about from her recent lachrymose condition. Her openness was heart-warming. Nothing could have pleased her hearers more.

The vicar gave her a mammoth hug. "Well, well, so it's to be Hanover Square, is it?"

"St. George's?" said Mr. Haverill. "No, sir. We want—indeed, we *expect* you to marry us."

"Here in Dolden Church, Papa," Caro said, and Mr. Haverill added:

"I will take my wife to Venice for a wedding trip and then we will settle at my manor in Surrey, for you see we are *also* agreed in disliking Town Life."

Mrs. Weldon, catching the special tone of Mr. Haverill's

voice when he said "wife," fell into a bemused and euphoric state, but Mr. Weldon, who had heard "disliking Town Life," and who detested city streets himself, immediately rallied him:

"Sir, if you dislike London, why did you live there?"

"I expect," admitted Mr. Haverill, "because one shops the Marriage Mart when one is looking—even if only subconsciously—for a wife."

Not knowing Mr. Haverill's long evasion of entanglements, nor the disappointment he had dealt predatory mamas for a decade, Mr. Weldon deemed this a fairly reasonable answer, although he could not resist pointing out its one flaw: "Not the place to find a country-minded lady, I would suppose."

"Very true. A foolish notion. I wasted years." He smiled at Carolina. "However, I have at last discovered what I want, and if you will remember, I found her in a ditch!"

ROMANCE FROM JO BEVERLY

DANGEROUS JOY   (0-8217-5129-8, $5.99)

FORBIDDEN   (0-8217-4488-7, $4.99)

THE SHATTERED ROSE   (0-8217-5310-X, $5.99)

TEMPTING FORTUNE   (0-8217-4858-0, $4.99)

WATCH FOR THESE REGENCY ROMANCES

BREACH OF HONOR (0-8217-5111-5, $4.50)
by Phylis Warady

DeLACEY'S ANGEL (0-8217-4978-1, $3.99)
by Monique Ellis

A DECEPTIVE BEQUEST (0-8217-5380-0, $4.50)
by Olivia Sumner

A RAKE'S FOLLY (0-8217-5007-0, $3.99)
by Claudette Williams

AN INDEPENDENT LADY (0-8217-3347-8, $3.95)
by Lois Stewart